To Terry,
With very best wishes
C. Rainsford
Tillingham
Essex
26th May 2007

666
and a
9 millimetre

by

Cornelius Rainsford

Grosvenor House
Publishing Limited

All rights reserved
Copyright © Cornelius Rainsford, 2007

Cornelius Rainsford is hereby identified as author of this
work in accordance with Section 77 of the Copyright, Designs
and Patents Act 1988

The book cover picture is copyright to Inmagine Corp LLC

This book is published by
Grosvenor House Publishing Ltd
28-30 High Street, Guildford, Surrey, GU1 3HY.
www.grosvenorhousepublishing.co.uk

This book is sold subject to the conditions that it shall not, by way of
trade or otherwise, be lent, resold, hired out or otherwise circulated
without the author's or publisher's prior consent in any form of binding or
cover other than that in which it is published and
without a similar condition including this condition being imposed
on the subsequent purchaser.

A CIP record for this book
is available from the British Library

ISBN 978-1-906210-02-1

*To my wonderful wife Joan,
who supplied me with thousands
of cups of tea during the writing of this novel,
and never once put anything more than milk
in them despite tremendous provocation.*

1

Everyone who knew Jack Blade liked him. He was the twenty nine year old landlord of a pub in the East End of London called The Raven, and he had an unequalled reputation for making his customers feel welcome as soon as they walked through the rare, hand-etched glass front doors. And because of this, a number of people came regularly from a great distance to enjoy the warm, cosy atmosphere of the pub, which they claimed could be found nowhere else in the cold and often unfriendly city that was London.

Jack was tall, edging just over six feet, with the lean powerful body of a professional swimmer. His hair was long, brown in colour, and had that baby soft look that many women found irresistible. His eyes were large and green, with grey dotted through them like tiny, though pleasing, imperfections. His lashes were long and curved, and his nose was what could be considered cute rather than perfectly formed. However, the one noticeable flaw in his almost physical perfection was his mouth, which was a little on the small side. But then again his lips were generous, and he had a remarkable resemblance to Robert Redford, or so it was often said by some of the younger female customers.

Another of Jack's attributes was that he was always scrupulously fair to his customers; no watering down of spirits for those too inebriated to tell the difference, for him. Everyone knew that you got your full measure from Jack Blade. And even when it was necessary to evict the occasional troublemaker, he never resorted to the use of bouncers. He always did the job himself, politely explaining to the offender as he gently escorted him off the premises, that he was very welcome to return the following evening when he had calmed down. And the remarkable thing was, the troublemakers always went quietly, because Jack had a gift, a way of talking that made others feel instinctively that he was just their big brother; looking out for them, and doing only what was in their best interest. Yes, everyone liked Jack, and many a local mother would say to their smitten daughter, *'you could do a lot worse for yourself than Jack Blade, Love.'*

But the truth was quite the opposite, because Jack was not all that he seemed to be. For, behind those engaging eyes and heart lurching smile, lay a cruel and ruthless mind; a mind with its thoughts focused entirely on just one thing - a fierce ambition to rise quickly and efficiently to the highest echelons of the London Underworld.

A long time ago Jack had decided that if he was to achieve his goal, no one must be allowed to stand in his way. And anyone who did was his enemy - ignorant of their crime or not. Yes, Jack Blade was ready to climb to the top, and you could either get out of his way, or suffer the fatal consequences.

But it wasn't only ambition that had brought Jack to London and The Raven five years earlier in 1964. The brutal fact of the matter was that he had no choice, because he left a great deal of trouble behind him when he moved down from Scotland. And there were more than a few people, including vengeful relatives of those he had killed, who had a very great need to see him at the bottom of a river - a Scottish Loch being the preferred choice of location.

Yes, Jack had indeed upset some very bad people who should never have been upset, before he left Glasgow behind, and he certainly wouldn't be going back to that particular city for his holidays any time in the foreseeable future. He had been incredibly lucky to escape with his life and a large bag of cash, and he promised himself that, come what may, he would never again put himself in a position where he would have to go on the run. A man on the run could only make plans for one thing and one thing only; how to stay alive for at least one more precious day.

Jack certainly knew how to live dangerously, but he also knew how to survive, and he was proud of the fact that he owed nothing of his survival to anyone. It was all done by his own ingenuity. And although he would admit to having learned from others, there wasn't a single person in the world that he admired or respected. However, there was another species of killer entirely that did command his respect - a certain type of snake called a Bambder, that lived in the humid interior of the South American Rain Forest.

The speciality of the snake that had caught Jack's attention some years ago while watching a TV programme on wildlife, is to coil itself up in loops, right out in the open on the forest floor, where it can be seen by all.

And there it stays, giving all the innocent appearance of a brown pile of animal faeces. And for up to three weeks that snake will remain there - not moving even the tip of its tail, and all the time waiting for its prey to come within reach. Now, the snake only uses a trail that leads to water, so there is usually a great deal of coming and going, and sometimes the chosen prey will pass by the Bambder perhaps two or even three times in a day; particularly if the weather is very hot. However, despite great temptation, the Bambder won't be drawn into any rash moves. It will already have invested a great deal of time in that particular prey, and it is not going to risk losing it. So, only when the prey is at just the right distance; feeling relaxed and at ease with the brown faeces, is the time right to strike - then *wham*, the snake launches itself at the prey - the fangs go in, and dinner is served – sometimes late, but never cold.

Jack felt a close affinity with the Bambder, but he knew he had to be even more cunning when hunting, because his prey was a seasoned survivor - an expert in avoiding attacks - perhaps even in counter- attacking. But Jack wasn't too worried. He had one great advantage over other ambitious killers, such as the psychopaths who didn't know when to stop killing, and are themselves eventually destroyed, and the criminals who believed the gun to be the answer to success, only to find out too late that they had shot the wrong people. No, Jack wouldn't end up like those misfits, because he had brains. He was smarter than the others and smarter than his prey - he had to be if he was to survive beyond his ambition.

Jack had selected his prey five years ago when he first moved to the area and bought the pub. However, unlike the Bambder's usual victim - a harmless little pig-like animal, Jack's selected prey was a far more powerful creature, who could probably destroy him without any effort at all if he found out what he was up to. Of course Jack understood this only too well, and that is why he has waited all this time - waited for the very best opportunity to present itself. And that evening, at precisely eight pm, on the twelfth of November, Nineteen Sixty Nine, the opportunity walked casually into his pub and leaned against the counter.

Freddy Boyle was a balding thirty five year old low life, who had the kind of face that even his own mother couldn't have forced herself to like. His large, crooked Roman nose and pink fleshy lips were far too prominent to allow any more pleasant facial features he might have to come through. His nickname at school had been Banger Nose, and the experience had left him with a sour disposition ever since.

Freddy worked for the biggest crime boss in London, who at this particular moment in time was right smack in the middle of a major police investigation. The heat was certainly on Manny Hemmings, and it was furnace hot. In fact it was so hot that it singed the eyebrows of the London Underworld, and so they kept well clear of him. The word was out. Manny Hemmings was very bad news at the moment.

Of course everyone knew about the serious trouble Manny was in: the Tabloids were keen to see to that, with headlines such as

*'HEAT FROM COPS PUTS
CRIME BOSS OUT IN THE COLD'
and
'MAN OF ILLICIT MEANS STEAMS
UNDER POLICE MICROSCOPE'*

However, no one dared discuss Manny in public, or even in private if they worked for him, in case someone in Manny's organization thought they were shooting their mouths off. And if you shoot your mouth off about what is strictly Manny Hemming's business, it is as certain as tax demands that he will send someone along to shoot your head off. So everyone kept quiet about Manny Hemmings and his problems, if they had any sense at all.

The Raven wasn't particularly busy just now; entertaining only a few regulars who liked the place best when it was quiet. But Jack didn't mind one bit. Come nine o clock and the place would be full of people buying rounds for newly discovered friends whose names they probably wouldn't even remember the following day, and rowdy young men holding drinking contests until Jack, or empty pockets, sent them home to their mortified parents.

Freddy Boyle glanced about him a few times. Then he called to Jack, who was replacing a large bottle of Bells whisky in the optics.

"What can I get you, Freddy?" Jack asked with a smile he reserved for people he didn't like.

"Just a quick word, if ya don't mind," said Freddy.

Freddy's secretive manner encouraged Jack to lean close to him.

"What's up?" he asked in a low voice.

"Manny needs a favour from ya, Jack," Freddy whispered. "A very *big* favour - if ya know what I mean?"

The sudden surge of excitement in Jack's chest almost chocked him,

666 AND A 9 MILLIMETRE

but he fought it down. *'Christ Almighty!'* his mind screamed. *"This is fucking well - it!*

"I don't know, Freddy," he managed to say calmly to the man. "I never get involved in funny business - too many local cops use this place."

"This ain't no funny business," said Freddy. "It's just somethin Manny wants ya to do for him until this fuckin trouble with the cops blows over. He wouldn't ask if he wasn't desperate. And he can be real generous to blokes who do him a favour."

"I don't know..." said Jack, pursing his lips thoughtfully. "If it gets out that I'm involved with Manny Hemmings, I'll lose credibility with a lot of my customers."

"Customers - who the fuckin ell are they!" Freddy hissed. "All I'm askin ya to do is help Manny out of a bit of bover, and you're poncin on about fuckin customers. Now listen here, Jack, Manny's known about ya ever since ya moved into his manor, and has he ever once leaned on ya – well, has he...?"

"No...I guess not," Jack replied.

"Too bloody right he ain't!" Freddy growled. "And I'll tell ya somethin else, Jack, more than half the fuckin businesses around here are payin protection money to Manny, but not this one! He left ya alone, and now it's time to return the favour."

"All right, just this once," Jack sighed. "So, what's the favour then? But it better not be hurting anyone. I don't hold with breaking legs or putting the frighteners on people."

A incredulous laugh shot from Freddy's ugly mouth. "Ya must be jokin, Mate. You - put the frighteners on someone. My sister Brigid is more scary than you. No, you're all right there, Mate. All Manny wants ya to do is look after a package for him, that's all."

"What kind of package?" said Jack.

"Naughty boy," said Freddy with a grin. "Didn't yer mommy ever tell ya not to ask the grown ups awkward questions?"

"As a matter of fact, no," said Jack.

Freddy's lips twisted in anger, and he jabbed a long finger at Jack. "Don't ya get fuckin lippy with me, Mate! This ain't no bit of fun! Manny wants yer help, and I aim to see that he gets it!"

"All right, all right, keep your flipping hair on!" Jack exclaimed. "I said I'll help didn't I! So, have you got the package on you...?"

"Christ all bloody mighty!" Freddy growled. "What the fuckin ell do ya think is in it - a couple of fuckin fivers and a bit of change! It's too fuckin big for my pockets, ya stupid git!"

"I didn't know it was money," Jack protested. "It could have been a book of names or something, couldn't it...?"

Freddy's eyes narrowed and he fixed Jack with a hard glare. "How did ya know about the fuckin book? Who's been blabbin? Tell me who it is and I'll cut his fuckin balls off?"

"It was only a guess!" Jack cried defensively. "Jesus Christ, Freddy! Calm down will you! People will notice! I just watch a lot of gangster films, that's all, and there's always a book with a list of names!"

Freddy straightened up; ran his fingers over what was left of his hair, then stroked his throat with bony fingers. "Yea., OK, Jack. Sorry about that. Got a bit carried away there. It's this fuckin investigation into Manny's affairs. It's makin us all as jumpy as a fox at Crufts. And just between the two of us, most of the gang would like to take to their heels, but they're too shit scared of Manny to try it."

"I understand," said Jack. "Have a scotch on the house."

Freddy watched as Jack walked to the optics and filled a glass with a triple measure of whisky.

Then Jack came back and placed the glass on the polished mahogany counter that had been there since 1896.

Freddy took the glass and held it up as a toast. "Cheers, Mate, you're a brick." Then he downed the drink in one go. He shuddered as the alcohol burned its way down into his stomach. "Christ, I bloody needed that! And do ya know what my dad used to call this stuff, Jack?"

Jack shook his head.

"Liquid Amnesia," said Freddy. "Because when he started drinkin it he forgot what an evil old bag he had waitin for him at home." Then Freddy pulled a sour face. "And she was a right cow she was, Jack. Oh, I know nobody should talk about their mother like that, but do ya know what she gave me on my tenth birthday?"

Again Jack shook his head.

"No, well I'll tell ya!" said Freddy. "She gave me a black eye and porridge for my dinner! Yea...that's right, Mate – a black eye and a bowl of fuckin porridge for my dinner! Now ya tell me, what kind of mother would do that to her only son on his tenth birthday – a right fuckin cow, Mate, that's who – a right fuckin cow!"

Jack felt like punching Freddy right in the face, but he resisted the temptation. "A sad story, Freddy," he said in an even voice. "Now have another drink. You'll feel better."

The offer seemed to snap Freddy out of his melancholy. "Thanks, but no thanks, Mate. I had a few too many before comin here. And if I turn up at Manny's place stinkin of booze, he'll set a couple of his Neanderthals on me, and ya should see the size of some of em, Mate; big as fuckin brick shit houses and twice as ugly. A couple of em could give King Kong hiself a good seein to."

"I'll take your word for it," said Jack.

Freddy's eyebrows arched in surprise. "Yea...of course. You ain't ever been invited to Manny's place at the top of Queensbury House - have ya. And ya know why, don't ya, Mate; not because he don't like ya, not a bit of it. In fact, the word is he admires ya quite a bit. No, the thing is that *you*, Jack me old son, are one of Manny's most secret investments. Ya see, Manny, bein the clever bloke he is, knew a long time ago that he had to have some place to stash his dosh when the cops were on the big sniff: somewhere they wouldn't even think of searchin. And who, in this wonderful fuckin city of ours, would even dream that the favourite landlord of old dears and thirsty down-and- outs, would have a stash of a million quid tucked away behind his shelves of dusty old bottles of stout."

Suddenly a look of utter horror - followed by sheer terror, appeared on Freddy's ugly, pock-marked face. "Oh my fuckin Gawd - I'm fuckin dead!" he wailed. "Me and my big mouth! If Manny finds out I told ya what's in the package he's goin to have me barbecued with a fuckin blow torch!"

"Take it easy, Freddy," said Jack. "I already guessed there must be a lot of cash, and there's no need for Manny to find out. I'll just hold on to it for him until his troubles blow over."

A weak smile of relief brightened Freddy's features. "Jesus, Jack, you're a real Mate – a twenty four carat diamond! You've just saved my bleedin life and I ain't about to forget it! And if ever ya need a favour, ya just ask! Freddy Boyle never forgets a good deed done to him!"

"Forget it," said Jack with a shrug. "You can buy me a pint if I ever end up on the streets. Now, about this package. Seeing as it's going to be a big one, I don't think it's advisable to have a couple of blokes humping it in past my customers. Someone might start asking questions."

"Manny thought of that already," Freddy replied, wiping sweat from his forehead with the back of his hand. "And the plan is for me to deliver it round the back after closin, and..."

Freddy stopped talking as Karen, a good looking, thirty five year old brassy blonde barmaid squeezed past Jack to get a box of tonic water.

"Scuze me, Sexy," Karen said to Jack with a coy smile. "I'm free at the weekend, so how about that date you keep promising me?"

"He's not good enough for ya, Karen," said Freddy with a leering grin. "Why don't ya come out with a bloke who knows how to appreciate a real woman?"

Karen squeezed back past Jack once more with the tonic. Then she stopped and stared at Freddy. "You know something, Love, I make it a rule never to date a man who has less hair on his head than I have on my legs, and eyes like a pet rat I once had. And another thing, that face of yours would scare the life out of my cat Tiggy, and he's jumpy enough as it is since they got that new dog next door."

Freddy went red with embarrassment and outrage. "Go fuck yerself, ya old crow!" he spat.

"You know, Jack," Karen said over her shoulder as she headed for the other end of the bar, "you really should do something about the vermin in this place. I hear Rentokil will give you a discount if they're particularly big and smelly."

Freddy threw an evil stare after Karen. "One of these days, so help me, Jack, I'm goin to cut out that nasty tongue of hers."

"You know she doesn't like you," said Jack with a grin. "So why keep asking her out?"

"Because I forget what an evil bitch she is, that's fuckin why. But she'll come round: I'll make her come round - ya see if I don't."

"You were saying about the package?" Jack prompted, leaning close once more.

"Oh yea, the package," said Freddy, putting Karen and her insults from his mind, "I'll bring it round after closin one night. Ya can give me a hand unloadin it."

Jack looked surprised. "You mean you'll be on your own - with all that money?"

"That's the plan," Freddy replied. "Ya see, Manny don't trust nobody, least of all those he's supposed to trust. I'm the only one that knows you're lookin after his dosh."

"Then he must trust you?" said Jack.

There was an edge to Freddy's voice when he spoke. "Ya fuckin deaf or what. Didn't I just say that Manny don't trust no one. Didn't I just say that."

"But you're delivering the package aren't you, and you know what's in it?" Jack protested.

"That ain't trust, ya stupid git!" Freddy snapped. "If ya must know, before he told me what his plan was, Manny took me for a ride in his Jag, and I was squashed between two of his Neanderthals for over a fuckin hour. And all the time I was pissin myself tryin to figure out what the ell I'd done. Ya see, I thought they were goin to slit my throat and dump me somewheres. Anyway, we pulled into this warehouse, and they had this bloke stripped naked and strapped down on a large table. He was all smashed up - ya know; black eyes, teeth missin, blood all over his face. He was a right fuckin mess I can tell ya, but he was still alive, and he was cryin like a baby - begging for his life. Then someone handed Manny a bottle of some liquid, and he began to dribble it slowly over the poor sod. Ya should have heard him scream, Jack. It was fuckin horrible. It must have been acid in that bottle because his body began to fizz - ya know, just like sherbet does when ya put water on it. I felt sick just seein it and I really wanted to get out of there, but they grabbed my arms and made me watch. And ya know somethin, Mate that poor sod must have been in a shit load of pain, yet he never passed out. He just thrashed around and screamed for half an hour before he snuffed it. Then we went back to the Jag - just me and Manny. Now at first he told me about his plan, but then he said that if I did the dirt on him, he'd do the same thing to me as that bloke in the warehouse. So, it ain't a matter of trust, Mate; it's a matter of sheer fuckin terror. No way would I touch what's inside that package. It ain't dirty money, Mate, it's fuckin agony money and I don't want no part of it."

"I don't blame you," said Jack.

"Just so long as Manny don't have no cause to either," said Freddy. "Right then, Mate, ya got a good hidin place for it?"

"There's somewhere in the cellar; a small room that must have held the proceeds from smuggling at one time, because the door is five inches thick."

"How many keys?" Freddy inquired.

"Just the one," said Jack. "It's about a foot long. Must be hundreds of years old."

"Ok. That's sorted then. I'll report back to Manny. Ya should have a delivery date in a few days."

"Looking forward to it," said Jack.

"Be seein ya, Mate, and thanks," said Freddy. "Manny knew ya wouldn't let him down."

"Oh, don't you worry about that," Jack said under his breath as Freddy headed for the door. "I won't let him down - until he's good and dead."

2

Manny Hemmings was a dumpy little fat man of fifty seven; balding, with a few dozen long strands of black hair plastered across the top of his scalp. His tiny piggy eyes peered out through folds of fat, and his thick rubbery lips protruding beneath his bulbous nose seemed perfectly designed to hold the unlit cigar that constantly extended from his mouth. In fact no one could honestly claim that they ever saw Manny without the cigar, and the joke was that it wasn't a cigar at all, but some mutation of a tongue; sticking out at the world in defiance. Because Manny Hemmings was certainly defiant. He had been defiant at school; in his first job, and his second, and all the others that followed, until he decided to work for himself. Yes, Manny was permanently defiant. He hated all authority, except his own. And anyone rash enough to stand up to him was always at two disadvantages from the very start. The first was that they could never win, because Manny would rather die than let them, no matter how trivial the matter. And secondly, it was a principle of Manny's to kill anyone that had the nerve to throw defiance his way. Manny secretly feared anyone with that kind of nerve, because they couldn't be trusted. It could be a case of giving defiance today and giving orders tomorrow, so they had to go, and go they certainly did, in ways only limited by Manny's imagination.

Freddy Boyle stood on the Chinese carpet before his employer, who was sitting behind a large desk with the ease of a slug resting on a cabbage leaf. The room was well furnished; a mixture of business and home style. Manny liked to sleep in his office when his nagging wife Jean allowed him to, which wasn't often enough for him these days.

"So," said Manny, "how did it go, Freddy?"

"Sweet as a raisin, Boss," said Freddy with a nervous grin. "Only too happy to do ya a favour."

"Excellent," said Manny. "Now, it's taken me half the day to put the money into the crate, so I'm a bit tired and not in the mood to be upset. And you're not going to do anything to upset me - are you, Freddy?"

"Christ no, Boss!" Freddy exclaimed, beginning to sweat, and praying to a god he didn't believe in that Manny hadn't found out about his slip up at The Raven. "What makes ya think I'd do anythin to upset ya...?"

"Relax, Freddy," said Manny. "Just making sure. So tell me, have you ever seen a million quid in ten pound notes?"

Freddy was feeling too nervous to even try to imagine such a huge sum. "No, Boss, I never have."

Manny smiled. "Well, let me tell you, it certainly is a beautiful sight to behold. And the paper they use - it's got that crisp feel to it. I wish I could get my hands on a whole five tonne roll of that paper. And do you know what I'd do with it, Freddy?"

"Print more money with it, Boss?" Freddy suggested.

Manny nodded his head slowly, and it reminded Freddy of a puppet he saw once in the rear window of a car. "Perhaps...if there was some of it left over, I might run off the odd few hundred thousand. But no, Freddy, I have something else entirely planned for that delicious paper should I ever end up with it. I'd have a different beautiful woman wrapped up in a sheet of it every night - right over there on that sofa-bed, so that I could unwrap her. And do you know what I'd do then?"

"No, Boss," said Freddy, wishing he was anywhere else but where he was.

"Well, if you don't, you're too old and ugly to learn now!" Manny then roared with laughter, and his podgy face turned purple-red with the strain.

Freddy laughed too, but it was hoarse and dry. His employer frightened him like no man ever had. And many times Freddy reminded himself how those German generals in the war must have felt when they stood before Hitler - and they were brave, military men.

Being in the room with Manny was like being locked in a cage with a wild bear. Sometimes you would be quite safe, but not always, because sooner or later you would do the wrong thing and that would be your lot. Sometimes Freddy felt he would prefer to be in the cage with the bear..

"You know, it's truly amazing," Manny went on as the humour left him, "how a nice crisp ten pound note *feels* like it's worth ten pounds. I mean, put a gold sovereign in someone's hand with their eyes shut, and for all they know it could be made out of lead. But just the feel of a bank note tells you it's something special. Don't you think that's amazing?"

"Sure is, Boss. Just amazin."

"And do you know why I'm telling you all this, Freddy?" said Manny.

"Because ya love money, Boss...?"

Manny leaned forwards and put both elbows on the desk. His expression had changed to one of such coldness that Freddy took an involuntary step back.

Then Manny did something that further unnerved Freddy. He took the cigar out of his mouth and held it between the thumb and index finger of his right hand.

"Now you listen to me, Freddy," Manny said in a low voice. "I love that money more than anything in this whole world; more than my wife, and even more than the two kids I adore. Understand? If anyone lays a finger on a single note after I have handed my money over to you, I'll have you screaming for six months before I allow you to die."

"Christ, Boss!" Freddy stammered. "There's no need to threaten me! I'll look after yer money like it was my own! No one's goin to touch it! And if they try, then I'll rip their balls off!"

Manny leaned back in his leather chair, put his cigar back in his mouth, and smiled. "That's all I wanted to hear. Now, you go back and tell Mr Jack Blade that he can expect the package on Sunday - that's four days from now in case you can't count that high. And tell him to have a trolley handy. That box must weigh nearly two hundredweight with a million pounds inside it."

"I'll get right on it, Boss," said Freddy, the tension leaving him at the thought of being somewhere else.

"And one last thing?" said Manny.

"What's that, Boss...?"

"I hope for your sake you haven't blabbed about the contents of my crate to anyone...?"

Fear drove through Freddy's body like a spear and he held himself ridged to suppress the shiver that was trying to give him away. "Christ no, Boss!" he cried. "I wouldn't do that!"

"OK, just checking," said Manny.

"Oh, and another thing..." Manny called out just as Freddy reached the door.

Freddy turned. "Yea, Boss...?"

"You better continue to keep your mouth shut, or I'll be finding out the answer to a question that's been bugging me for years."

"What question's that, Boss?"

"What the screams of a man who has had his tongue pulled out with a pair of pliers, sounds like."

Freddy shuddered. "Sure thing, Boss. Mum's the word."

"It better be," said Manny.

3

"Hold the fuckin thing steady!" Freddy snarled as he allowed the wooden crate to slide out of the van towards the waiting trolley.

"I'm trying!" Jack snarled back. "But I can't hold the bloody trolley and help you with the crate as well!"

"Then put yer fuckin foot behind one of the wheels, ya stupid git!" Freddy shot back when the box knocked against the top of the trolley, nudging it away from the van.

Jack, both hands taking some of the crate's weight, stuck out his right foot and pulled the trolley back. Then he placed his foot behind one of the wheels. Suddenly the crate slipped and dropped down on to the trolley with a loud crash that sounded like the worst thunder bang either men had ever heard. And they even heard it echo a few times in the dark and empty streets.

"Christ all fuckin mighty!" Freddy cried, glancing around him nerviously. "What are ya tryin to do - invite every fuckin copper in the neighbourhood to come and watch!"

"It wasn't my fault," Jack replied. "Manny should have sent someone to give us a hand. He knows how heavy it is."

"Then fuckin tell him, not me!" said Freddy.

"I will, if I see him," said Jack. "Now let's get this inside. I saw a curtain move over there."

With Freddy's help, Jack steered the trolley through the back door of the pub; along a narrow corridor, then down a dozen stone steps to the cellar. At the far end of the cellar was a small empty room. The crate only just scraped through the room's narrow doorway, and it was with great relief that Jack finally locked the door with the twelve inch long key.

"Fuck me!" said Freddy, struggling to catch his breath. "Money ain't so attractive when ya have to shift it around like this!"

Jack grinned. "You're just knackered, Mate. You want to lay off those Woodbines. They've got more tar in them than the A1."

"I packed up six weeks ago, ya stupid sod!" Freddy snapped. "Anyway, where are ya goin to keep that bloody great key; not on yer fuckin key ring, I hope…?"

"I've got a good hiding place," said Jack. "Don't worry, it will be safe."

Freddy became instantly suspicious. "What hidin place…?"

"Don't be daft," said Jack. "It won't be a hiding place if anyone but me knows about it, now will it."

Freddy's teeth showed through angry lips. "Don't get cocky with me, ya fuckin bastard, or I'll bash yer stupid brains in!"

"Hey, take it easy!" Jack exclaimed. "Can't you take a joke!"

"This ain't no jokin matter! Now, show me the fuckin hidin place!"

Jack sighed loudly. "And I thought you were a mate."

"I'll be yer mate when this business is over, and I have reported back to Manny," said Freddy. "Now show me…and it better be good."

"Fair enough," said Jack. "It's through here."

Freddy followed as Jack went through another door; up twelve different stone steps, and out into a thirty by twenty foot enclosed yard. It was just before midnight, and a few dark clouds obscured the full moon. Jack then stopped and spread his arms. "This is it," he said with a smile.

"Ya mean yer hidin it out in the open!" said Freddy. "Yer fuckin crazy!"

"I don't see why not," said Jack. "We're not overlooked here, and quite by chance I discovered a loose brick in that wall over there. Behind the brick is a leaver; pull that and it opens a trapdoor right where you're standing. We can hide the money in the room below. It will be safer there. I'll start shifting it tomorrow night."

"So what's a room doin under a yard?" Freddy asked, looking at the paved area around his feet.

"This pub is two hundred years old; maybe even older. And it has a long history of smuggling. You see what we consider cheap drinks today such as coffee and tea were really expensive at one time and it was worth bringing them in without paying customs duty. This place was perfect for hiding the proceeds of that smuggling because who would ever think of searching out here. All a customs man would have seen were a few empty barrels. And it works the same now. Anyone snooping around here would find nothing. They certainly couldn't even imagine that in a room under their feet was a stash of a million quid."

Freddy grinned. "Hey...yer right, Mate! It's a fuckin fantastic place! So let's have a look at this smuggler's room. Which brick is it?"

Jack walked over to one of the lime-washed walls and pointed to a brick about six feet above ground level. "That one."

Freddy joined him and peered at the brick in the poor light. "Christ, Jack, I can't even see the fuckin join."

"That's the beauty of it," said Jack. "Have a go, but be careful...don't pull any of the mortar away; it's a bit on the crumbly side and it could make the brick stand out."

"Gotcha, Mate," said Freddy. Then he reached out and pulled at the brick with his fingers, but it didn't move. He grunted as he then attempted to loosen the mortar around the brick, but despite Jack's warning, the mortar remained fixed in place. "Fuckin solid enough here, ain't it, Mate," he complained. "You sure this is the right brick?"

Jack stood behind Freddy. "Course I am. And it takes a little bit of practice. So try again, Mate. It'll come out if you pull both ends of the brick at the same time. Use both hands."

"OK," said Freddy with a sigh. "But it don't look loose to me."

Freddy began pulling at the brick with both his hands now, but still the brick resisted. "Fuck this for a game of ludo!" he growled. "You get the bleedin thing out before I take a fuckin sledgehammer to it!"

"OK," said Jack.

But as Freddy was about to move aside there was a soft thud. His eyes went wide with shock, and his mouth opened, releasing a gasp. He staggered back from the wall, and slowly turned - both hands still raised.

Jack was smiling at him, and there was an expression on the landlord's face that Freddy had never seen before. It told him everything.

"Ya fuckin bast...!" said Freddy, but his words were lost in a long gurgle and the bubbles of blood that dribbled from his mouth and down his chin.

"Just look on the bright side, Freddy," Jack sneered. "You won't have to buy me that pint after all, and you definately won't have to listen to Karen telling you what a low life you are. In fact I think I have just done you a big favour. Aren't you going to thank me."

Freddy moved slowly forwards like a drunk; trying to get his outstretched hands around Jack's throat.

Jack slowly retreated, still smiling. "That's it, Freddy. Let's see how tough you are with a carving knife in your back. Here, I'll make it easy for you. I'll even let you grab hold of me so that you can show me how a cocky little shit, who usually has the backing of Manny Hemmings, manages when he's on his own."

Freddy continued on, his balance getting worse by the second. Then his fingers finally slipped around Jack's throat - but there was no strength left in them.

"Awww, you're not giving up already, are you...?" Jack cooed in disappointment as Freddy's legs buckled and he slipped slowly to the ground in a sitting position. "Shame on you, Mate. Mind you, I always suspected you were a quitter, and that's why I've never liked you, Freddy. You're just something that crawled out from under a rock somewhere and latched on to someone who had power and position in the community, because you could never achieve those things for yourself. And if that wasn't bad enough you then had the nerve to upset my staff and treat me like dirt. However, despite all that I'm going to give you a present; just something personal from me to you."

Jack suddenly kicked out with his right knee, smashing Freddy full in the face.

Freddy was thrown on his back by the blow, but he managed to force himself into a sitting position once more – blood from his broken nose mixing with the blood from his punctured lungs. Then he began sobbing and pleading for his life...a number of agonizing coughs seperating each word as it came.

"Shut up, you whining bastard – you'll wake the neighbours!" Jack ordered. "Now that one was for giving Karen some of your lip! But this one is for treating me like a wanker!"

Jack then kicked Freddy in the stomach, and a spray of blood shot out of his mouth.

"Oh Gawd...Oh Gawd!" Freddy cried between coughs - hanging on to Jack's trouser legs. "I didn't mean it, Jack! Please, get me a doctor! I'm dyin...!"

"You got that right," said Jack, shoving Freddy over on to his back. Then he stamped on his victim's left hand. The sound of thin bones snapping could be heard above Freddy's fresh cries.

"I think you liked that...didn't you," said Jack, pushing his foot into Freddy's face and twisting it. "Then you can have some more."

Freddy grabbed Jack's foot with his good hand. "No more – no more, Jack! Please, for the love of Gawd, don't hurt me no more! Take the money...I don't want it! And I won't grass on you to Manny – honest to

Gawd I won't! I'll say I was attacked by a gang before I got here! Please...Jack...get me a doctor! I'm bleedin all over the place!"

"You're telling me," said Jack. "I'm the one who has to clean it up, you selfish bastard."

"Please, Jack!" Freddy continued to beg. "Get me to a doctor!"

"Sorry, Mate," said Jack, "but allowing you to live would rather complicate my plans, and they're complicated enough already."

Freddy saw the terrible, almost inhuman expression that then appeared on his attacker's face, and he knew it was the look of death approaching. He screamed out in absolute terror.

Jack cursed, and lifting his right foot, he stamped repeatedly on Freddy's face until the screaming finally stopped for good.

Exhausted by his efforts, Jack reached down and pulled out the seven inch carving knife from between Freddy's shoulder blades. He then wiped the weapon clean on the dead man's jacket. And by morning, not a single sign was left that Freddy Boyle had paid a visit to The Raven the night before.

4

Manny Hemmings was mad; teeth grinding, cat strangling mad. But most of all he was a very worried man. Something terrible had gone wrong with his plans to outwit those interfering cops - he just knew it. In fact, he had it on good authority, because from the day he first got into the business twenty five years ago, he realized that the elbow of his left arm always tingled when something had gone wrong. And his elbow was always right. Manny called it his Spider Sense - just like the one Spider Man had, except in the super hero's case it was the back of his head that tingled - but Manny didn't see the need to split hairs over the anatomical difference. What did it matter what part of your anatomy tingled, just as long as some part of it did when trouble was heading your way.

Manny's elbow was throbbing as well as tingling now. And that could only mean that he had suffered a disaster. And since it wasn't his death, then it must be something nearly as bad, and that could only be the loss of his million pounds.

It was nine thirty on a Monday morning. It was drizzling out, and a few pigeons were sheltering on the window sill of Manny's nineteenth floor office. He hated pigeons; they always seemed to be making fun of his cigar as they pecked away at some cigarette butt on the ground. They never actually ate the bloody things, but they were constantly pulling and flicking the butts around, and why would they do that if not to annoy him. But the pigeons didn't have it all their own way, because whenever the opportunity presented itself, he would drive his car straight at them. Usually they were too quick for him and got out of the way in time. But just occasionally there was the satisfying thump as he hit one. Then he could enjoy the rest of his drive, happy in the knowledge that, at least temporarily, a measure of justice had been awarded to him.

But Manny wasn't interested in pigeons this morning. He was interested in the whereabouts of one Freddy Boyle - a crate containing a million pounds, and a small black book of names and addresses the crime squad would give their pensions for.

The door to Manny's office opened, and two handsome burly men entered. They were both dressed in hand made, pale blue suits without lapels that had been the fashion years earlier when worn by The Beatles. Some would say that at thirty five years of age, the Flynn brothers were not only out of date, but too old to be wearing such clothes. However, no one was stupid enough to put them straight.

"Well?" Manny demanded. "Have you found him...?"

"Sorry, Mr Hemmings," said Andy Flynn, the older of the twins by two hours. "No one's seen hide nor hair of him since yesterday."

"Damn!" Manny's fist slammed down on the desk. He chewed on his cigar for a few moments and watched the pigeons through the wet glass. Then he turned his attention back to the men. "I want you to pick up Jack Blade. He's the landlord of The Raven pub."

"Right you are, Mr Hemmings," said Andy, turning to leave.

"Not now, you idiots!" Manny retorted. "The cops are watching me round the clock. Pick him up after dark, and go easy on him. I don't know if he's involved yet."

"You mean in that crate of special magazines you told us was missin?" Pat Flynn asked in a strong Irish accent.

"No - in the disappearance of the crew of the Marie Celeste!" Manny spat. "Of course I mean the magazines!"

"Sorry, Mr Hemmings," said Pat, looking sheepish.

"Just get out!" Manny snapped, shaking his head in disgust.

In his living accommodation above the pub, Jack slept soundly. Most men would have been pacing the carpet by now, waiting for the wrath of Manny Hemmings to descend like a lightening bolt from Zeus. But Jack was made of sterner stuff than most men. His five year plan was at last in motion, and for him it was something to celebrate, not fear. And so he lay tucked up in his bed, with his eyes closed, thinking fond thoughts about a girl he knew back in Glasgow.

A single tap on the window pane opened Jack's eyes. He sat up when the sound was repeated. He looked at his watch. It was five minutes past three am. He climbed out of bed and walked across the room to the window. He pulled back the curtains and lifted the catch. The cold wind hit him in the face as he opened the window. He looked down into the dimly lit street. Two men stood looking up at him.

"What do you want!" he growled. "Can't you see the pub's closed!"

"We don't want a drink, Jack," said Pat Flynn. "Manny wants to see you."

Jack yawned and scratched his head. "It's three in the morning, Mate. Call back at a more reasonable hour. And what does he want to see me about anyway?"

"That's his business," said Pat. "Now, are you goin to come down, or do me and Andy here come up and get you?"

"There's no need to take that attitude," Jack muttered. "Hang on a minute. I'll put some clothes on."

When Jack came out of the pub a few minutes later, a grey Volvo car was next to the twins. Jack was firmly guided inside the back, where the two men sat either side of him. The driver, a swarthy looking man with a crooked nose, stared at him in the rear view mirror for a moment, then accelerated away.

"So…?" said Jack, staring at each of the men in turn. "What's this all about…?"

"You'll soon find out," Pat answered without looking at him.

"Is it about Freddy by any chance?" Jack asked. "Because if it is, I want a word with him. He said he'd meet me about something on Sunday night and he never showed. I hung around for nearly two hours, and I think it's taking a liberty changing your mind and not sending word. He could have phoned, couldn't he…?"

"I guess he could," said Pat, still staring fixedly ahead.

"You know something," Jack said after a while. "I've never been to Manny's office. Freddy tells me it's really comfortable, and Manny even sleeps there sometimes, on a sofa bed. Mind you, according to Freddy it's not one of those cheap store ones, but those fancy ones you only get from Harrods. I'm going to get myself an expensive sofa bed like that one of these days. Obviously not as good as Manny's, after all, he has more money then I have, and anyway I'll bet his room is a great deal bigger than mine so he has more…"

"Shut the fuck up, will you!" Pat snapped, turning to glare at Jack. "You're doin my fuckin nut in!"

"Sorry, Mate," said Jack. "Nerves I guess. You see, I can't help wondering what Manny wants me for at this hour of the morning."

"You'll soon find out! Now shut your gob!"

"Right..." said Jack, and he stayed silent for the rest of the journey. He must make sure he didn't over play the innocence card. He was dealing with professionals and they were probably expert at getting the truth out of people.

About ten minutes after leaving the pub, the Volvo turned right into Fletcher Street, then left through a pair of peeling industrial doors. Jack heard the doors pulled closed as the car came to a halt inside. And before he had time to take in his surroundings, he was bundled out of the car; through a small door, and into a huge derelict room which had a dirty concrete floor and at least three dozen metal framed windows with cracked panes. A bare bulb was suspended from the ceiling above the centre of the room, illuminating a single wooden chair and a small table with things on it. Next to the table stood a man dressed in a fine suit and overcoat. Jack recognized him immediately as Manny Hemmings.

"Glad you could come, Jack," Manny said. Then he indicated the chair. "Make yourself comfortable and we can have a chat."

The men escorted Jack across to the table.

Jack stared at the chair. "I'm fine standing, Mr Hemmings. Thanks anyway."

The smile that formed around Manny's ever present cigar wasn't friendly – it was too fixed for that. "Oh, but I insist, Jack. After all, what sort of host would I be if I didn't offer my guest a comfortable seat."

Jack slowly sat down. The thin chair creaked and altered shape under his fourteen stone weight.

"That's fine, Jack," said Manny. "Now, I know it may seem rather unusual, but I'm going to have to tie you up for a while...just so as to have your undivided attention. After all we wouldn't want distractions keeping us in this rather unsavoury building any longer than absolutely necessary."

Before Jack could protest, his hands were pulled hard behind the back rest, and secured with thick string. His legs were then tied to the chair.

"Comfortable...?" said Manny.

Jack nodded, and a trickle of sweat ran unseen down his back.

"Excellent." Manny then moved until he was standing before Jack, looking down at him. The smile was gone from his face, and there was a hard look in his eyes. "I have invited you here, Jack, because I'm faced with a problem which I'm sure you can help me with."

"Of course I'll help…if I can," said Jack.

"I know you will," Manny replied. "Now then, Jack, you know Freddy Boyle, don't you?"

Jack nodded.

"Of course you do," said Manny. "And last Wednesday he called into your nice little pub to ask a favour on my behalf, didn't he?"

"About the package you mean…?" said Jack. "Well, as a matter of fact I was just saying to…"

A sharp tut from Manny cut Jack off mid-sentence.

"Now don't interrupt me, there's a good chap," said Manny. "You just answer yes or no to my questions and that should be easy enough for an intelligent young man like you. But to continue, Freddy reported back to me that you were willing to look after a certain package for me - correct…?"

"If something's happened, I don't know anything about it!" Jack shot back. "He never showed up…!"

Manny's eyes narrowed. "Jack…Jack, I thought I told you not to interrupt. A simple yes or no will suffice."

Then Manny threw a look at Pat Flynn, who responded by punching Jack on the back of his head. The hard blow knocked his vision out of focus for a moment, then clarity returned.

"You shouldn't have made that necessary," said Manny. "But you see, Jack, I really do need my sleep. And yet here I am in this abandoned warehouse in the middle of the night discussing problems with you, when I should be tucked up in my bed. So, as you can imagine, I'm feeling a bit cranky. Now, you just answer yes or no to my questions, and then we can all get some sleep. Agreed…?"

"Yes, Mr Hemmings," said Jack.

Manny reached down and patted Jack's left shoulder. "That's fine, Jack, that's fine. So, on Sunday night I sent Freddy to deliver to your pub a large crate of very special magazines. Do you know what special magazines are, Jack – no, then I'll tell you. You see, they come from America, and they contain a great deal of pornographic images. They also contain something else - something not to everyone's taste, and certainly not to mine. But there are a lot of very bored rich people who will pay over a hundred pounds each for those magazines, so you can see how I would want them back. As I said, they're not to my taste. Having the cast of a film actually killed on camera is not my thing at all. But, if the demand is there, the goods must be made available, and like any good businessman

I try to provide for that demand. But my question to you, Jack is, where are my magazines?"

"I don't know, Mr Hemmings," Jack replied, his voice trembling.

"I think you do know, Jack," said Manny. "And it makes me very angry when someone not only steals from me, but then tells me lies to my face as if I was some gullible corner shop owner dealing with kids nicking his sweets."

"Honest to God, Mr Hemmings, I'm not lying to you!" Jack wailed. "Freddy never turned up!"

"Of course he turned up," said Manny. "After all, I sent him, and he certainly wouldn't have taken it into his simple head to go somewhere else. Freddy is loyal to me. True enough it is loyalty exacted from him by fear, but loyalty nevertheless. And therefore he will go any place I send him, and since I sent him to your pub with my property, then it stands to reason that he delivered that property into your hands. So where are my magazines, Jack? Come on now, I'm losing all patience with you?"

"But he never showed up, Mr Hemmings!" Jack shook his head in desperation. "Honest he didn't! I waited for over two hours and he never showed! Honest to Christ he didn't!"

"Oh dear," said Manny, clicking his tongue a few times. "Is this going to be your answer every time I ask you? You're being very uncooperative you know, and I have to confess that I'm becoming a little peeved with you."

"But I don't know what else to say, Mr Hemmings!" said Jack. "It's the truth! I wouldn't do anything like that! Ask anyone - they'll tell you! I don't get involved in that kind of business! I'd be too scared! All I want to do is run my pub! I wouldn't steal any magazines from you - honest I wouldn't!"

Manny looked hard at Jack for a few moments, seeing the sweat on his face, and the wide, staring eyes. He knew fear when he saw it, and this man was afraid.

Manny turned his attention to the small table on his left. He reached down and picked up a stainless steel dentist tool. It had a long round handle, with a fine hook at one end. He held it up, scrutinizing the workmanship with half closed eyes. Then he looked at Jack once more.

"I have to tell you, Jack that Pat and his brother Andy are keen to show me a new trick they have invented with this little implement - something to do with teeth and nerves I believe. However I suspect it would be far too gruesome for my sensitive nature. And you know something else,

Jack, I believe you're telling me the truth. I believe that no matter what we do to you, you will stand by your story because it's the truth - isn't it?"

A broken laugh shot from Jack and he began nodding his head frantically. "I am, Mr Hemmings! Honest to God I am! That's what I've been trying to tell you all along! I wouldn't steal from you - honest I wouldn't!"

Manny dropped the tool on the table. "Then we won't be needing this little lot. However, you have presented me with a fresh problem, Jack. You see, you're an honest man - aren't you?"

"I try to be, Mr Hemmings," said Jack.

"Of course you do; that's one of the reasons Andy and Pat are not demonstrating their new technique on you at this very moment. I would only allow them to do that to someone who is keeping something from me, and since you are clearly not, what would be the point. The most we could do is to force you to tell me lies. However, I regret to say that the honesty that has protected you from some very unpleasant torture, has also put me in a rather awkward position."

Jack stared at Manny with tear filled eyes. "How do you mean, Mr Hemmings?"

"I mean," said Manny, "what does an honest man do when someone hurts him?"

Jack shook his head.

"Why, he goes to the police of course, and tells them what the nasty men did to him," Manny continued.

"I wouldn't do that!" Jack replied with a nervous laugh. "You didn't hurt me, Mr Hemmings!"

"But your head, Jack?" said Manny with a serious expression. "Pat hit you? I saw him do it?"

Jack laughed again and shrugged. "Well I won't tell if you won't, Mr Hemmings. Anyway that was nothing. I've had a harder punch than that from Karen when I slapped her behind before she got to know me."

Jack heard a shuffle behind him and flinched.

"No more of that, Pat," Manny warned. "I don't believe Jack was insulting your prowess with your fists. He's found himself in a very difficult position and just trying to get himself out of it as best he can You can't blame him for that, now can you?"

"I guess not, Mr Hemmings," came the grumpy reply, and Jack relaxed a little.

"Now then, Jack," said Manny, "as I was saying, you might go to the police, and to be honest I just can't handle any more trouble at the moment. I know a certain high ranking policeman who would just love to have me banged up while they are free to go through everything I own with a fine toothcomb. And with me not around to thwart their efforts, who knows what they might find. I would not see daylight again for at least twenty five years. And at my age, that would be a death sentence. So you can see my dilemma, can't you Jack. I just can't afford to take the risk."

Jack's head darted around in panic. "What do you mean, Mr Hemmings? What are you going to do to me…?"

"I'm sorry, Jack. You're a good chap, and in a way I admire you. But you're dangerous to me now, and I can't allow you to hang around that pub of yours, deciding whether or not to go to the police when your courage returns. That would be very foolish of me."

Manny then moved away from the table, and Jack's breath caught in his throat when a cold liquid gushed down on top of him; soaking his hair; his clothes, and spreading in a pool around his feet. Then the strong smell of petrol struck his sinuses, and a fit of violent coughing overtook him.

Pat Flynn appeared in front of Jack and placed a small black box in the pool of petrol on the floor.

"That little device is on a timer, Jack," said Manny, rolling his unlit cigar around his mouth. "In five minutes it will generate a tiny spark and you will go up in flames. But don't worry too much. I'm told that if you can breath in the fumes, you'll die a lot quicker. There won't be so much pain."

Jack screamed, and rocked himself violently from side to side.

"Shame on you, Jack," Manny tutted. "At least have a little dignity."

"No - please!" Jack begged. "You can't do this! I haven't done anything to you, Mr Hemmings! Please! Oh God, I don't want to die! I won't say anything! I won't!"

"But you might, and I can't take that chance," said Manny.

"I'll do anything – anything, Mr Hemmings! Please don't burn me! You can have my pub! The key's are in my pocket! Please, Mr Hemmings, I don't want to die like this!"

"We all have to die sometime," said Manny. "And I suppose more than a few others will join you before this business is over with. Now, goodbye, Jack Blade. And think on this. Honesty isn't always the best policy – especially in a business that doesn't know the meaning of the word."

Jack began crying as Manny and his men left the room. His sobs filled the huge space with a ghostly, haunting echo.

The minutes passed and Jack went on with his struggles to break free. His efforts tore the flesh from his wrists and stained the string with his blood, but still he could not free himself. And when he tried to bounce himself away from the petrol he discovered that the chair was secured to the floor with a loop of chain.

He called out a few times, making all kinds of promises, including working for nothing for Manny. But each time there was no reply.

Then there was a click from the device.

Jack screamed at the top of his voice and threw himself backwards. The chair toppled over, dropping him into the large puddle of petrol.

He thrashed about trying to move away, but the heels of his shoes slipped on the wet floor.

He then stopped moving and tried to look at the device, but his legs prevented him from seeing it. But where were the flames? He couldn't even smell any burning? What was going on?

Then realization came to him and a huge surge of relief rose up inside him.

He laughed out loud. The device had gone off; he had heard the click. But nothing had happened. It didn't work. There was no spark. They had made a mistake. *He wasn't going to burn! He was going to live!*

"You'll do yourself a mischief, Jack," said Manny's voice from behind. Then powerful hands were righting the chair.

Jack stared in confusion as Manny's smiling face appeared in front of him.

"Sorry about that little charade, Jack," said Manny. "But I had to be absolutely sure that you didn't have my magazines. And if you had you would most certainly have been offering me a deal by now. And don't worry, this stuff is ninety five per cent water, and the devise is harmless."

"Jesus...Jesus...Jesus!" Jack cried, sagging in his chair.

"Cut our friend loose and give him a shot of whisky, will you, Pat," said Manny. "I do believe he's had a bit of a fright."

Jack snatched the quarter bottle of scotch that was handed to him, and took great long gulps of the fiery liquid.

"He *has* had a fright, hasn't he," Manny quipped.

A sudden fit of coughing racked Jack's body.

Manny laughed. "Take it easy there, old chap. I have a great deal invested in you, so I don't want you turning up your toes on me just yet."

Jack quickly recovered, and stood up unsteadily. Pat supported him.

"Now don't you fret," said Manny. "I'll make it up to you soon. And

Ronnie will drive you back to your pub where you can get into some dry clothes and get some rest."

"Thanks, Mr Hemmings," said Jack. "And I hope you find your magazines."

"It's good of you to care, Jack," Manny replied. "Now you get going. But you will be hearing from me soon."

As Jack let himself into the pub, he closed the door behind him and heard the Volvo drive off. He then made his way to the bar and poured himself a double measure of scotch from the optics. He downed it in one go, and then he began to laugh.

"Sweet, fucking shit!" he exclaimed, pouring himself another drink. "Sweet fucking shit, it worked! What a performance! Jack, my old son, you could show Paul fucking Newman himself a thing or two about acting!"

Then still laughing he grabbed a bottle of Bells and sat at one of the tables. He was ecstatic. Things couldn't have gone better. It was obvious that Manny was going to send for him when his money disappeared, and he was relieved that Manny hadn't tortured him - at least not physically. Of course he could have taken the torture, he was no stranger to pain, but it was great that he didn't have to. And that business with the petrol - what a gamble. He had heard about big time gamblers putting their homes on the table - boasting afterwards about the risk they took. Risk - what fucking risk? They should try sitting in a gallon of petrol tied to a chair, and watch their captors leave the room as a timer counted the minutes to ignition. They should try keeping stumm and take the risk that it was all for real - *that* was gambling! And now that he was beyond suspicion, he could continue with his plan.

From carefully orchestrated conversations over the years, he had found out that Manny had about seven hundred people working for him. However, most of them were just low paid help; running errands; delivering packages and generally keeping their eyes open and their ears to the ground. These people were of no interest at all to Jack. His interest was fixed solely on those closer to Manny; men such as Andrew Winterton. - an ex bank manager who now advised Manny on the intrinsic workings of the financial system, and who wasn't afraid to get his hands into some dirty dealings. Then there was Phil Braddon, one of Manny's greatest assets; an ex Detective Inspector with the Met. Phil had been forced to resign after an internal investigation into corruption, but he still had friends in the Force. Manny paid Phil forty pounds a week more than anyone else - he considered him that valuable.

The brothers Andy and Pat Flynn were valuable to Manny in quite a different way to Phil. They were what the Mafia would call the Enforcers of the organization. And when you saw them coming, you knew you were in serious trouble.

The brothers were twins, but not identical - except in their love of violence. They both stood at six feet three inches, with the kind of physiques javelin throwers had - broad shouldered and with tremendous upper body strength. Twenty hours a week at a local gym kept them looking like that. They went everywhere together and even shared their women who were many, since they were thirty five year old, blond haired, blue eyed Adonis's. A few people liked them, but not anyone who really knew their true nature. Andy and Pat had six men working for them directly, because despite the brother's confidence in dishing out punishments, there were occasions when they had to go in mob handed. It was amazing how many fathers, brothers, nephews, and cousins came out of the woodwork to help some stupid sod who had decided that he wasn't going to pay protection money any more. Not that their support ever did the stupid sods any good. The Flynn brothers had never lost a fight in their entire lives, and would never allow anyone to change that. And that's where their six subordinates came in – violent men who enjoyed hurting people nearly as much as the Flynns.

Lastly there was Jimmy Tanner. Now Jimmy was something of an enigma. No one knew anything about his background; not even Manny. He turned up one day in Manny's office after a discussion between mutual acquaintances, and the next thing everyone knew Jimmy Tanner was the boss's right hand man. If you desperately needed to talk to Manny, and he wasn't available, then Jimmy was the one to see. His words were Manny's words; his decisions were Manny's decisions, and his displeasure was Manny's displeasure. Jimmy Tanner may be a thirty nine year old, five feet five, seven stone strand of soggy spaghetti, as someone once described him, but he could scare the shit out of men twice his size with a stare from those dark eyes of his that looked like they belonged to the devil himself.

These were the men that Jack Blade decided years before that he must eliminate before he could finally take over the organization from Manny. Because any one of them could already be harbouring a secret desire to replace their boss, and they would never tolerate an outsider beating them to it. No, Manny's Inner Circle must be done away with first, so that when he eventually took the reigns of the organization that controlled much of the prostitution, illegal gambling, and drug running in that part of London, there would be no one left with teeth to oppose him. The cuckoo chick had the right idea, Jack frequently reminded himself; push everyone else out of the nest so that you got all the food on offer.

Of course Jack realized that he couldn't achieve his plans alone. And when he had told Freddy Boyle that he watched a lot of gangster films, he wasn't lying. It was an inspiration to Jack how the films and books often reflected events in real life, and it was clear that the greatest danger to any crime boss was the informer; the squealer; the snitch; the Judas; the enemy within. No matter how well you treat some people, they will drop you in the shit the first chance they get, because they have no loyalty or principles. They would have you sent down for twenty five years to save them from three months without their freedom. Yes, the grass was the problem, but Jack believed that he had found a way to overcome that particular problem. And his method was to vet his possible recruitments, like no recruits had been vetted before. He had already chosen his men, but only after talking to them for five years. Every time they came into his pub, he made time for them; gave them free drinks when they were down on their luck, or he would bung them the odd fiver. Of course he always allowed them to pay him back when they were flush once more. This was important if he was to allay suspicion, and give the unquestionable impression that he was simply a nice chap who was always willing to help those in trouble. And it certainly worked, for two of his new employees had told him they considered him a member of their family.

'Jesus Christ, Jack, you're a fucking saint - a real fucking saint!' one grateful recipient had once declared as he staggered towards the door with two fivers in his back pocket.

Jack had smiled at the comment. Little did the man know that he would soon be given the chance to really show his gratitude.

5

It was seven fifteen pm on the Wednesday following Jack's ordeal in the abandoned warehouse. The Raven was reasonably busy and Jack had brought in his other female member of staff Mandy to give Karen a hand. They were coping well, selling the drinks and keeping the customers happy.

Jack looked at his watch for the fourth time within the last five minutes. The man he was expecting was late, which was unusual for him. Then the man came through the door, and sat on a stool at the bar.

"Hey, Tom!" Jack shouted above the noise. "Come down this end - it's a bit quieter!"

Tom Smith approached and flopped on to a stool opposite Jack.

"Usual?" said Jack.

"Make it a fucking double will you, Mate," said Tom, with a weary tone to his voice. "I certainly need it after the poxy day I've just had."

Jack placed a double brandy on the counter. Tom took the drink down in one loud gulp.

"I bet that hit the spot just right," said Jack grinning. "Another...?"

"In a minute," said Tom. "I've got all night to relax and I'd rather it wasn't by being flat on my back."

A loud burst of laughter drew Jack's attention. A group of lads were messing about But since it seemed good natured and Karen, who was serving their drinks, was laughing also, he didn't intervene. He turned his attention back to Tom who was staring into his empty glass as if he might just find something he needed inside it besides alcohol.

"Fancy a game, Mate?" said Jack.

Tom shrugged. "Fine by me."

"Karen," Jack called out. "We're going upstairs for a game of cards. Hold the fort will you."

"You two go and play," Karen grinned as she served a customer. "And no fighting over who wins the most matches. I'm too busy to sort out any squabbles between naughty boys."

Jack laughed and took a bottle of brandy, scotch, and two glasses with him as he and Tom went up the back stairs to the flat. In the living room, Jack cleared a small table that had two chairs by it. The chairs were old with thick padding and high backs. They were also falling apart with the fabric worn in places, and a few of the joints were loose. But Jack couldn't bear to throw them out. They were there when he bought the pub and somehow seemed to have more right to be there than him. Anyway, they were still extremely comfortable to sit in so long as there wasn't too much moving about.

"Poker?" Jack inquired as they sat down.

"Deal em up, Pardner," said Tom, pouring himself a drink.

"So, how are things?" Jack asked, dealing out the cards.

"Same as usual," Tom replied. "Sandra wants us to go on holiday to the Canaries with the new neighbours. She knows damn well we can't afford it, but she will keep on."

"I can help you there," said Jack, pouring himself a whisky.

"You've helped us enough already, Mate," said Tom. "If it wasn't for you, I'm sure me and Sandra would have split up by now. We love each other, but Sandra wants to go places; you know - see Europe; visit the pyramids for Christ Sakes. All that way to stare at a fucking great rockery. She must think she's married to a bloody millionaire."

"She could be..." Jack said slowly, fixing his eyes on Tom.

Tom picked up his cards. "What's that supposed to mean?"

"I don't mean an actual millionaire," said Jack. "But I could fix it so that you and Sandra and the kids could have at least one great holiday a year - any place in the World that takes your fancy."

Tom stared back at his friend. "That would be a miracle, Mate. So, does God owe you a favour or something...?"

"Fraid not," said Jack. "But I could still make it happen."

Tom sighed. "Look, Mate, I'm finding life a bit tough at the moment. The boss at the security firm has been on my back about the way some of the staff under me are turning up late some mornings. Sandra has been shoving holiday brochures under my nose when I'm trying to eat my breakfast or dinner – I can't remember the last time I actually saw the food I've been eating. And the kids are going on about being laughed at by their friends because they don't even have a second hand bicycle. So if you have something to say, just give my poor old brain a break and spit it out nice and clear will you?"

"All right then," said Jack. "I'm going to kill Manny Hemmings; take over his organization, and I want you to help me do it."

Tom continued to stare at Jack. Then he blinked a few times. "Listen, Mate, how much did you have to drink before I showed up tonight, because you are definately not making any sense?"

"I'm serious, Tom," said Jack. "I've been planning this for five years - waiting for the right time to make my move. And that time came when Freddy Boyle walked in to my pub last week and told me that Hemmings needed my help."

"Don't talk so fucking stupid!" Tom retorted. "Manny Hemmings is a vicious killer, and you think you can just knock on his door, and do what - shoot him with a machine gun, and then shoot all those hundreds of scumbags he has working for him, just like you've seen in the film The St Valentines Day Massacre! You're cracked, Mate, so shut up and play cards. I'm in the mood for giving someone a good pasting, and you have been elected."

"I *am* going to get rid of some of his employees as a matter of fact," Jack replied, "but not in the crude way you put it. It will take careful planning."

"Planning my fucking arse!" Tom snapped. "Just get on with the game, and stop pissing around!"

Jack suddenly swept his arm across the table, and the cards, glasses and bottles of drink flew across the room. "I'm being fucking serious, Tom!" he spat.

The silence between the two men that followed, was eventually broken by a female voice from downstairs.

"I thought I told you two boys not to fight over matches!" Karen shouted. "Now sort it out or I'm coming up! You've been warned!"

"It's OK, Love!" Jack shouted back. "Tom had a few up his sleeve! You go back to the bar!"

Tom had hastily retrieved the now half empty bottles, and placed them back on the table. "That Karen's a lippy cow," he said with a grin, refilling the glasses which had been saved from destruction by a thick carpet.

"Couldn't run this place without her," said Jack.

"Then marry the girl if you think so much of her," said Tom, "or do you think she's a bit too old for you. Because if you do, then you're wrong. Sandra is six years older than me and it makes no difference at all. In fact

I sometimes think *I'm* too old for *her*. And you know very well that Karen fancies the pants off you, so what more do you want."

"She's not too old, but she is too bossy," said Jack. "She'd have me in a pinny within a month – I swear she would."

"All right, Mate, you win?" said Tom in a firm voice. "You have my attention now? Let's hear it?"

Tom's expression was granite hard as Jack explained everything to him - about killing Freddy - the million pounds, and the visit to the warehouse. And when Jack had finished, there was a strange look in Tom's eyes.

"So, what do you think?" Jack asked.

"I think," said Tom in a flat tone, "that I haven't the faintest idea who the hell you are."

"What's that supposed to mean?" said Jack, taken back by the answer.

"I mean, I seem to be *looking* at good old Jack Blade: I seem to be *listening* to good old Jack Blade. I even seem to be *talking* to good old Jack Blade. But the strange thing is it's fucking obvious that it *isn't* good old Jack Blade sitting across the table from me; rather some raving lunatic who has taken it into his head to sacrifice his ownership of one of the best pubs in London, and his life, for no bloody good reason at all that I can see."

"Never mind all that crap!" Jack growled. "I'm offering you a chance to improve your life; a chance to give Sandra and the kids what they deserve. What right do you have to deny them that?"

"And what about giving Sandra a dead husband, and my kids a dead father?" Tom retorted. "Well, come on, good old Jack Blade, what about those insignificant little details....?"

"Do you think I would involve you if there was any danger to your life?" Jack demanded.

A grunt shot from Tom. "Yesterday I would have said no way! But now I see that our so called friendship was all just a con on your part! All you wanted was someone who you thought was as crazy as you to help you go after Manny Hemmings!"

A sarcastic tone then entered Tom's voice.

"What did you say to me so many times in the past – oh, I remember now *'Have a few free drinks until you get back on your feet, Tom! What, in a bit of trouble, Tom! Go on, have a few quid on me! After all, what are Mates for!'* But when it comes right down to it, Jack, you're just full of shit!"

A loud sigh came from Jack. "Look, Tom, I admit I knew for a long time that I was going to need your help. But that doesn't mean our friendship isn't Kosher. All I did was put off asking for that help until the time was right. For all I knew the opportunity to carry out my plan might never have presented itself. Don't you see, I had to wait for Manny to approach me. If I had involved myself in any way with him, I would now be under suspicion about the million pounds."

"You are under suspicion, you stupid pratt!" Tom replied. "You just told me he poured petrol over you in a warehouse and threatened to send you up in flames! Now, in my books that means he's suspicious!"

Jack leaned forwards on the table. There was an excitement in his eyes Tom had never seen before. "You're wrong, Mate, Manny was never really suspicious of me, but who else could he pull in about it! It's a bit like when you're looking everywhere for the kitchen towel say! You end up looking in the fridge - not because you think it's in there but you're desperate and can't exclude any place! I gambled that he would still need me in the future, and I was right!"

"And what if you had been wrong?" said Tom.

"All gamblers lose sometime, Mate! But my instincts told me I had a winning hand!"

"All right," said Tom, some of his anger evaporating. "Say I accept your explanation for now? What about that time last year when you helped me out over that bit of trouble I had at Robert Taver's betting shop? And I want the truth now; no lies or I'm out of here for good? If you weren't going to need me, would you still have got me out from under?"

"OK, Tom, I'll level with you," said Jack. "If it had been during the first year of my taking over this pub, then no. I'd have sympathised with you, but two hundred pounds is a great deal of money. But when you told me last year, I was only too happy to do what I could, because you're a mate, Tom. No matter how this turns out, you're a mate. And that's why we will still be friends, even if you want nothing to do with my plans. All I would ask you to do is keep stumm about them."

"Just one other thing," said Tom. "Does all this have anything to do with the fact that Lynda's pimp was working for Manny Hemmings?"

Jack was caught out by the directness of the question. He shifted uncomfortably in his seat. "I suppose it does," he said in a quiet voice. "I know you blame Manny for Lynda taking the overdose that killed her, and that it burns you up inside knowing he will never be brought to account."

Tom's expression was cold as he stared into Jack's eyes. "I see you plan things well when you put your mind to it, good old Jack Blade. So, what's in it for me?"

Jack's expression brightened. "Well, I've got a million quid put aside for a start. Of course I can't touch it, expect for a couple of thousand for expenses. You would be immediately on the payroll at seventy five pounds a week. Mind you, you'll have to keep your old job for the time being. Outwardly, nothing must change. But when I eventually take over from Manny, you can run the organization with me, or you can have a two hundred thousand pay off. And you will have had revenge for Lynda."

"It could never be revenge enough for my daughter's death," said Tom, "And I'll admit it's a great offer, but I'm still not sure – it's a very big step to take."

Jack stared at Tom. He liked the man. There was a certain quality about him that invited trust at first sight. And he didn't at all look anything like the sort of man who would go up against a villain such as Manny Hemmings. Yes, he was tall, with a solid build. But he was also edging over forty and had little previous criminal experience. Yet Jack knew he needed Tom. He couldn't proceed without him. He just had to say yes; he just had to!

Then Tom grinned. "You got yourself a deal, Mate!" he declared.

Jack slapped the table and laughed. He stuck out his right hand. "That's excellent, Tom! You won't regret it; I promise you!"

Tom grinned and shook hands. "Don't you worry, good old Jack Blade - I won't. So where's the money, and what have you done with that little rat, Freddy Boyle?"

Jack stared at his friend for a few moments, as if undecided. Then he poured them both a drink. "Come back just after twelve tonight, Mate. I want to show you something very special."

6

The courtyard at The Raven pub wasn't particularly large, being just over thirty feet by twenty. It was completely surrounded by two storey buildings belonging to the pub, and no windows looked down on it. The only access to the courtyard was through the cellar, and therefore not that many people knew of its existance. Therefore it was perfect for what Jack had in mind.

It was ten minutes past midnight. There was a stiff breeze blowing, and the sky was overcast. Out in the courtyard, Tom scratched the back of his neck as a gnat had a go at it.

"What the hell are we doing out here?" Tom complained when something far larger then buzzed in his right ear.

"Showing you what must be one of the best kept secrets in the area," Jack replied. "Now, point that torch on the wall - just there next to the flower tub."

Tom placed the beam of his torch on the brick wall, about two feet above the paved ground. And as he watched, Jack knelt, and using a knife, teased one of the bricks out.

Jack threw a grin at Tom, then pulled out five more bricks, until there was a square hole in the wall.

"Come closer and shine the light in here," Jack ordered.

Tom knelt beside Jack and shone the light inside the dark hole. He saw a iron wheel about the size of a saucer sticking out of the inner brickwork. It looked very old.

Jack reached in with both hands and began turning the wheel clockwise, but slowly, because it was clear that great effort was required. And as Jack turned and turned, he eventually began to grunt with each effort.

"This fucking thing doesn't get any easier," he complained. "I must have poured a gallon of lubricating oil on it but it's just as stiff as ever."

"Want me to have a go?" Tom asked.

"You're alright, Mate," said Jack. "Almost got it."

Finally, after about six more turns he relaxed. "Done."

"So what the hell is it?" said Tom.

"You read Alice in Wonderland when you were a kid, didn't you?" said Jack.

"So...?"

"Well, I'll be the rabbit and you can be Alice. Now, fetch me those two crowbars over there by the door."

Tom was soon back with the crowbars, and commented that one end of each of them had a very long straight blade that was six times wider than any he had seen before. The blades were also very thin. The crowbars also looked very old.

"They were made for a specific purpose," said Jack, taking them from Tom. "Now, watch and all will be revealed."

Tom followed as Jack then moved to the centre of the courtyard. He handed Tom a crowbar. "Right, Mate, you stand on the other side of this flagstone and do exactly as I do. And whatever happens, don't get fucking heavy handed. I could never replace one of them exactly if they got damaged."

When Jack carefully slipped the thin blade of the crowbar between the join of the flagstone and the one next to it, Tom did likewise, and was surprised to see the blades go down at least twelve inches.

"Go careful here, Tom," said Jack. "Just slowly push back on the handle until it's resting on the ground."

Tom had to throw all his weight on the crowbar before it would move. And as it went down, the flagstone slowly came up.

"Now, put your foot on the bar and give me a hand," Jack ordered. And between them, they managed to lift one end of the ten inch thick flagstone up and over, so that it lay upside down.

"Fucking thing must weigh a tonne!" Tom panted.

"Good as," Jack panted back. "Probably had to be that thick so that it wouldn't sound hollow if tapped by a customs man."

Tom saw two half rings of metal set into the underside of the flagstone. "What are those for?"

"That wheel in the wall draws back a long bolt that holds this flagstone down," Jack replied. "With that bar in position you could never lift it out. It was a clever idea for those days. Now, let's get on with it."

Tom shone his torch on to the spot where the four foot by four foot flagstone had sat. But instead of solid ground, there was a square hole that was just a bit smaller than the flagstone, and the sides were smooth. It was obviously man made. Tom saw metal rungs descending down one wall.

"It's a bit of a squeeze because of the size of the rungs," Jack said as he lowered himself into the hole. "People must have been a hell of a lot thinner in those days. Now, follow me down, and watch your step. I don't fancy you dropping on my head."

"How deep is it?" Tom asked.

"About twenty feet." Jack's voice sounded hollow as his head vanished into the shaft.

A couple of minutes later Tom found himself standing in a small room about ten feet square. On an old oak bench against one wall were eight bulging knapsacks.

Tom's eyes were wide with excitement. "Is that the money?" he asked. "Is that really a million pounds…?"

"Look for yourself," Jack laughed. "It won't bite you."

Tom walked over to the bench. He tentatively reached out and unbuckled one of the sacks, which he noticed was the waterproof canvas kind. He reached inside the sack and pulled out a six inch thick wad of ten pound notes with a paper band around it. His torch illuminated the money, and Tom took a deep breath.

"Fuck me with a toilet brush, Jack! How much am I holding?"

"What - that little bundle," said Jack. "Hardly worth bothering about, Mate. Can't be more than six thousand."

Tom gasped. "Six thousand quid - just in this one pack! And how many packs in each sack?"

"Since I could hardly complain to Hemmings if I'm a bit shy of a full million, I didn't bother to count them. Anyway, when you've seen one bundle of six thousand pounds, you've seen them all. I just filled up the sacks from the crate and stashed them down here for the time being."

"A fucking million quid!" Tom laughed with fresh excitement. "I'm actually standing next to a *million quid!* I can't believe it! Wait until Sandra hears about this!"

"If you want to keep her alive you won't tell her…at least not yet," Jack warned.

Some of Tom's excitement faded. "Of course. Sorry, Mate, just got a bit carried away. It's not every day a working man like me gets anywhere near a stash of money like this."

Jack grinned. "I felt the same way myself when I first opened the crate."

"So," said Tom, gazing at the money in his hand as if it was his new born child, "what did you do with Boyle and the crate?"

"I put the crate in the back of Freddy's van, and took them both for a long drive. I also took along a motorbike so that I could get back and get rid of any incriminating evidence."

"I haven't heard of his body being found?" said Tom. "You must have found a good place?"

"Hid him and the van in Epping Forest," Jack answered. "He'll be found eventually I suppose. And I put him in the driver's seat so they'll think his passenger killed him."

"Won't forensics discover that he was killed elsewhere?" said Tom. "I hear they're getting pretty clever in finding out such things these days?"

"Not after what I did to him with a lump of concrete, I shouldn't think," said Jack.

Tom slowly put the money back in the sack and buckled it up. "You know something, Mate," he said without turning round. "You're beginning to scare the shit out of me now."

"Naaa…" said Jack. "That's just opening night nerves. Now, let's get back up top."

Tom felt a sudden draft on the back of his head. He shone the torch around the room, and saw a five foot high door set in the wall opposite him.

"That leads directly to the river," said Jack. "Don't forget, this was used by smugglers."

"You ever been in there?" Tom asked.

Jack pulled a face. "Couple of times, but it stinks like a down and out's underpants."

"Any chance of anyone getting in from the other end?"

"Doubt it. Part of the tunnel fell in a few years back. Don't worry, Tom, the money is safe down here."

"I wasn't just thinking about the money," said Tom. "I'm sure plenty of people know we are friends, and if Hemmings finds out that you have all this I'm bound to end up in the same deep shit you will definately be in."

"Guilty by association," said Jack. "Well you can stop worrying. I haven't spent five years planning this only to have it all come to nothing because someone blundered in here. There's only one way to reach this room, and you just used it."

7

Manny Hemmings sat comfortably on his sofa bed, sipping a glass of fifteen year old single malt whisky, without taking the cigar out of his mouth. His feet were resting on a stool, and he was watching a TV set on the other side of his office. He was in a depressed mood. A million pounds of his money was gone, and the only man who knew where it was had vanished from the face of the Earth. His contacts at the airports had reported nothing - nor had anyone at the ports of Dover, Southampton, Harwich, Liverpool or any of the others. Of course he still had quite a bit of cash left, but that was mostly for the police to find if they were good at their jobs. On the other hand his million pounds was to give him a fresh start if the investigation went badly for him. Now it was missing, and so was Freddy Boyle.

The newscaster began the news by reporting something about the Prime Minster. But his second report sent Manny's cigar flying out of his mouth, and his drink slopping on to his lap.

"Andrew...Andrew!" he screamed at the top of his voice. "Get your poncy arse in here now, you lazy fucker!"

The door quickly opened and a forty six year old dandy of a man stepped into the room.

"I do wish you wouldn't use such coarse language at me, Manny," he bemoaned in an educated accent. "You know how much it offends me."

"Shut the fuck up and listen to this!" Manny spat.

The newscaster reported how the police forensics team were still at the crime scene, and that all that could be said at the moment was that the victim was in the driver's seat of a red Ford van, and that he had been battered to death with a lump of concrete. The only content of the van was a large wooden crate, which was empty.

"It seems that we now know what happened to Mr Boyle," said Andrew, as if discovering the fate of a missing sock.

"Who the fuck said it was Freddy!" Manny snapped. "For all I know that little shit killed whoever was helping him, to throw us off the scent! I'll bet you a bottle of fifty year old malt that whoever was found in that van has had his face smashed up so that he couldn't be identified! And why would the killer take the time to do that if not to make it hard to prove that it wasn't Freddy. And the only person I know who would want me to think it was Freddy Boyle is Freddy Boyle himself! Well, I'm not falling for it! I'd rather watch that money go up in flames than let that little shit spend a single penny of it!"

"But I thought you said that Mr Boyle was far too frightened of you to carry out such an audacious theft?" Andrew replied. "After all, his fear was the very reason you chose him to approach Mr Blade in the first place?"

"That was before *this*, you moron!" Manny retorted pointing at the TV. "Now get out there and find Boyle and my money!"

Andrew made a disapproving pout. "Me? But I wouldn't even know where to start…?"

"Start by getting on with it!" Manny roared. "I pay you two hundred a week! Earn it for once!"

Andrew was still defiant. "May I remind you, Mr Hemmings," he declared haughtily, "that you employ me for my financial expertise, not to chase errant employees around the country."

"All right!" said Manny. "I pay you to give me financial advise! So what the fucking hell do you think a million pounds is – fucking pie and liquor! Do your fucking job and advise me where my money is!"

Andrew straightened his back. "I have just explained that…"

"Get the hell out of my office, you fairy cake!" Manny screamed, throwing his glass at Andrew.

Andrew ran from the room with whisky stains all over the front of his latest Savile Row suit.

8

By Friday of the following week, Jack had recruited two others. There was Pete Crofter - an ex SAS soldier, now working as a bouncer for a famous London club, but who dreamed of owning his own pub. And Henry Dane, a school caretaker harbouring an ambition to be a champion weightlifter. They were fit men, and still in their prime. They also wanted to own a business connected with their ambitions.

When Jack first approached them with an offer to realize those dreams, Henry Dane had jumped at it. But Pete Crofter had reservations. He had explained that throwing out the odd troublemaker was a far cry from taking on Manny Hemmings and his organization. He had asked for a few days to think about it and Jack had obliged. However, he eventually joined the group, saying that all of a sudden being a bouncer had lost its appeal.

Of course the pay of the late recruits was less than Tom's. They were paid fifty pounds a week, and the promise of a top job when Jack replaced Manny, or a one off payment of ten thousand, if they decided to call it a day. The offer was just too good to turn down, but they both made one point clear to Jack as they joined. And that was that they would not rob any banks, or security vans. Those were criminal pursuits, and they were certainly not criminals. However, doing away with Manny Hemmings was carrying out a public service, just as was any job involving ridding the streets of rubbish, and they were glad to do it.

Jack and Tom were having another card game in the flat above the pub. Tom had been happy with Jack's choice of men since he knew them both and considered them the reliable sort. He was even more pleased when he was told that his pay was a great deal more, because it proved in his mind that Jack thought of him as a close friend.

"Then we're all set to go," said Tom, picking up his drink and asking for another card. All he needed was another King and that would be four games in a row he had won.

"Seems so," said Jack, flicking a card across the table.

"Just like Elliot Ness and his Untouchables," Tom muttered. "Bladers..."

"What's that?" said Jack, scrutinizing the poor hand he had dealt himself.

"Bladers," said Tom with a smile. "That's what the three of us decided to call ourselves. Jack Blade and the Bladers. Has a ring to it don't you think?"

"You're having me on!" Jack laughed.

"No," said Tom indicating he wanted a second card. "We discussed it and we're all agreed."

"Sounds like a group," said Jack, flicking yet another card at his friend.

"It is a group," said Tom, hiding a smile that wanted to form when he realized it was a King.

"I mean a pop group," Jack chuckled.

"Oh, I think we'll be doing a fair bit of singing when this is all over with, don't you?" Tom replied.

"Ok. But don't go spreading that name about or we're all dead."

"Relax, Mate. It's just a name between ourselves. Now, who's the first to be Bladed?"

"That will have to be Jimmy Tanner," said Jack. "And it has to look like an accident."

"Why him?" Tom asked, taking a drink from his glass.

"Because he's too clever. I don't want someone like him giving good advise to Manny when we start piling on the pressure. All Hemmings is worried about at the moment is his missing money and the police investigation he's under. But once we add to his problems I want the cracks in his smug exterior to open up so wide that they swallow him up. Tanner could fill in those cracks so he has to go."

"Fair enough," said Tom. "But why make it look like an accident? I thought the whole idea was to turn up the heat on Hemmings?"

"It is, and Tanner's death will do just that. But I need a few days more before I let him know that someone's after him. I don't want any more visits to an abandoned warehouse."

"Tanner it is then," said Tom. "Hit and Run be OK?"

"Too risky. An accident in his home would be better."

"Be more complicated than a Hit and Run," said Tom.

"And I'll probably have to go back over my old crime novels for a few ideas. Mind you, it could be fun."

"Just as long as it looks like an accident," said Jack.

"Don't you worry, Mate," Tom replied. "It will be as if God himself decided to just reach down and take his soul…delivering it straight to hell of course. Now, how much are you prepared to bet on the hand you have there?"

9

It was late; just after two in the morning. Jimmy Tanner cursed Manny's name as he climbed the stairs to his first floor flat. Ever since Manny's blasted magazines had gone missing, he had been more demanding than a pregnant woman with multiple cravings. Jimmy couldn't understand what all the fuss was about. Ok, so Freddy Boyle had done a bunk with some valuable goods, and that was certainly something to be pissed about. But there was no need to go ranting about the place day and night, making everyone's life a misery - especially Jimmy Tanner's. After all, according to the latest reports, the body in the abandoned van was Freddy's, so he had already been punished for his thieving little ways. It was time to move on.

Jimmy was about to insert his key in the lock when he noticed the damage to the wood next to it. It was obvious that someone had forced it. He put down the carrier bag of shopping he was holding, and reaching inside his coat, he pulled out a small silver plated automatic. Then he slowly pushed the door open. And reaching in with his free hand, turned on the light switch. The large room filled with illumination.

Jimmy stepped inside, the gun held about a foot from his body.

Except for a few bits and pieces scattered on the carpet, there didn't appear to be much damage done. The TV was still there and so was his collection of china figurines in the mahogany display cabinet that had been his grandmother's.

Jimmy checked the bedroom, where he discovered that a Rolex watch, and a few gold rings were missing from his bedside table. He then checked the kitchen and bathroom. There were no signs of disturbances there.

"Fucking kids!" Jimmy growled as he tidied up. Then he wedged a chair against the front door handle and made himself three mugs of strong coffee over a thirty minute period. And after reflecting on what it sometimes meant working for Manny Hemmings, he climbed wearily from his leather settee and made for the bedroom. He felt extremely tired and a little light-headed. He also hadn't enjoyed his coffee one little bit and this only served to sour his mood further.

He turned on the bedside lamp.

"That fucking prick is working me to death!" he growled as he undressed. Then he pulled back the eiderdown and climbed in. The top quality mattress felt good beneath him. He needed his rest and comfort, but what would a slaved river from the slums like Manny Hemmings care about that. Once they became rich their greed turned them into monsters. But his torment wouldn't last forever. Having no family to support, or a need for any vices beyond the best coffee, he was being paid far in excess of his needs. And his bank account reflected this beautifully. His last statement had informed him that he had just over forty thousand pounds saved. And with the hundred thousand he planned to relieve his employer of sometime in the next year, he would be in a position to live abroad in the lifestyle he had always dreamed of. Yes his day would come, but not yet. He had to be patient, and that was something he had plenty of.

Jimmy reached for the packet of John Players cigarettes and lighter resting on the little table next to the bed; thought better of it, and left them there. Then, still cursing Manny's name, he fell into a very deep sleep - and never woke again.

In Manny Hemming's outer office, two Irishmen were arguing.

"You fuckin tell him!" Andy Flynn retorted. "You were the one who heard first, so it's down to you!"

"Fuck that!" his brother Pat snapped. "Since when do you make the rules! Just because I told you that Jimmy has been burnt to death in his bed is no fuckin reason to expect me to pass on the bad news to Manny! You know very well he'll go fuckin ape when he finds out! He can't even take a shit without Jimmy's help these days!"

"Well, someone's got to tell him Jimmy's been barbecued!" Andy shot back.

"Hey!" said Pat. "Maybe he knows already...!"

"Don't be such a fuckin turnip!" came the reply. "Have you heard any shoutin - or screamin comin from his office? Have you heard glasses flyin or fuckin swarin?"

"No..." Pat admitted.

"Then he aint fuckin heard yet!"

The two brothers were sitting in a smaller office next to Manny's, as they usually did each morning, waiting for their boss to give them their orders for the day. It was a varied job - one of the main attractions for them. One day it could be putting the frighteners on some bloke who was falling behind in his payments. Another day it might be breaking someone's legs - or neck if their crime was serious enough. Then again they might be on bodyguard duty if Manny decided to pay a visit to an old rival. The brothers loved these particular visits, because as often as not they resulted in a fight - Manny's bodyguards against the other bloke's. And Pat and Andy took great pride in the fact that they always won. They also got an extra bonus from Manny when fights happened. Because as Manny once told them it was common knowledge amongst those involved in criminal activities that only the best worked for the best. And when they won a fight, they were also paying homage to him and therefore deserved to be rewarded. The Flynns liked the way their employer's mind worked. It was very good for their wallets.

Manny's office door opened and he stuck his head out. "Has Jimmy turned up yet?" he asked.

"No, Mr Hemmings, not yet," said Pat.

Manny looked at his watch. "It's bloody ten o clock! What the hell is he playing at!"

"Maybe he got a bit hot and bothered last night when he lit up," said Pat. "So he had a lay in this morning."

"Lay in - hot and bothered?" Manny retorted. "What the fuck are you talking about, Pat?"

"I'm just guessin why he might be late, Mr Hemmings," Pat replied, ignoring the look of thunder his brother was throwing at him.

"Well, when he shows up, tell him to come straight to me!" Manny ordered. "And no stopping to chat up my secretary either!"

"Right you are, Mr Hemmings," said Pat. "Straight in to see you it is."

Manny retreated back into his office, and a laugh burst out of Pat.

"You stupid bastard!" Andy hissed in a low voice. "He'll remember what you said when he finds out how Jimmy died!"

"Aaa, you worry like an old woman," Pat replied. "He'll have too much on his plate to remember what the likes of us said to him."

"The likes of you, you mean," Andy grunted.

"Whatever…" said Pat, picking up a morning paper.

Andy watched his brother read for a few moments, then he stood up and went to Manny's office door.

"Where the hell are you goin?" said Pat.

"To get you out of the shit you're too fuckin stupid to know you're in," said Andy. Then he knocked.

"Come in - and it better be you, Jimmy!" Manny shouted from the room beyond.

Andy opened the door and stepped inside. Three minutes later he came rushing out with the sounds of screaming and glass breaking following him. Andy pulled the door closed behind him and dropped wearily into his seat.

"It's my guess he knows now," Pat said with a grin.

"That he does," said Andy, loosening his dark blue tie.

"Do you think Manny will give one of us Jimmy's job?" Pat asked after a while.

"Would you?" said Andy.

Pat looked thoughtful. "No."

"Then there's your answer."

"Pity," said Pat. "I could use the extra cash. But, you know sometin, Andy, Manny's organization has had a bit of bad luck lately. It's almost as if someone was having a go at it - don't you feel that?"

"No."

"Aaa, me neither," said Pat, going back to his paper. "As I said, it's just a bit of bad luck."

10

"Never mind the hand you've got," said Jack. "I know you're dying to tell me how you did it."

Tom had a smug expression on his face as he examined the cards in his hand. Then he laid them carefully on the table, face down. He poured himself a drink, and raised his glass. "A toast to the recently departed Jimmy Tanner!" he cried. Then he swallowed the brandy and put the glass down. He looked firmly at his friend.

"It worked a treat, Jack. You see, the first thing I did was to make a few discreet inquiries about our friend Jimmy. I found out where he lived; that he only drank coffee at home, and that Manny has been keeping those close to him even closer; well into the small hours as a matter of fact; probably afraid to let them out of his sight for too long in case they do a Freddy Boyle on him. Anyway, I forced the door of his flat; doctored his coffee; took a few items, and left. Then I paid a second visit when he was unconscious in bed; set fire to him, and Bob's Your Uncle - no more Jimmy Tanner."

"Now hold on a minute!" Jack said incredulously. "You mean he left the door open for you…?"

"Of course not," said Tom. "He wasn't that obliging. You see, when I broke the lock on the door, I knew he'd probably do what most of us would do - at least those of us who never put the police on our Christmas list - and that is, stick a chair under the handle with the intention of phoning a locksmith the following morning - have a nice cup of coffee, and then fall into bed. And that's exactly what he did."

"So how did you get in?" Jack asked.

"It's amazing what you can do with a one metre metal ruler pushed under the door. Once you feel a chair leg, a few good shoves and the chair slides away."

"With a bit of noise I should imagine?" Jack added.

"Not much since there was a shag pile carpet," said Tom. "Anyway, as I said, I had already drugged his drinks. What I did was I paid a visit to one the chemists and bought myself a few bottles of those herbal tablets that make you sleep better. Then, at home I dissolved some in a concentration of coffee, and dried it out so that it took on the colour and texture of coffee powder. I put an empty bottle of the herbal sleeping tablets in his bathroom, and a half full jar of decaf in the kitchen. I also replaced the drugged jar of coffee with a normal one – not forgetting to wash the mug and spoon he used of course."

"Why the empty bottle in the bathroom, and the decaf?" Jack inquired.

"So that the police will think he had a bit of a sleeping problem," said Tom. "That's why they won't be surprised to find a powerful dose of sleeping tablets in his blood - not enough to kill him of course, but certainly enough to put him right out. The police will assume that he overdid it. Anyway, I left a bottle of the sleeping tablets next to his bed, minus fifteen.. Then, as he snored away, bless him, I sprinkled just enough lighter fluid on him and the duvet to give the flames a good start. And finally I lit one of his cigarettes, and dropped it on the bed. Then I reset the chair and left."

"How did you do that?" Jack was intrigued.

"With a very long piece of string placed around the chair and looped over the door. Mind you I had to practice for a couple of hours at home. Sandra thought I'd finally cracked, but the kids had the time of their lives."

"Clever bastard," Jack laughed. "I'm glad you're on my side."

"We Bladers are the best…didn't you know that," Tom replied, trying to look aloof and proud.

"Seriously though, Tom, you did a great job," said Jack. "But you also took a great risk. I can see three or four things that could have gone wrong."

Tom shrugged his shoulders. "Just like you, Jack, I gambled, and won."

"Well, you won't have to gamble any more, Mate. The next death will convince Manny that someone's after him, so there's no point in trying to make it look accidental. At least we still have a few days without being under pressure, and yet we have already weakened him considerably. Pretty good going wouldn't you say."

"So who's next?" said Tom.

"Andrew Winterton - Manny's financial adviser. I don't want him convincing Manny to transfer his assets abroad. They will come in handy when I'm running the organization."

Tom's expression became stern. "Do me a favour, Mate - when you take over, I mean. Get rid of the drugs and the prostitution, will you?"

Jack smiled. "I was going to anyway, Tom. Manny has plenty coming in from other enterprises. That's no problem."

Tom visibly relaxed. "Thanks, Jack. It's just the thought of all those young kids like my…"

"I understand," said Jack as Tom's voice trailed away. "I only wish I could have done this a couple of years back, before Lynda got involved."

Tears welled up in Tom's eyes. "I know you do Mate…and thanks."

"Aaa, forget it. Now, are you going to just sit there or are you going to play cards."

A smile appeared on Tom's face as he picked up his hand from the table. "When you see what I've got, my friend, you will regret those words - you surely will."

11

Andrew Winterton settled back in the lavish settee with a contented sigh. It had been a hard day. Manny had been particularly difficult since Freddy Boyle ran out on him, and he expected the rest of his staff to work off his debt. But the rest of the staff were lucky, because they didn't have to suffer the stress of knowing that Manny was attempting to hide a million pounds. And as far as Andrew was concerned, this was a secret he most certainly did not want to share with his employer. He had seen far too many pirate films when he was a child, where the pirate captain always killed the men chosen to bury the treasure once they had completed their task. He felt it was only a matter of time before Manny came to the conclusion that his money would never be safe while one other person knew of its existance. So of course he had attempted to do something to alter the situation. He had tried desperately to convince Manny to include as many people as possible in the secret. But Manny had said that most of his staff couldn't be relied on to keep their mouths shut, and if Jimmy Tanner knew about a million pounds sitting in some landlord's cellar, he was bound to have a crisis of loyalties, and Manny didn't want to put him in such a difficult position – especially when he had a very good idea what the outcome of that crisis would be.

Now the money was missing; Jimmy Tanner was dead and Andrew was feeling very vulnerable indeed.

However, life had to go on, and there were smaller concerns to contend with, and one of those was attempting to get home to his family at nights. At least for the last few days Andrew had been managing to talk Manny into letting him go home early - if eight pm could be called early. And perhaps when Manny recovered from the shock of Jimmy's death and the loss of his million pounds, he would be more reasonable to his staff. At least it was something to hope for in these tough times.

"Dinner at the table or on your lap, Darling?" said his blonde-haired wife Mary.

"My lap will be fine, Dear," he replied warmly. "I've had enough of sitting on hard chairs. Manny doesn't notice because he sits on something much more comfortable."

"Then why don't you tell him," Mary advised through the serving hatch.

"Gracious, Dear," Andrew declared, "I couldn't do that! All Manny Hemmings wants to hear from me these days is the location of his money. And you know something, I think, deep down, he blames me."

"That's ridiculous," Mary replied, opening the oven door and wincing as a blast of heat hit her in the face. "You're his financial adviser. What has the missing money got to do with you, for heaven's sake?"

Andrew sighed. "You try telling him that. But you won't get very far, Dear, I assure you."

As Mary came into the living room with a tray containing her husband's steak and asparagus dinner, she almost tripped over her nine year old son's feet as he lay on the floor watching a programme on TV.

"Michael, will you please sit on the settee!" she scolded. "Why don't you behave more like Rosemary!"

Michael turned his head to look at his eight year old sister who was relaxing on one of the armchairs. She stuck out her tongue at him.

"Rosemary!" Mary exclaimed as she rested the tray on Andrew's lap. "Wherever do you get such rudeness from!"

"He started it!" came the shrill reply.

"No I didn't!" Michael declared.

"Yes you did!" Rosemary wailed. "You made a horrible face at me because you know it frightens me!"

Michael's expression became fierce. "I only *looked* at you! You're a liar! *Liar liar house on fire!*"

"Right...that's it!" said Mary, storming over to the TV and turning it off. "It's early to bed for the two of you tonight! And I don't want any tantrums! Your father has been working very hard lately and he needs to be able to eat his dinner in peace!"

The doorbell rang with the sound of a Westminster Chime.

"I'll get it!" Michael shouted, jumping up and running out of the room.

"Who is it, Michael?" Mary asked after a few moments of silence.

There was no reply.

A frown creased Mary's forehead. "Michael, who's at the door...?"

Michael came slowly into the room, walking backwards. He was looking up at something.

"What's the matter, Dear?" said his mother. "Is it someone collecting for...?"

The words caught in Mary Winterton's throat as two men wearing balaclavas followed her son.

Andrew jumped to his feet - the tray spilling its contents on to the white carpet.

"Sit down, Mr Winterton," said one of the men, pulling a gun with a long silencer, from his overcoat pocket.

Andrew dropped back in his seat, looking pale and shocked.

"You too, Mrs Winterton."

The gun swung towards Mary.

Dazed she sat next to her husband, and they held hands.

"What do they want, Mommy?" Rosemary cried, sliding off the armchair and running to join her parents.

"Go sit with your sister, Sonny," the man ordered, looking at Michael.

"No I won't!" Michael replied firmly.

"Do as you're told!" the man barked, but Michael stood his ground, his chin stuck out in defiance.

"Come over here, Michael!" Mary ordered. "Immediately, Young Man!"

Walking backwards once more, the boy reluctantly approached the settee and sat next to his sister.

Andrew licked his dry lips. "Look here, whoever you are! Please don't hurt my family! You can have my wallet - it's in my coat on a hook by the front door! There's about thirty pounds in it! And in a small safe in our bedroom, there's fifteen hundred pounds in cash! Please, take it all and leave!"

"Take him upstairs," said the man who hadn't spoken yet. "You know what we want."

"Come with me, Mr Winterton," said the man with the gun. "And if you do exactly as you're told, and don't give us any trouble, everything will work out fine."

Throwing a look of desperation at his wife, Andrew joined the gunman and led the way up to the bedroom. He went immediately to a painting hanging on the wall next to the bed and removed it - revealing a small, circular metal door. Andrew spun the lock a few times and the door swung open. He reached inside and withdrew a pile of money. He turned to the gunman - holding out the money. "Please, take it and leave!"

"Keep it," said the gunman. "All I want are any papers you have concerning Manny Hemming's organization."

Confusion mingled with the fear on Andrew's face. "I don't understand...?" he stammered.

"You don't need to. Just hand over the papers and we're gone."

Andrew placed the money on the bed and reached inside the safe once more. He withdrew two small ledgers. "There isn't much, I'm afraid, just the records of a few of his accounts abroad."

"You sure that's everything?" the gunman demanded, taking the ledgers.

Andrew nodded, drops of sweat sliding down his cheeks.

"Good." said the gunman. "That wasn't too difficult, was it?"

"What happens now?" said Andrew.

"Now I take you back down to your family. But we'll have to cut the phone line you understand. We wouldn't want any silly calls to the police."

Andrew took off the glasses he was wearing and wiped sweat from his eyes. "I won't call the police," he replied. "After all, no one has been hurt, and only a few books have been taken."

"That's the spirit," said the gunman. "Now, before we go, you better put that money back in the safe where it belongs; lock up, and replace that fine old painting."

"Of course," said Andrew, collecting the money from the bed. Then he placed it inside the safe - and a large calibre bullet blew part of his brain and skull in with it. There was a thump as his body hit the floor.

Downstairs, everyone looked up at the ceiling.

Mary's fear turned to panic. "What was that?"

"Probably dropped something," said the man.

Then came the sound of someone running down the stairs. "Let's go!" a voice shouted.

"My husband!" Mary cried, jumping to her feet and following the man out into the hall.

"He's just locking up the safe, Mrs Winterton," said the gunman.

Then the intruders were gone.

Two minutes later the men climbed into their car. The gunman started the engine and handed the weapon to his partner.

"Telephone...?" the partner asked.

"Seen to!"

The car screeched as it shot away.

Jack pulled off his balaclava and put it and the gun into a holdall.

The driver pulled his off and handed it to Jack. "I didn't enjoy killing that man," said Tom. "I thought I would, but I didn't."

"Were you supposed to?" said Jack.

"You know what I mean," said Tom. "I know he was high in Manny's organization, but he seemed just an ordinary family man. I suppose that's why I made sure he didn't see it coming."

"Dead is dead," said Jack. "What does it matter."

Tom threw a quick glance at Jack, and deep down he wondered if he really liked him as much as he thought he did.

"So far we have destroyed the wisdom and the financial bedrock of Manny's organization," Jack went on. "Now we must get rid of its strength."

"The Flynn brothers?" said Tom, his tone filled with reservation. "They won't be as easy as the others."

"And it will take more than just the two of us," Jack added.

Tom tightened his grip on the steering wheel as the car flew through the night. "Decided on the means yet...?"

"I have a few ideas, though nothing definite," said Jack.

"Well, I wouldn't tackle them in any physical way," said Tom. "From what I've heard, they take to violence like dolphins to water."

"You're probably right," said Jack. "Although we take a great risk each time we carry them, we'll have to use guns again. And I think we should bring Pete and Henry along when we go after them."

"That's two of your rules you'll be breaking," said Tom. "Never use the same weapons on two jobs in a row, and never have more than two of us working together at one time – those were two of the first things you drummed into us."

"And for good reasons," said Jack. "But as you said, the Flynns are going to be difficult. The guns will give us an edge, and Henry's weight-lifting experience and Pete's SAS training could come in handy if anything goes wrong."

"I'll arrange it with them when I have the place and time," said Tom.

"Don't worry, Mate," said Jack. "You'll have them soon enough."

12

The Raven was busy. The drink was flowing out of the barrels, and the cash was flowing into the tills. Jack was happy. He sat behind the quietest part of the counter in his usual place where he could observe customers and staff. In a way he thought of the staff as the male dancers in a ballet, supplying the lifts and the energy and the customers as the female dancers; impetuous; demanding, and prone to tantrums. But all was in harmony in the ballet tonight, so he allowed himself to relax.

Then a customer sitting at the middle of the bar drew Jack's full attention. The man had arrived some twenty five minutes earlier, but had refused to be served. Jack guessed the man to be about fifty years of age, and at least six feet two inches tall. He was lean, but muscular, and his hands were unusually large. Jack noticed the shock of coal-black hair combed back on his head; the chiselled features that were a mixture of handsome and rough. He reminded Jack of a baddie character in a comic he used to read when he was a child; but what was the character's name? Then it flashed in his mind. Of course, he was *'The Cutting Man.'*

Jack smiled at the memory, but it instantly left his face when the man waved Karen away for the fourth time.

Jack moved up the bar.

"Not drinking tonight, Mate?" he said to the man. "Drinking is usually compulsory in a pub – especially this one?"

The man turned dark eyes on Jack. "Maybe later, Buddy."

An American. Jack was intrigued. He didn't get many Americans in his pub.

"Call out when you're ready," said Jack.

"Hey, Buddy?" said the man as Jack made to move back to his former position.

Jack stopped and turned.

"You wouldn't happen to be Jack Blade by any chance, would you?"

"That's me," said Jack, moving back opposite the man. The almost imperceptible change in the man's expression when he had acknowledged his identity hadn't escaped Jack's notice. "Why do you want to know?"

"Well, I'm here on business; more as a favour for someone really, and I always like to know who I'm dealing with."

"Are we having dealings?" Jack inquired.

"Well now," said the man, "that remains to be seen, Jack. You don't mind if I call you Jack do you. Us Yanks tend to be more informal than you Brits. And my name's Frank by the way."

"So, what kind of work are you in, Frank?" Jack asked.

"I run my own business back in the States. It's a pretty big enterprise. I probably employ about thirty thousand people; you know, buying; selling; borrowing - lending, and such like."

"And do you have something over here already, or are you hoping to open up a branch?" said Jack.

The man scratched his jaw. "Nope. Got a brother in London in the same line of work. Anyway, I couldn't work in England; I'd suffer from claustrophobia within a month, so I'll just sort out my brother's little problem and get back to the wide open spaces."

"Well, I hope you manage to help your brother out," said Jack.

The man smiled - a perfect white teeth smile. "Why thank you, Jack. Manny will sure be happy to hear you say that."

'Manny...Christ Almighty, this is trouble fucking big time!' Jack's mind shouted, but outwardly not even the smallest facial muscle twitched.

Frank stared fixedly at Jack. His eyes were intense; as if searching for a pinhead of fear in an expression of casual interest. "Maybe you know my brother? His name's Manny Hemmings?"

"I know him," Jack replied.

"I thought you did. And, although he's a few years older than me, I consider him to be my little brother. And like all big brothers, I come down hard on any bastard giving him grief. Yep, real hard; know what I mean, Jack?"

"That's the way it should be," said Jack. "Family always come first."

"And you know something else," said Frank. "Back in the States we have these hunting dogs; bloodhounds as a matter of fact. And once those dogs pick up your scent there ain't nothing you can do to shake them off. Why, you might just as well give up there and then. Well, I've been called a bloodhound by some people because I'm always sniffing around; trying to find out what's what; trying to find out who's being clever. But there's one big difference between me and those bloodhounds back home. When they eventually run down their prey they just get real excited and holler and howl something fierce. But me, well, once I catch up with my prey they find that I have fangs worse than any hunting dog. Get my meaning, Jack?"

"I get your meaning," Jack replied.

"Glad to hear it. Now, I better get going. Be seeing you real soon, Jack - real soon."

Jack watched as the American ambled out of the pub, and for the first time in five years, doubt about his final goal began to niggle at the back of his mind.

Later, when Tom turned up, Jack took him upstairs for their usual game of cards.

"I didn't know Manny had a brother," Tom said once Jack had filled him in. "That's going to complicate matters. Know anything about him?"

"Only what he told me. And I gather he's a big time crime boss."

"Shit!" Tom retorted, suddenly slamming his fist down on the table. "Shit...shit...shit!"

"Hey, take it easy," Jack smiled. "We can find a way round this problem."

"How?" Tom demanded. "When Manny has a powerful crime boss for a fucking brother, what can we do; take on the whole fucking Mafia...?"

"I'm not convinced he's part of the Mafia," Jack countered. "He sounds like an independent to me. But even if he is with them, I'm not going to let him or anyone else get in my way. I've invested too much in this to stop now. Anyway, what have you found out about the Flynn brothers?"

"Not a great deal more than we already know, except that they have a few deals going on the side - nothing too big mind you."

Jack sat back in his seat and stretched. "Anything we can use to set a trap?"

"Maybe. They sometimes meet up with a few others for a game of poker in the Swan - you know that pub on the corner of Kerby Street. It seems the pot can run into hundreds."

"Right," said Jack. "See if you can find out what dates they meet - if it's always on the same day, and with the same people. And fill in the others about Manny's brother will you. I don't want anyone being taken off guard."

Tom's eyes narrowed. "You think this Frank knows it's you?"

"I don't think he knows exactly. Up to now I've been above suspicion because of the front I've built up over the last five years. But Frank doesn't know me from Adam. He'll have come in to this with an open mind, and that could be very dangerous for us."

Tom stood up and swallowed the remaining drink in his glass. "You be careful, Mate. This American is an unknown quantity."

"Our whole future is an unknown quantity," said Jack, "and it hasn't caused us any real problems up to now."

A minute after Tom had left the room, Jack let out a roar of frustration and threw a bottle across the room.

Karen shouted up, but was ignored.

13

"So what do you think?" Manny asked, handing his brother a glass of whisky.

Frank reached up from the sofa bed and took it. "Hard to say. He's certainly a cool one, and I'm sure he isn't the placid guy you say he is. But that don't mean he's involved with your missing dough. He may have a few deals on the boil and just suspicious of a new guy in town."

"Well I think you're barking up the wrong tree suspecting him, Frank," said Manny, taking his seat behind the desk. "I've known about him for five years, and he's never done anything to make me distrust him."

"Hmm," said Frank, swirling the golden liquid around in the glass. "Wasn't it that private detective guy Sherlock Holmes who said that *'when it ain't the possible, then it must be the impossible,'* or something like that."

Manny sighed. "I believe what he said was, *'When all that is possible has been considered and rejected, then whatever remains, no matter how improbable, must be the truth.'* Anyway, it's a work of fiction, Frank, and it won't help me get my money back."

"What about the guys who work for you?" Frank asked. "Would any of them have the balls to cross you?"

"The ones with the brains and the guts to even think about it are dead," said Manny.

"You should have asked for my help earlier," Frank replied, looking a bit cross.

Manny shrugged. "I thought I should try to sort it out on my own."

Frank suddenly got to his feet and walked to the drinks cabinet. He poured himself a large scotch, then turned to face his brother. "It seems pretty clear to me that the missing money and the deaths of your guys are connected. Someone is trying to do more than just rip you off - otherwise it would have ended when the money was taken."

"What are you getting at," Manny asked, "that they're trying to get my organization away from me?"

"Worse than that, Little Brother," said Frank. "They took out your second in command and your financial adviser; that to me sounds like a military campaign - a campaign to weaken you before moving in for the kill."

"What?" Manny spluttered. "You mean they're after me personally...?"

"Yep...you and your organization – the whole shebang, Little Brother," said Frank. "I mean, it must be worth something by now? How much would that be – two; two and a half million dollars...?"

Manny did a quick mental calculation. "Nearer six," he replied proudly.

"Not bad, Little Brother," Frank replied, genuinely impressed. "Not bad at all. And to think that dad used to say that you would never amount to anything. *'Your trouble, Manny is you spend too much time thinking about filling your belly instead of your pockets.'* He used to say that to you all the time."

"I remember!" Manny spat, suddenly angry. "And the bastard died before I could prove him wrong!"

"Well you know dad!" Frank laughed. "Never did like to lose an arguement!"

Manny then let out a loud sigh. "What am I going to do, Frank? People have tried to kill me before, but I've always known who they were, and I've always done something about it. But this is different. Someone is after me and I don't know who the bastard is?"

"What about the opposition?" said Frank. "Anyone come to mind?"

"I can't see it," said Manny. "I'm under the police microscope at the moment, and everyone's keeping well clear. At any other time I would have suspected them, but not now."

Frank pursed his lips. "Then we must be dealing with someone very cunning, Little Brother; someone who has been waiting a very long time for the cards to fall his way; someone not known to the police but known to you – though not suspected."

"You mean Jack Blade?" said Manny.

"Could be," said Frank. Then he finished his drink and poured himself another. "Tell me something? Blade's pub is some distance from here. Do any of your guys use it?"

Manny looked thoughtful. "I've been there a few times, and so have one or two of the lads I believe."

"Is that so," Frank said frowning. "Pat Flynn's outside isn't he. Get him in here."

Manny pressed a button on the intercom on his desk. "Susan, send Pat in, will you."

A minute later Pat Flynn marched into the room, leaving the door wide open.

"Door, you ignorant Mick!" Manny barked.

"Sorry," said Pat, running back to close it. Then he was standing at Manny's desk. "What's up, Mr Hemmings?" he asked.

"The Raven," said Manny. "Do you ever use it?"

"Jack Blade's pub," said Pat. "Sure I do. Good place to hang out. You can pick up some decent crumpet there, and the beer's OK too."

"And do any of the others use it?"

"We all do, Mr Hemmings. As I said, it's a good place."

"How well do you know Jack Blade?" Frank inquired, coming round to look at Pat.

Pat shrugged his broad shoulders. "Not a great deal. He rarely serves customers himself. He usually leaves that to his female staff. We like it that way."

"Do you know if he has any family - friends...?" said Frank.

"Haven't heard about family, and as for friends, don't seem to have any close ones - except for that bloke Tom Smith, maybe. They play cards together in his flat above the pub."

"Just the two of them?"

"No one else is ever invited, accordin to one of the bar staff," said Pat.

"OK, thanks, Buddy," said Frank, turning away.

"Anythin you want done, Mr Hemmings?" Pat asked Manny.

"Hang around outside. I may need you later."

"You still interested in Blade?" Manny asked when Pat left the room.

"I guess so, because there is one indisputable fact concerning him that can't be ignored," said Frank.

Manny threw his brother a blank stare.

"You had no business dealings with The Raven for five years," Frank continued. "And when you do, you get robbed and three of your guys are wasted. Some coincidence, wouldn't you say?"

"So I'll send the Flynn brothers to pick him up and get the truth out of him," said Manny. "Those two could make a rock talk."

"That could solve one of your problems," said Frank, "but it won't get your money back. I have a strange feeling that Jack Blade would never tell you where it is, no matter what you did to him. And another thing, that book of names and those ledgers; for all we know they could be on the way to the cops five minutes after we bring him in."

A desperate look appeared in Manny's eyes. "Then what can I do to stop him?"

"We play him at his own game," said Frank. "Now Mrs Winterton said that two men came to the house and shot her husband. They could have been Blade and this guy, Tom Smith. However, there could be others, and that's what we must find out first."

"But that will take time!" Manny cried. "What if his next target is me?"

"I don't think so," said Frank. "It's my guess that he will leave you until last, otherwise you would have been the first target. This guy's smart. He knows that if he gets rid of the boss, he will be forever watching his back…waiting for those hatching their own plans to kill him. No, this guy wants a clear field when he moves against you. You're safe for now."

"You bet my life on that do you?" Manny quipped.

Frank gave his brother a strange look. "If this guy Blade is who I suspect he is, then I'm betting both our lives on it, Little Brother."

14

"Fuck me, Pat, you just have to be chitin!" Andy Flynn exclaimed, throwing his cards on the table in disgust.

A great big grin lit up Pat's face as he drew the substantial pot towards him with both hands. "Aaa...you're just jealous of my talents. I told you I wasn't bluffin. And out of brotherly love and all that shit, I did warn you that I had a great hand."

"Well, I didn't believe you, you fuckin bastard, and you knew I wouldn't!" Andy protested.

"Gentlemen, please, can we get on," a well dressed man in his late fifties said. "And do we have to have a post-mortem each time one of you wins."

"Keep your toupee on, Bert," Pat laughed. "I'll take the rest of your money soon enough, but don't rush me. I want to savour my growin winnings."

The back room in The Swan pub was dusty and grimy. A heavy oak table rested in the middle of the floor. At the table were the Flynn brothers and two other men - Bert Mitchell and Teddy Hart. Both were old friends of the Flynn's, although they weren't involved in criminal activities. Bert owned a chain of butcher shops, and Teddy had three hair salons to his name - two more to be added in the near future. Both Bert and Teddy were doing very well in business, and had plenty of spare cash to indulge their passion for the game of poker. And since as often as not they all won, there was rarely animosity between the players. But it seemed tonight that Pat Flynn was having an exceptional run of good luck. He had won the last nine games, and was now over six hundred pounds ahead. It was going to be a very costly game for the others if they didn't reverse that luck.

Andy Flynn suppressed a scowl as he looked at the new hand Pat had just dealt him. 'He's fuckin cheatin, I swear he is!' he said to himself. 'I'll break his fuckin legs if I catch him at it!'

The single door to the room flew open, and four men wearing balaclavas rushed in. Two of the men held guns with silencers.

"Stay where you are!" one of the gunmen shouted. "And don't make a fucking move!"

Bert and Teddy dropped their cards in fright, but the Flynn brothers simply stared back at the men.

"It costs twenty quid to sit in, Mate," said Pat to the gunman. "If you don't have it, why not just own up."

"Shut your fucking mouth!" the gunman spat. Then he prodded Bert and Teddy with the end of the gun. "On your feet, and do exactly as you're told!"

As the terrified men climbed from their chairs, they were taken out of the room by the second gunman.

"This is cosy," said Pat, weighing up the three men. The one with the gun seemed well built and fit. He had the commanding voice of a leader. The other two were armed with baseball bats. One was of slight build, but the other was something else. Huge muscles bulged on his arms, and his broad shoulders looked as if they were used to carrying great weights.

"What the fuck do you want?" Andy Flynn growled. "This is a private game?"

"We want the two of *you*," said the gunman.

"And can a couple of ignorant Irishmen inquire why they are wanted?" Pat asked. "Or is it that your wives are findin you a bit borin in the bedroom and want a bit of excitement?"

Pat heard the powerful looking man with the baseball bat swear softly to himself, and grinned. Here was a chance; a very slim chance, but a chance nevertheless.

"Cut the lip," said the gunman. "We're here to get rid of you."

"Now why is that?" Pat asked.

The gunman shrugged. "Simple, Mate. You're in the way."

"Is that so," said Pat. "Then why not be a polite bastard and ask us to move out of the way, instead of gate crashin our innocent game of poker?"

"Because I don't think you'd oblige us, Mate."

Pat grinned again. "Probably not, *Mate*. So, what now?"

"We shoot you."

"Then why the baseball bats? You have guns, so why bring Twiggy and Tubby along?"

"Watch your mouth, Paddy," the big built man warned, "or I'll come over there and take the greatest pleasure in shoving those words down your throat."

"Did you hear that, Andy!" Pat declared. "Tubby can actually talk! Now out with it, Tubby, who taught you to put a long sentence like that together. It's a well known fact that big blokes like you are strong but retarded. And yet here you are, at least as clever as a three year old, talkin joined up words to me. But then I have to admit it's just amazin what the latest teachin techniques can do for morons these days. A blessed miracle it is."

The large man dropped his bat on the floor. "Want to back up those words, you fucking Mick!"

"Leave it!" the gunman warned. "He's just winding you up!"

"Just let me have five minutes with him!" the large man begged. "Just five minutes!"

"Five minutes, Tubby," Pat replied. "It would take you longer than that tryin to figure out which fist to use first - you dumb brain."

"For God's Sake, Jack!" the large man cried. "I can't let him get away with talking to me like that!"

"I said leave it!" the gunman barked. "He's going to be dead in a minute, so what does it matter!"

Pat's mouth dropped open in surprise. Then he laughed. "Well I'll be a tit on a boar! You know, I thought that voice sounded familiar! Jack Blade - well now, ain't you a deceivin little devil! And I suppose you are the one who nicked Manny's magazines and did in Winterton and Spooner?"

"I wouldn't waste my time on magazines," said Jack, taking his balaclava off. "But a million pounds is a different matter entirely."

Pat's eyes widened in disbelief. "*A million...!*" But a roar of laughter from Pat cut his own words off mid-sentence.

"I'm glad you find it so funny," said Jack as the Irishman's body shook, "seeing as you're going to be dead in a minute."

Pat then managed to stop laughing. "You know somethin, Boyo, I would have given anything to have seen the expression on Manny's fat face when he found out that a million pounds of his money had gone. Sweet Jesus...*a million quid!* What me and Andy could do with that kind of cash..."

Henry Dane and Pete Crofter pulled off their balaclavas. "Let's get on with it, Jack, for Christ's Sake," said Pete. "All this talking is doing my head in."

Jack immediately levelled the gun at Pat Flynn's chest and tightened his finger on the trigger.

The brothers moved with the precision and speed of trained athletes.

The heavy table flew through the air and slammed into Jack and Pete. They went down under it.

Pat leaped for a startled Henry Dane, raining powerful blows into his face that drew a lot of blood. But Henry fought back, driving his forearm into Pat's chest. Pat was thrown backwards.

Andy charged at the strong man and kneed him in the stomach.

Henry grunted and doubled up.

"Where's your fuckin brave talk now, Tubby!" Andy laughed, driving his elbow down on Henry's neck with tremendous force.

Henry's legs gave way and he crumpled to the floor.

Suddenly strong arms encircled Andy's body - pinning his arms to his sides.

Andy snapped his head back.

There was a thud.

Pete Crofter staggered from the blow, blood pouring from his broken nose.

Andy turned. "Have another one, Twiggy!" he cried, head butting the former SAS man.

This time Pete went down.

Tom Smith came running into the room, still wearing his balaclava. He aimed his gun at Pat Flynn who was rolling around on the ground with Jack.

Andy Flynn's foot kicked out and Tom's gun was knocked from his grasp. Then the Irishman's fist slammed into the side of Tom's face. Tom fell sideways, then toppled over the fallen table.

Andy dived for the gun.

A chair smashed against his head, and a great weight forced him to the floor, face down. Andy managed to turn his body, and saw Henry Dane sitting astride him - his bloodied face glaring down at him. Andy grunted when huge hands encircled his neck. He kicked and struggled as his breathing was cut off.

Henry's white teeth showed through the blood around his mouth. "Here's another long sentence I learned, you fucking Mick! I'm going to choke the life out of your rotten Irish body! So what do you think of that, you fucking bastard!"

Andy's hands shot up and two thumbs drove deep into the soft tissue of Henry's throat. The strong man gagged and rolled away in a fit of violent coughing.

Andy leaped to his feet and stomped on Henry's groin with the heel of his right foot as the big man lay on his back struggling for breath. "And what do you think of that, you fuckin fat pig!"

Leaving Henry moaning in pain, Andy looked about for his brother.

Pat was trying to hold his own against Jack and Tom, who were both attacking him at the same time.

Andy threw himself at Jack, slamming him face first against a wall.

Jack jabbed his right elbow backwards, catching Andy in the face.

The Irishman staggered back with blood pouring from his nose.

Jack struck again, delivering an uppercut to Andy's jaw. Andy's legs gave way and he fell to the floor. But in an instant he was up and punching. Jack retreated before the assault. Then he stood his ground and traded blow for blow.

Each blow was powerful, and each blow did some damage. But so focused and determined were the two men that even punches which would have finished them on many other occasions, did little to even slow the furious pace of the battle.

Meanwhile, Pat and Tom were furiously punching and kicking each other, but it was clear that Tom was getting the worst of it. A massive fist crashed into Tom's stomach and he dropped to his knees. Pat picked up a chair and raised it above his head.

There was a loud putt sound.

Pat staggered.

Another putt followed.

A small red hole appeared on the side of Pat's left temple. The chair fell from his grasp, and he toppled over Tom.

"Get up from that, you fucking Mick!" Henry Dane roared, still pointing the gun at Pat's body.

A loud cry of despair shot from Andy Flynn and he broke off his fight with Jack. And picking up an empty whisky bottle from the floor, he hurled it directly at Henry. The big man staggered when the missile caught him in the chest, but he remained standing.

"I'll kill you for that, you fat bastard!" Andy cried. Then he ran for the door.

Henry aimed the gun at him and fired twice.

The bullets missed.

Andy flew through the doorway and into the empty bar beyond.

"Come on!" Jack cried. "He knows who we are! We have to stop him getting back to Manny or we're finished!"

Henry and Tom followed Jack out through the door and into the bar. The front doors were wide open.

Andy Flynn's feet splashed on the wet pavement as he ran for his life. He had only noticed just in time that the tyres of his parked car had been slashed, otherwise he would have wasted valuable time on the useless vehicle.

The drizzle of rain that had descended was keeping people inside, and so his desperate bid for freedom went unobserved.

Running was nothing new to Andy. Long hours on the treadmill at the gym meant he could keep running for hours; something he didn't expect his attackers to be fit enough to do. But he would not forget that they had killed his brother. He knew who they were now, and he would pay them back.

"Fuckin murderin bastards!" he growled as his blood boiled with rage. "I'll get every fuckin one of them - especially that fat sod!"

Then his voice rose almost to a scream. "You're dead, you bastards, do you hear! You're all fuckin dead!"

The sound of an approaching car drove Andy's rage from his mind.

He dived for a dark shop doorway as headlights illuminated the pavement around him.

He flattened himself against the side glass of a window and held his breath.

A red Ford Cortina roared past.

Andy began to breath again.

But the screech of protesting tyres on wet tarmac sent panic blasting through his body. He shot out of the doorway and ran back along the street. He would have to be quick. They might reverse instead of turning round. He had to get to Manny.

"There's the bastard! I'll get him!" a voice cried out.

Andy heard the sound of a car turning and footsteps coming behind him.

Suddenly there was someone in front of him. He stopped.

The figure was Henry Dane, and he was standing with both arms spread out at about thirty degrees from his huge powerful body. His face was still covered in blood, and there was a maniacal grin on his face.

"Right then, you fucking Paddy!" Henry snarled. "It's just you and me now!"

Andy threw a desperate look behind him. The red Cortina was rolling slowly towards him, and in front of it, Tom Smith was walking with a gun held low in his right hand.

"Shit!" Andy cursed.

"That's right, Flynn," said Henry. "There's no escape that way. I killed your bastard of a brother, and now I'm going to kill you."

"You can try, Tubby," said Andy, concentrating his attention on the big man.

"Oh I'll do more than that," said Henry. "I'm going to break nearly every bone in your body, then I'm going to break your neck."

Henry began to move slowly towards the Irishman, his powerful hands open and ready to break bones.

Andy began to retreat, then suddenly he rushed at Henry.

Henry was caught out by the tactic.

Andy slammed his right foot between Henry's legs, but the blow was slightly off.

Henry grunted and dropped on one knee. And when Andy dashed passed him, he reached out and grabbed his left ankle in a powerful grip.

Andy grunted, lost his balance and fell over.

Henry reached for Andy's right ankle with his other hand and gripped tight. "Got you now, you fucking Mick!"

Andy found himself sliding backwards along the wet pavement - face down, as the hugely powerful hands of a gleeful Henry Dane pulled him. Then he was grabbed by the collar of his coat and turned so that he was sitting face to face with his captor. Andy's right fist shot out, and two of Henry's front teeth disappeared.

"Is that the best you got, Paddy," Henry grinned, spitting blood and teeth on the pavement. "Well, it's not enough."

Andy hit out again when Henry raised a massive fist to strike.

The Irishman's knuckles drove deep into Henry's throat, the impact instantly crushing his larynx.

A gurgling moan came from Henry's wide open mouth. He grabbed his throat. Blood spilled down his chin. Then his eyes turned back in their sockets and he slumped sideways.

In an instant Andy was on his feet and running along the dimly lit street - renewed hope of survival urging him on.

Tom Smith ran to Henry's side. "You stupid bastard!" he cried, kneeling down beside him and supporting his head. "I told you not to take any chances with these people! I told you that lifting weights in the gym wouldn't do you much good against street fighters like the Flynns!"

The loud noise of a car shooting past drowned out words of revenge from Tom.

At the far end of the street, Andy Flynn turned right down an unlit alleyway.

He was lost.

Although he had been coming to The Swan for years to play cards, he didn't know the back streets of the area. So he just ran - letting fortune take him where it may.

He heard quick footsteps behind him - gaining on him, and it was only then he became aware that he was running with a bad limp.

"That fuckin fat pig has crippled me!" he growled as the pain where he had been grabbed by the strong man, revealed itself. "Fuck that bastard! Fuck that ugly fat bastard!"

Suddenly his leg gave way and he fell.

He grunted when his forehead slammed against the paving.

The footsteps in the darkness grew louder, then stopped.

Andy rolled over on his back and sat up.

He could only just make out the figure that was standing a few feet away. He knew it was Jack Blade. He sensed rather than saw the gun that was pointing at him. He grinned.

"You know, Jack Boyo, you had us all fooled. You wouldn't have Irish blood in you by any chance?"

"No," said Jack in a cold voice.

"Pity," said Andy. "So what's the gripe with Manny then; revenge; money, or maybe you don't like his brand of cigars?"

"Power," Jack replied.

"You don't seem the type, Mate," said Andy. "But I can understand a man wantin to better himself. Now, if you need a good bodyguard, I'm your man. Give me a few days and I'll be as fit as a flea?"

"Afraid not," said Jack.

"Now fair's fair, Jack!" Andy exclaimed. "We ain't had a run in before, have we! At least nothin serious! Alright, we were a bit rough on you in the warehouse, but that was nothin personal...just business! Manny was our boss, and he told us to do somethin so we did it. Now, you're a boss yourself, and you expect those under you to carry out your orders don't you! Anyway, surely you wouldn't go shootin a mild mannered Irishman who's lyin injured in a stinking English alley; grievin over his poor departed brother, and him bein such a long way from home...!"

The first bullet from Jack's Nine Millimetre took Andy in the chest, going straight through his heart. The second went through his forehead and blew the back of his skull off.

His lifeless body flopped backwards.

"Yes I would," Jack said. Then he turned and went back to where he had left the car.

15

The waiter poured a little of the wine from the bottle into the empty glass on the table.

Manny picked up the glass; sniffed, then tasted the rich, dark red liquid. "That's excellent, Michael."

The waiter nodded and filled the glass, and also the glass of Manny's guest at the restaurant – ex Detective Inspector Phil Braddon. Then he placed the bottle on the table and left.

"That tip-off you gave me the other day turned out to be spot on, Phil," said Manny. "If it wasn't for you warning me about that police raid, I'd have lost a warehouse full of valuable goods."

"Glad to be of service," said Phil, taking a sip of the wine. "But things are getting pretty difficult now. My contacts in the Force are getting twitchy. I had to pay them fifty quid each this time."

"And worth every penny," said Manny cheerfully.

Phil's heavy set face became serious. "Mind you, I don't know how much longer they can be relied on. There's too much going on with your name on it. You know they're trying to gather enough evidence to put you away for a long time, and all these deaths aren't doing you any good at all."

A fork full of rare steak paused half way to Manny's mouth. "You say that as if I *wanted* them dead!" he hissed in a low voice. "I've lost two of my best people, and that's not doing me any good either!"

"I know, I know!" Phil protested. "But they've got to stop, Manny! And I take it from your behaviour that you haven't heard yet?"

Manny put his fork down, and his eyes narrowed. "Heard what...?"

Phil shifted uncomfortably in his chair. "Well, Pat Flynn's body was found in the back of a pub called The Swan last night, and Andy's in an alley not far from it. Both of them had been shot."

Manny leaned back in his seat, and stared at the other diners for a moment. His face was a blank mask.

"The police know they were working for you," Phil went on. "They might try and make a case against you from their deaths."

"What the hell do you mean?" Manny snapped, glaring at Phil. "I don't know anything about it? You've only just told me for Christ Sakes?"

Phil leaned closer and his voice dropped low. "They could claim that because of this investigation into your affairs, you've decided to get rid of what could be the most incriminating evidence of all - your top people."

Manny's eyes widened in disbelief. "What are you saying - that I'm behind all these killings...?"

Phil couldn't hide the uncertainty in his voice. "No, Manny, of course not!" he said hurriedly. "I know you wouldn't do something like that.! All I'm saying is that the deaths look suspiciously like an internal cleansing. Think about it for a minute. The first to go was the man who knew most about you - then the man who knew your financial situation, and now the men who were stuck to you like Siamese twins wherever you went. They were all privy to your deals to some extent, and now they're all dead. It looks bad for you, Manny. That's all I'm saying."

"But that's because someone is trying to destroy me!" Manny shot back. "Just ask Frank! He'll tell you!"

"Frank..." said Phil, averting his eyes.

"What?" A laugh erupted from Manny. "Now you're saying my brother's behind it? Are you crazy...?"

"No, of course I'm not!" Sweat began to form on Phil's brow, and he dabbed at it with a very white handkerchief. "It's just that..."

"What?" Manny demanded "Come on - spit it out, you over-suspicious bastard?"

"It's just that your troubles started just before Frank turned up," said Phil.

"He turned up, as you put it, to help me out!" Manny snapped.

"I know! But think about it! Your organization is worth over two million pounds, and...!"

Manny's laughter cut Phil off mid-sentence. "You know what, Phil, that's something like Frank said about Jack Blade. But I think to myself, maybe Blade's being clever - or maybe it's Frank who's being clever, or maybe you're the clever one, Phil. Yea, maybe I should have all three of you killed - just to be on the safe side."

Phil paled and began to tremble.

"Christ Almighty, Phil!" Manny hissed. "Don't give yourself a heart attack! Can't you tell when someone's pulling on your dick! And don't go to pieces on me now! I need you calm and focused! Anyway, I thought you DI's were hard bastards!"

"I wasn't in the Sweeney, you know," Phil replied. "And in case you haven't noticed, I'm not a DI any more - just a criminal working for a criminal."

"Fair comment," said Manny in a calmer voice. "But if it'll make you feel any better, you can have an extra five hundred this week - call it a bonus for the tip-off. And now you can get that Rolex watch you've always wanted."

"Thanks," Phil replied, sounding anything but grateful. Working for Manny had been quite easy up to now, but lately things had become very complicated. And at fifty four, he was too old for complications. Maybe it wasn't safe to be in the same building as Manny Hemmings anymore. Perhaps it wasn't safe to be even in the same city. .

"Come on, Phil," Manny prompted with a smile, "cheer up for Christ Sakes, or everyone will think we're a couple of queers having a tiff and get us arrested."

Phil managed to smile too, but things had gone far beyond Manny's jokes and Rolex watches. It was time to get out, but how to do it without Manny knowing.

"Look, Phil," said Manny, worried that his dinner guest was getting cold feet. "There's no need for you to worry about anything. Maybe Frank's right and Jack Blade is behind all this. Then our problems will soon be over. I had hoped to use Blade and his pub as a safe house, but I have to go along with Frank now. He's bringing a few of his friends over from the States to help him."

"Jesus, Manny, not more killing!" Phil cried. "What are you trying to do - convince the police that an international gang war has started up - that the Mafia has designs on the East End of London!"

Manny suddenly lost his temper, and crushed a serviette in his right fist. He leaned forwards across the table. "What the fuck do you expect me to do! Some bastard is trying to take over my business - a business I've built up and kept for nearly thirty years! And if you think I'm going to sit back and give him free rein, then you've got fucking shit for brains! It's been tried by others, you know, and what are they doing now, well I'll tell you, shall I, Phil; they're propping up new buildings; fertilizing park flowerbeds; sharing coffins with some dearly departed, and feeding the fish in the sea! So, you just think on this, Phil, no one moves in on my territory and lives to enjoy one second of it! And I don't care who I hurt, maim or kill in the process, but stop them I will! Now is that clear? Do you get the fucking message, *Philip...?*"

"I get the message, Manny," Phil replied, gulping down his glass of wine.

Manny straightened up and looked around him. No one seemed to have noticed his outburst.

"That's good, Phil," he said in a calm voice. "That's very good. Now eat your dinner; it's getting cold."

16

"What are we going to do with Henry?" Pete Crofter asked, pouring himself a drink with shaking hands. "I don't want anything disrespectful, like chucking him in the river, or burying him in a wood somewhere?"

"Don't worry, we won't do anything like that," said Jack. "I don't think he has any family, does he?"

Pete shook his head. "I've known Henry for ten years, and he never mentioned any."

Jack looked round the bar of his pub, and wondered if maybe he should have been satisfied with what he had. He wasn't too bothered by Henry's death - the man was a bungling fool. In fact, Pat Flynn had been right about him. And if he hadn't risen to the bait the way he did, he would still be alive. But events were happening that he hadn't planned on - the arrival of Manny's brother being the main one. If he succeeded in killing the both of them, would even more relatives turn up looking for revenge?

"You've gone very quiet, Jack," said Pete.

"Just thinking about our next move," Jack replied.

"Which is…?"

"Getting rid of Phil Braddon."

"Won't they be expecting us to do just that…?" Tom Smith asked.

Jack frowned. "So…?"

"Nothing. It's just that I don't like the idea of Manny knowing that we are going to try for Braddon in the near future. He could set a trap."

Jack smiled. "But we know that he knows…"

"And so does he. So where does that leave us?"

"Maybe it leaves us with an alternative."

Tom frowned. "What alternative?"

"We kill Frank Hemmings first. Then we kill Phil Braddon."

"But you don't know anything about this Frank Hemmings," Tom protested, "except that he's some big time crime boss in the States and Manny's brother? And what if you do kill him? I mean, does he have family, or partners? I can't see him ending up dead over here and nobody coming looking for him? For all you know, you could start a bloody war?"

"Maybe we should," said Jack. "Let Manny and Frank's lot fight it out, then we can move in and take over."

"That's fucking crazy!" Tom retorted. "If you think the Yanks would just pull out and leave Manny's organisation to you, then you're a penny short of a full shilling!"

"Perhaps," said Jack after a short pause. Mentally he told himself off for even thinking such stupid thoughts, but the fact was that he was getting worried. Frank Hemmings was probably a real obstacle to his plans and the truth was he couldn't see any way around it. At the very least he would have to change his plans. But for now he must get some sleep. Henry Dane's body was down in the cellar, and since he was a friend of Pete's, he couldn't just dump him in the Thames as he would have liked to. As Pete had put it, 'Henry must have a dignified send off.'

Sending Tom and Pete home, Jack locked up. He needed to think and he always did his best thinking when he was alone.

Three days had passed since the killing of the Flynn brothers, and Manny Hemmings was in a good mood for a change. Frank had brought over a top Private Investigator from America, and already he had made a few important discoveries.

At this very moment Frank was working on that information, and Manny expected to hear from his brother any time now. And after all the bad news he had had lately, it would be a relief indeed to see the tables beginning to turn on his as yet unknown enemy.

It was eight am at The Raven pub, and Jack was having a wash in the bathroom. The phone rang. The voice on the other end was Pete Crofter's, and he sounded very frightened.

"For the love of God, Jack, give them what they want! They're going to kill me if you don't!"

"Calm down, Pete," Jack urged. "Just tell me what's happened."

"Frank Hemmings sent some of his men to my place!" Pete wailed. "They kicked down the door! My son Tommy was knocked over! Christ, Jack, he's only three years old! He might have been hurt! They wouldn't let me see him! They shoved Brenda around and ripped out the phone! I tried to stop them, but they knocked me out and brought me here!"

"Where are you now?" said Jack.

There was a muffled sound, and a few seconds later Pete was back. "I can't tell you, Jack! They said they'll break all my fingers if I do! They know everything! I don't know how they found out, but if you don't tell them where the money is, they're going to kill me!"

Jack cursed under his breath. How did Frank find out about Pete? And Tom - they couldn't have him yet because he knew where the money was. He better warn him.

Suddenly there was an unfamiliar voice on the other end of the line; someone with an American accent.

"Mr Blade. It would appear that we are both in a position to help one another. I have your friend, and you have Mr Hemming's money. Now, I suggest that you tell me where the money is, and as soon as it has been recovered by its rightful owner, Mr Crofter will be returned to his family unharmed."

"Look, Mate; whoever you are!" Jack said forcefully. "I don't know anything about any money, so there's no point in hanging on to Pete!"

"I was afraid you were going to take that attitude, Mr Blade," said the voice. "So, if you could stay on the line for a moment."

There was silence, then Jack heard a thud and a prolonged scream, followed by sobbing.

"I am afraid," said the voice, "that Mr Crofter has met with an accident. Unfortunately he has suffered a broken arm and requires hospital treatment. And since he is likely to meet with further accidents, I suggest that you reveal the location of the money, Mr Blade, so that we can conclude our business."

"Fuck off, Yank!" Jack roared, and slammed the phone down.

He poured himself a generous whisky, and began pacing up and down. He ignored the phone when it rang a dozen times over the next hour. His hands were shaking, and his stomach felt as if he had eaten something bad. He cursed Pete Crofter's name time and time again. The idiot must have done something to give himself away. How could he have been so stupid. Now what was he going to do? Manny knew he had the money, and realized after that business with the petrol in the warehouse that torturing him wouldn't work. So he must have decided to go after his friends instead. Well let him. When it came to it he had no real friends; just a few blokes willing to help him out for more money than they could have dreamed of. And they knew the risks. There had to be risks when anyone with very little talent was offered that kind of money – even idiots knew that. It was their choice whether or not to accept the job, and the consequences of their acceptance had to be theirs also. But what about Tom? He knew where the money was. He had to warn him about the danger before they grabbed him as well and ruined everything.

Jack dialled Tom's number. A woman answered - a sobbing, frightened woman.

"Who is it…?" she asked in a trembling voice.

"Can I speak to Tom, please?" said Jack.

"I don't know where he is! Who is it?"

"Just a friend of his, Mrs Smith."

A loud sob came down the phone. "He didn't come home last night! Please…if you know where he is, tell him to stay away! Some horrible men came here last night looking for him! I called the police after they left, but they said they couldn't do anything! Please, tell him to phone me as soon as he can!"

"Does he have another place where he might stay?" Jack inquired.

"I tried all the places he might be, but…" the woman's voice suddenly stopped. And when she spoke again, her voice was stronger - more controlled. "Who are you? You didn't say your name? You say you're a friend, but you didn't say your name? You're one of them, aren't you - one of those horrible men who called here last night? Well I'm going to call the police and tell them that you…!"

Jack gently allowed the receiver to rest back in its slot. At least that was something. Tom probably realized that the men had called to his house. But where was he hiding? And why hadn't he called?

Jack started as something clicked against the window. He turned out the light - went to the window and carefully pulled back one end of the curtain. It was light out. The street was quiet. Then Jack saw a figure that must have been crouching behind a car, dart out and throw something up. The small stone bounced of the glass. Jack opened the window and leaned out.

"Tom!" he hissed. "Get round the back!"

Jack closed the window; went downstairs and let Tom in. As soon as they were in the living room, Tom poured himself a scotch with shaking hands. He looked dishevelled; frightened and edgy.

"They're on to me, Jack!" he cried. "Jesus Christ…they even know where I live! If I hadn't turned up just as they called at the house, I'd have walked straight in on them! And I don't know if they've hurt my family! I know I should have gone in and checked, but I just took off! Anything could have happened to them! I didn't know whether to phone home or not! I thought if I did the men might still be there and start hurting my family to make me give myself up! But if I didn't phone then there would be no point in hurting them! Was I wrong, Jack? Did I do the right thing?"

"Calm down, your family is OK, Tom," said Jack. "I phoned a few minutes ago. Sandra's a bit shaken up, but otherwise she's fine. "

Tom dropped heavily onto the settee, spilling some of his drink in the process. He began to sob quietly to himself. "Oh, thank God! Sweet Jesus...thank you!"

Jack sat in an armchair opposite and allowed Tom's emotions to run their course. And when his friend seemed calmer he decided he could take some more bad news without going into a panic.

"Look, Tom," he said, "I suppose you might as well know. I've had a call from the people who came to your house. They've got Pete. They know I took Manny's money and they want it back."

"Then give it to them for God's Sake!" Tom retorted. "There were four men at my house! I didn't recognize three of them, but I did recognize Micky Peach!"

"Never heard of him. Who is he?" Jack asked.

"Let's put it this way," said Tom. "If you want someone to break a few legs; kidnap a child, or carry out any other work that involves pain and misery, he's your man. If I hadn't recognized him, I'd have assumed they were the police at my house. But I'll tell you this, Jack, Micky Peach has been linked to a few disappearances over the years, and he isn't cheap. If he's with the men who took Pete, then Pete's in big trouble."

Jack ran his fingers through his hair a few times, then he punched his fist into the palm of his hand in frustration.

"I know it's bad luck, Mate," said Tom, "and you gave it a good go. But you have to give back the money now, and get out of here as soon as you can. You must have money of your own surely. After all this is one of the best pubs around. You can make a fresh start somewhere else, and when everything settles down you can get an agent to sell this place for you."

Tom saw something in Jack's expression and a niggling doubt sprang up inside him. "You're not thinking of running off with the money are you...?" he asked in a low voice. "Because if you are, Mate, then I have to tell you...?"

"Course not!" Jack interrupted with a laugh. "I wouldn't do something like that to Pete!"

Tom visibly relaxed, and took another sip of his drink. "So, have they left you a contact number, or are they going to call you back?"

Jack stared hard at his friend. "If you must know, Tom, I hung up on them, and I haven't answered the phone since."

Tom was confused. "What do you mean...?"

"I mean that nothing's changed. I'm going on with the plan. I'm keeping the money, and if I have to I'll hire all the help I need."

"What about Pete?" Tom exclaimed. "What's going to happen to him while you're hiring a new set of friends to replace the old ones...?"

"Of course I'll try and help Pete," Jack replied. "But it has to be said that he knew the risks as well as the rest of us. Or did he think he was being paid all that money because I liked his personality."

Tom gritted his teeth. "I think you'll find that he thought that you paid him the money first and foremost because you are friends, and secondly because you wanted him to help you get rid of a scumbag who has ruined thousands of young lives with prostitution and drugs. And, just like me, he doesn't mind a bit that you're planning on taking Manny's place because, as you promised me, you were going to get rid of those elements. We're not saints. We have no objection to someone making their way in the world using iffy gear and gambling. But we do expect you to keep your promises and help us out when we're in serious trouble. You know we'd do the same for you."

"I know you would," said Jack with a sigh. "But I can't do very much for Pete at the moment, at least not without giving up all my plans, and I won't do that, Tom. An opportunity like this only turns up once in a lifetime, and I'm not going to let it pass by just because someone got careless. I should be able to help Pete in a few days if everything works out, but not now. Sorry, Mate but that's the way it has to be for the time being."

"That's what you think," said Tom in a firm tone.

"What do you mean by that?" Jack asked, his tone equally firm.

Tom placed his drink on the small table in front of the settee. "I mean I'm sorry about your plans, Jack, I really am. But you can't leave Pete with those thugs...even for a couple of days. I won't let you do that. God knows what they might do to him. Now you have to be reasonable about this, Mate. You must give Hemmings his money back. And I hate the idea every bit as much as you do because the thought of doing that scumbag a favour makes me feel sick to my stomach. But this isn't about my daughter or your ambitions now; it's about a friend who's relying on us to save him from some horrible death. Surely you can see that. And if you don't, then you're not the man I thought you were."

Jack jumped up and crossed the room to pour himself a drink. He knew that he had to conceal his true feelings on the matter from Tom. Tom was a tough man, but he was also a sentimentalist who would hand back a fortune without thinking about it if it meant saving the life of a friend. He had to be handled very carefully.

"Look, Tom, giving that money back is no guarantee that they will let Pete go. And do you really think Manny is going to forget about what I did - in a pig's ear he will."

"I know he won't, Mate," said Tom. "Scum like him never do. But that's exactly why you have to clear out after getting Pete free. Just close the pub for a couple of years, and who knows, you might even be able to come back and reopen it. Someone else will probably be running Manny's organization by then. Greedy bastards like him only employ his own kind, and I'll bet there are at least a hundred people at this very minute who want to take his place. Or maybe someone who hates his guts will catch him on his own one night and do him in when he's least expecting it."

"I can't rely on that happening," said Jack.

A hard look came into Tom's eyes. "Oh yes you can, Mate. I can't guarantee the takeover, but there's no way that man is going to live on into old age after what he's done to my family. I'll see to that."

"I don't know, Tom," Jack replied, walking to the window and peering through the curtain. "I feel there's no going back now. Once I took that money, I committed myself all the way. I can't back out now."

"Then I'll have to tell them where it is," said Tom.

Jack's grip tightened on his glass. "I told you already, Mate, they didn't leave a number."

"That doesn't matter," Tom replied. "I'll go straight to Manny Hemmings with half the money. And when Pete's free, I'll tell them where the rest of it is."

Jack turned to look at Tom. "You're spoiling things for me; you know that, don't you?"

"And I'm really sorry," said Tom, genuine regret showing on his face. "I know how long you have been planning this and I wanted you to succeed every bit as much as you when you told me what you were up to. But I can't put your ambitions before someone's life. Pete has to be saved, and that's the bottom line. And to tell you the truth, Mate, I'm more than a bit disappointed that you don't feel the same way. Now I couldn't save Henry, but I'll be dammed if I'll let Pete go the same way."

Jack went back to his seat. He watched as Tom reached for his glass. He said nothing as Tom downed the drink, and then settled against the back rest. He seemed very tired.

"You're serious about this, aren't you?" Jack said after a while.

Tom nodded slowly a few times. "As serious as life and death, Mate."

"And there's nothing I can do to change your mind...?"

"Not a damn thing."

"Then do me one favour, will you?" said Jack.

"Anything, Mate, so long as it's nothing to do with that money and what I'm going to do."

"Well, it is in a way," said Jack. "Hold off on telling Manny where the money is; just for a day, so that I can come up with a plan to get Pete free without giving it back."

A humourless laugh shot from Tom. "And give you time to move it. You may have all the brains, Mate, but I wasn't born yesterday you know."

Jack suddenly left the room and returned a few minutes later with the special crowbars.

A concerned look appeared on Tom's face and his body tensed.

"Now, you know there's no way to lift that paving stone without these," said Jack, placing them on the table. "You hang on to them. And if I can't come up with an alternative plan by morning, then you're free to go to Manny and tell him where the money is. I'll even help you and prove that you are wrong about me."

"I don't know..." said Tom, not convinced he should wait. "How were they treating Pete? They didn't hurt him did they...?"

Jack grinned. "Pete said they hadn't done anything except give him a bit of a fright; something about dangling him out a window. That's why he told them everything. But as for anything physical, that's no concern at the moment. And don't worry, they'll phone again and I'll string them along for a while."

"I'm still not sure..." came the reply.

"Come on, Tom!" Jack cried. "At least give me a chance! And remember the kind of man I stole the money from and what he will probably use it for – all that prostitution and drugs going around because no matter what the police find, they won't get their hands on that million pounds of his when he gets it back! He won't be so careless again!"

"OK," said Tom reluctantly. "I don't want to see your plans go up in smoke any more than you do. So, you come up with something to get Pete back, if you can. But make it good will you, or we're all likely to end up like Henry if it goes wrong."

A smile softened Jack's stern expression. "Thanks, Tom. I knew you would give me a chance. You won't regret it."

"I hope so, Mate. Now, I didn't get any sleep last night, so do you mind if I get my head down for a few hours? I'm shattered."

"Course not. Use my bed."

Tom climbed wearily to his feet, and taking the crowbars with him, walked towards the bedroom. Jack watched as he entered the room and closed the door behind him.

Jack then leaned back in his seat and absentmindedly tapped the side of his head with the fist of his right hand. He had to come up with a plan, and soon. Tom wouldn't give him any more time than the following day.

An hour later the phone rang, and an American voice said. "Ahhh, Mr Blade. I trust you have calmed down. And you will be pleased to hear that no further accidents have befallen Mr Crofter. However, our patience is not without its limits. If we do not come to a satisfactory agreement during the course of this conversation, then I regret to say that matters will deteriorate to a point that will be unbeneficial to Mr Crofter's health and well-being."

"It's all right," said Jack. "I've come to a decision."

"That's good, Mr Blade. That's very good indeed."

17

It was seven am when Tom came out of the bedroom. He found Jack asleep on the settee. Tom scratched his head and yawned loudly.

Jack opened his eyes and sat up. "What time is it?" he asked.

Tom stared at his watch with bleary eyes. "A minute after seven, Mate. And sorry about taking up your bed. I only meant to have a few hours kip."

"That's all right," Jack replied. "I didn't feel like sleeping until gone five. Anyway, I had to wait up until they phoned."

"And did they?"

"Yes," said Jack.

"And have you come up with an alternative plan?"

"Not exactly."

"I see," said Tom frowning. "So what's the deal with the kidnappers?"

"We take the money to a warehouse later on this morning where we do a swap – Pete for the million; simple."

"And what if they try and do us in?" said Tom.

"That won't happen," said Jack with a smile. "I told them I'm going to put small bottles of petrol inside each bag and keep a lighter handy. One wrong move and whoosh, a million quid goes up in flames."

"I like it," said Tom. Then he gave Jack a puzzled look. "I must admit, I'm surprised you're taking it so well. I was sure you would try and talk me out of it at least one more time. Not that it would have done you any good. And you know I'd do the same for you as well…don't you?"

"Course I do, Mate," said Jack. "And the reason I'm pretty laid back about what we're going to do is because it isn't all bad news for me in the financial sense."

"No..?" said Tom, becoming instantly suspicious.

"No…because I told them I had already spent a hundred and fifty thousand. Of course they created hell about that for a while, but eight hundred and fifty thousand is better than nothing, so they accepted it. Anyway, I've been working it out. So far I've spent six thousand out of the money. That leaves me with a hundred and forty four. And as you say, it wouldn't be safe for me to hang around here, so after the deal is done I'm off to pastures new. There's a great pub I've always fancied, but the owner wanted more than I could pay. So once I place fifty five thousand in his greedy fat palm, the pub's mine. I can use the other fifty seven thousand on providing myself with a very comfortable life."

"Don't you mean the other eighty nine thousand?" said Tom.

"Naaa..." said Jack. "Look, Tom, you and the lads have done your best for me and I don't see why you should walk away with nothing. So, I'm giving Pete ten thousand and you twenty two. That should give the both of you a great start in your new lives. And as for me, I'll have a pub I've always wanted and a fortune to spend. So don't you dare feel guilty about taking your share, because you deserve it, you selfless git."

"Jesus Christ, Mate!" Tom exclaimed. "You're the most generous bastard I've ever come across! So, where is this pub anyway...?"

"No offence, Tom," Jack replied, raising his hands defensively, "but when I disappear I *really* disappear. It's best that you don't know where."

Disappointment appeared on Tom's face. "You're right, of course, Mate. But I'll sure miss you."

"You never know though," Jack laughed. "You might get a postcard and an invitation through your letter box one day when things cool down a bit."

"If the Post Office can find it," Tom replied. "I'm getting out myself and taking my family with me. Now, what's first - the money?"

"Nope - a good old English Breakfast, and I'm cooking!" Jack declared, rubbing his hands together in anticipation.

18

An hour later breakfast was over. Tom and Jack made their way to the courtyard. Jack explained that they would first remove their share of the money and leave the rest in the cellar until the knapsacks could be fitted with the bottles of petrol and loaded into a van Jack had asked a friend to deliver later that morning. Jack had also phoned his staff, telling them that he wouldn't be opening up for the next week or so due to a serious problem with the electricity supply in the bar. And that he had already posted five hundred pounds in cash to each of them.

Having turned the wheel to draw back the locking bar, Jack and Tom lifted up the paving slab using the special crowbars.

Tom grunted with the effort. "Christ, Mate, how the hell did you manage to do this on your own. You wouldn't get me doing this every time I wanted to check on the money, no matter how many millions were stashed down there."

"Don't you worry," Jack laughed, wiping sweat from his forehead. "This will be the last time. Now you climb down first. But watch yourself. It rained a bit last night, and the rungs will probably be slippery."

Tom stepped down on to the first rung, and nearly lost his balance when his foot came off.

"I said watch it!" Jack barked. "I'll have one hell of a job trying to get a solid bugger like you back up if you knock yourself silly!"

Tom grinned and began to descend once more.

But just as he was shoulder deep in the shaft, he looked up to ask for the torch he'd forgotten. Jack was standing like a statue - staring down at him with a terrible expression on his face.

"What's up, Mate?" Tom asked with some concern. Then the awful truth of his situation tore through him. He cried out and began to clamber back up. But he was too late.

A metal crowbar arced suddenly through the air and struck Tom on the head - caving in his skull. His body dropped back into the shaft. There was a thud when it hit the ground below.

"You stupid, fucking bastard, Tom!" Jack growled. "Did you really believe for one second that I would hand back a million pounds, just to save the life of a careless prick like Pete Crofter - like hell I will, Mate, like fucking hell I will!"

Twenty minutes later the body of Henry Dane joined Tom Smith's under the courtyard. Then they were carried through the door and along the tunnel to the river.

Far from being blocked, the tunnel was as perfect as when it had been dug out hundreds of years earlier. An old fisherman's hut at the other end kept the tunnel from prying eyes, and this hut formed part of the pub's property.

In the courtyard once more, and cursing his latest victim's stupidity, Jack walked over to the wall, and reaching up, took hold of two chains that were hidden in a covering of Russian Vine. Then, as he stepped back and pulled, a metal hoist that was fixed to the wall some twenty feet up, swung out.

Satisfied that it was in the right position, he went into the cellar and returned a few seconds later with an elongated steel grab that had two blades the same length and thickness as those of the crowbars. Jack smiled smugly to himself at his cleverness. Within two weeks of purchasing the pub, he had the hoist custom made. He knew that he would probably have occasions when he would need to remove the flagstone cover on his own. And although he trusted Tom with the secret of the hidden room and the crowbars, he kept the hoist a secret.

Having attached the grab to one of the chains, he positioned the blades into the groves in the flagstone. Then, slowly pulling on the other chain, he took up the slack. Gradually the flagstone lifted and flipped over - right way up. Then it was a simple matter to lower it into position, and set the locking bar once more.

Jack unhooked the grab; reset the hoist, then walked back to the cellar. His next task was to find a room to rent for a few days before visiting his mother-in-law. So far everything was going well. He hoped his luck would continue.

19

Detective Chief Inspector George Mandell of the Wapping Crime Squad sat at his desk, thoughtfully rolling a pen between his fingers. The case he was working on was becoming more and more complex by the day, and he was at a loss at what to do about it.

There was a knock at his door.

"Yes!" he answered, a little sharply.

DI Ken Hanson - a thirty four year old Scot, came into the office.

"What have you got?" Mandell demanded.

"Not much more than we already know, Guv. The Flynn's were shot with the same gun as Andrew Winterton, and the two men that played cards with them still claim they have no idea who the killers were. But I think they're lying, Guv. They know all right, but they're not talking. Probably been told they'll get the same as the Flynns if they open their mouths."

"We could threaten them with being accessories to the murders?" said Mandell.

Hanson shrugged. "Tried that already, Guv. No joy I'm afraid. And I checked their backgrounds. Not so much as a parking ticket between them. We've got nothing and they know it."

DCI Mandell applied pressure to the pen - bending it. "Send someone to interview Manny Hemmings. And while you're at it, find out what you can about his brother Frank."

"You still think Hemmings is doing a bit of spring cleaning in his organization?" Hanson asked.

"Maybe. But Frank Hemmings turning up now is putting a new slant on it. He could be here to help his brother with the clear out, or to help him against some outside agency that's trying to take over. I take it Manny is still under observation?"

"Round the clock, Guv. But he's managed to give us the slip a few times."

A hard look appeared in Mandell's eyes. "Then make sure he doesn't! The Commissioner wants results, and so far all I've given him is a load of dead bodies and a lot of suppositions! Manny Hemmings has had things his own way for too long! It's about time he was brought to book!"

"Right, Guv," said Hanson. "Oh, and by the way, that business with the warehouse. We now know there was a tip off, and who's responsible. You want me to arrest him?"

"Who is it?" said Mandell.

"DS Chalmers. Seems he's been paying a few too many visits to the bookies, and the word is he owes about seventy quid; or did, until he paid it off the other day."

"That's all I need – a dishonest police officer on my patch having links with one of the biggest criminals in London!" Mandell exclaimed. Then he pursed his lips. "Hold off on his arrest for now. But warn everyone not to discuss any more plans involving Manny Hemmings in front of him. We could use him ourselves when the time is right."

"Yes, Guv," said Hanson, and he left the room.

The phone rang and Mandell frowned as he lifted the receiver. It was bound to be trouble.

"That's how it went," said Frank Hemmings to his brother as he sat at his office desk.

"What a fucking bastard!" Manny exclaimed.

"You can say that again," Frank replied. "When he put the phone down on Marty yesterday, I knew he would answer sooner or later when we called back. I mean, hearing a pal of yours screaming as a guy breaks his arm is enough to rattle anyone. But it wasn't until the early hours of this morning that he did answer, and made a deal. He said that he would hand back the million, less the hundred and fifty grand he had already spent...what the fuck on; Buckingham Palace? The guy's obviously determined to get out of this with something for the future. But I thought, what the hell; you're getting most of it back. Anyway, the plan was that we would meet behind a warehouse on Sanderson Street at 11.30 this morning, but he never showed. I sent a few guys to his pub, but he wasn't there. His clothes were gone from his apartment, so I guess he's taken off. I've left someone watching the place just in case he shows, though I doubt he will. The bastard's too clever for that."

"What about his accomplices?" Manny asked, trying not to think about the one hundred and fifty thousand pounds of his money being spent by some pub landlord - all those crisp Tenners; it was unbearable.

"He wasted them, and dumped their bodies in the Thames," said Frank.

"The fucking bastard!" Manny spat.

"So you said," Frank replied. "And I could use someone like him back in the States. Anyway, I've brought over a pretty smart PI to look for Blade, but it might take some time and plenty of dough."

"Just so long as I get my money back and Jack Blade ends up dead, I don't care what it takes!" Manny growled. "And I want that hundred and fifty thousand as well!"

"I'll see what I can do, Little Brother," said Frank.

20

The doorbell rang at No 24 Russell Street. A lady of fifty years of age answered it. She smiled warmly at the visitor. "Jack…!"

Jack stepped inside and kissed his mother-in-law Marion on the cheek. "How are thing's, Mum…?"

"Oh, same as usual, Love," she replied, taking his coat. "Go on through."

Jack moved down the long hallway and turned right into the living room. It was well furnished with quality items, and Jack smiled to himself. Cheryl's family always did have good taste.

Sitting on the floor watching television was a ten year old girl with long straight blonde hair. She had a pretty face, but although the programme she was watching was a cartoon full of humour, her expression was blank. Her name was Sally.

Jack squatted down beside his daughter and placed the brightly coloured package he carried on the floor in front of her. "I've brought you something, Darling. I think you'll really like it."

Without saying a word, Sally pulled the parcel towards her and returned her attention to the TV.

Jack frowned. "Aren't you going to open it, Darling?"

There was no reply.

He tenderly stroked her head with his right hand, but again there was no response.

The mad antics of the most famous cat and mouse on TV continued - fuelled by the skills of the finest humour masters in Hollywood. But they were being watched by wide open eyes that didn't see that humour – that didn't understand.

Marion came into the room. "She hasn't been doing very well the last couple of days," she said with sadness in her voice. "But don't worry about it. The doctors say that autistic children go through particularly bad patches from time to time. Now you make yourself comfortable, Love, and I'll put the kettle on."

Jack hugged and kissed his unresponsive daughter. Then he sat in a nearby armchair.

There was pain in his eyes as he watched his daughter staring fixedly at the television. He thought back to the day, just six years ago, when the police called to his home in Glasgow to say that his wife had been killed in a car crash, but that his daughter had survived without a scratch. He had been grateful and devastated at the same time. Fortunately, Cheryl's mother Marion Peterson and father John were only too delighted to look after Sally, which allowed him time to run his rather underhanded business buying and selling quality goods that had fallen off the backs of quite a few lorries.

He had heard of a revolutionary treatment for autism developed in America, but it was long term treatment and hugely expensive. He had been informed that the total cost of treating Sally could exceed thirty thousand pounds, because it meant more than a year in a special hospital. And from that day he swore to himself that whatever it cost he would provide the funds for that treatment. Now he had the money, but with Frank Hemmings sniffing around, he couldn't risk sending his daughter at the moment. What if the newspapers heard about it? They were bound to mention his name, and then Marion and John were certain to have unwelcome visitors.

"Hear we are, Love," said Marion ten minutes later, placing a tray of cakes, sandwiches and cups of tea on the coffee table in front of him.

Jack helped himself to a ham sandwich.

"So...?" said Marion sitting in her own chair with a cup of tea and a slice of sponge cake. "How are things in London...?"

Jack grinned. "Hectic as ever."

"But you're doing OK...?"

A stern expression appeared on Jack's face. "If you mean am I squandering the profits from the pub on gambling and women instead of saving for my daughter's treatment, then you'll be glad to know that I expect to have the funds to send her to America in a few weeks!"

Marion frowned. "Now don't you take that tone with me, Jack Blade!" she declared firmly. "I know very well that there isn't a day goes by without you thinking about Sally! I was simply asking how you are doing in yourself!"

"Sorry, Mum," said Jack sheepishly. "Things have been pretty intense this past week, and it's getting to me."

"Anything I can do?"

"No. It'll sort itself out. So, how's dad getting on?"

Marion's face lit up. "He was promoted to manager last month."

"I'll bet he's pleased about that," said Jack with a grin. The death of his only daughter had hit John particularly hard. Cheryl had always been particularly fond of her father – *Daddy's Little Shadow* Marion used to call her because she used to follow him everywhere when she was young. Depression had been a problem for a while after the funeral. Obviously he was now completely recovered.

Marion laughed. "He wouldn't shut up about it for over a week. And I'm really glad for him. He'd been passed over so many times, he thought he'd never get the promotion."

"That's because they're jealous of his intelligence," said Jack. "He always was a clever so-and-so."

Marion laughed again. "He certainly believes he could do a better job at running the country than the current Prime Minister, that's for sure. Now then, Love, you said that you expect to have the money soon to send Sally to America?"

"That's right, Mum. She could be on her way by September."

Marion looked surprised. "But I don't understand that, Love? How can you have raised such a huge sum of money? Surely the pub isn't doing that well…?"

"That and a few good investments," Jack replied. "But do me a favour, Mum. Keep it to yourself for now. I don't want to get Dad's hopes up before I'm ready - just in case."

"I won't say a word," Marion replied. "You'll stay the night, won't you? He'll be delighted to see you when he gets in. He's always talking about your last visit when you two stayed out till all hours. I think he would like to do that again, so be warned."

A sadness suddenly entered Marion's eyes. "He misses having a son you know."

Jack smiled. "As a matter of fact, I was hoping to spend a few days here this time…if that's all right?"

Marion instantly cheered up. "Course it is, Love." Then she became serious. "It's not like you to sit around listening to John and I boring the pants off you. What's up, Love…and no lies now? In my house we only speak the truth."

Jack shifted uncomfortably in his seat. Marion was the only person in the world that could make him feel like a naughty little boy trying to hide the fact that he was concealing something important from a grown up. "Yes, you're right, Mum," he replied. "I'm trying to get away from a bit of trouble."

"Trouble...?" Marion's expression hardened a little. "What kind of trouble? I thought you said everything was going well with the pub...?"

"Nothing serious - just a couple of blokes cheesed off with me. It will soon blow over."

"Then I better prepare the spare room," said Marion, standing up. "You just relax and finish your tea."

Jack helped himself to a slice of cake, and wondered if hiding out in Chigwell was such a good idea. Somewhere farther from the East End of London would be preferable, but he was loathe to move very far from his newly acquired fortune. He had done a great deal to get that money.

Sally turned her head to look at her father. Her eyes were large and round, like those of a baby's. But when Jack smiled at her, she simply turned away and continued watching the television.

Jack suppressed a surge of grief that threatened to overwhelm him. Then he cursed himself for being so weak. How many times over the years had his daughter responded with indifference to him. He should be used to it by now. But, like an old wound that had never quite healed, it would always be there – ready to flare up when he was at his most vulnerable.

21

DCI Mandell's office door opened quickly and DI Hanson rushed in. "Another body found, Guv!" he exclaimed. "Pete Crofter – a regular at The Raven!"

"Damn!" Mandell swore. "Not another one! So where was he found?"

"In the Thames at Chiswick. Seems he was just dumped. No attempt made to weigh him down or anything like that."

"A friend of Jack Blade by any chance?"

"According to an informant, he's been helped by Blade on a few occasions."

"Coincidence...?" Mandell stroked his chin with the fingers of his right hand. "How much do we know about Jack Blade?"

"There isn't much to know, Guv. Turned up about five years ago. Paid cash for The Raven. No record, and never been in any trouble since he got here."

"Yet most of Manny Hemmings employees have drunk in his pub?"

"It's a popular place, Guv," said Hanson. "Most of our lads know The Raven quite well too."

"That's as may be. But this informant of yours? You say he told you that Manny Hemmings had Blade picked up one night?"

"That's right, Guv. The driver of the car is his brother-in-law and told him how Blade was taken into an abandoned warehouse. And when he drove him back later, he was in a right old state and stank of petrol."

"That's what's been bugging me since you told me this yesterday," said Mandell. "Why would Manny Hemmings take such an interest in the honest landlord of a pub?"

"Maybe he fell behind in his protection payments?" Hanson offered.

"Is there any evidence he's paying protection?"

"No, Guv. But it stands to reason. Most of the business's around that area are, although we can't prove it. So why would The Raven be excluded?"

"You could be right, Ken," said Mandell. "Anyway, I think it's time we paid Honest Jack Blade a visit."

"No point at the moment, Guv. He's away."

Mandell frowned. "Oh…?"

"According to the staff, he phoned them last week saying he was closing due to some electrical problem in the bar."

"Any sign of work being done?"

"Nothing, Guv. But we did notice that the back door has been forced. We checked inside. Someone obviously had a good search but nothing seems to have been taken. His TV and stuff are still there, so it's unlikely to have been burglars."

Mandell stared fixedly at his DI. "Now how many landlords do you know who would close down their pub for nearly a week, and not call in anyone to fix the problem; then go away and leave the place unattended without warning anyone?"

"I'd say he was in hiding," Hanson answered.

"But from whom, Ken, and why…?"

"Don't know, Guv. But it seems to be boiling down to something going on between him and Manny Hemmings."

"I agree. But what. There's no way someone like Blade could muscle in on Manny Hemmings. He just doesn't have the backing, and if he did we would know about it. So what are we overlooking?"

"Maybe he's got something on Hemmings," Hanson offered. "Maybe he overheard one of his men say something revealing in the pub and tried blackmailing Manny. And maybe he then panicked and went into hiding."

"That could explain Blade's friend ending up in the river, but not what has been happening to Hemming's men. This smells big time to me, Ken. Someone else must be involved."

"Another gang you mean?" said Hanson.

"At least someone with brains and cash."

"Frank Hemmings…?"

"He's the only one in the picture with both that I can see."

"Want me to pick him up, Guv?"

"Invite him in for an informal chat," said Mandell. "But no pressure. If he refuses to come, then don't press it."

"Right, Guv."

The instant DI Hanson left his office, Mandell stared fixedly at the telephone on his desk. He wondered how long it would be before his irate superior called again, demanding progress in the Manny Hemmings case.

Three hours later, Frank Hemmings was sitting in an interview room. Sitting opposite him were DS Angela Wilkinson and DI Ken Hanson.

"Thank you for coming, Mr Hemmings," said Hanson.

"Think nothing of it, Buddy," said Frank with a smile. "I've always wanted to see British bobbies at work."

Hanson and Wilkinson threw each other a glance that said *'we have a right comedian here.'*

"So," said Frank, still smiling. "What can I do for you?"

"Well," said Hanson, "as I'm sure you know, we're looking into your brother's affairs, and we were wondering if you could tell us why you are in the UK at this particular time?"

"Wouldn't any time be a particular time," said Frank.

"Please answer the question, Mr Hemmings," said Hanson.

"To see my little brother, of course," said Frank. "Nothing wrong with that is there. At least there isn't in the States. But then again this is not the States but good old England. And from what I hear, before the war your government allowed some fascist and his followers to go parading about the streets, whipping up support for Hitler. So who can be sure just what is allowed on this little island."

"Thanks for the history lesson," said Hanson with a wry smile. "Now there have been a lot of killings taking place recently, and this is of great concern to us."

"Of course it is," said Frank. "I mean, you wouldn't want good old London turning into Chicago, now would you."

"I'm referring to killings associated with your brother, Manny!" Hanson replied testily.

Frank frowned. "Associated with Manny, Detective Inspector Hanson? Are you saying that my little brother has something to do with the killing of these people? Because if you are, I would certainly like to see the substantial evidence you must have to make such a serious accusation?"

"You know very well your brother is involved!" Hanson snapped. "So let's cut the baloney, shall we!"

"The baloney...?" Frank looked puzzled. Then he smiled. "Oh, you mean the bullshit. Right you are then, Buddy, let's cut the baloney. My brother has nothing to do with anyone being killed. Got it."

"And do you?" Hanson asked, trying hard to keep his temper.

"Hey, Guys - come on!" Frank exclaimed. "I told you! I'm here paying my brother a visit! What could I know about what goes on in London any more than you could know what's going on in my home town! Be reasonable…!"

Hanson looked at an open folder on the table. "I see that a couple of people connected with The Raven pub have been murdered since you arrived."

"And may I ask if anyone was murdered *before* I arrived?" said Frank, clearly bemused by the proceedings.

There was no reply.

"I thought so," said Frank. "Now listen, Guys, I agreed to come here out of respect for the British police force, but I did expect to be treated with a little courtesy. So, if you don't have any more questions…?"

"What's your connection with Jack Blade?" said Hanson.

"Don't know the guy."

"You were seen talking to him?"

"And when was that exactly?"

Hanson placed his elbows on the table and leaned closer to Frank. "You were seen talking to him in The Raven pub as a matter of fact, and it was clear that you weren't discussing the weather?"

"Oh, you mean the guy behind the bar," said Frank. "So what. I spoke to the stewardess on the plane coming over; a guy at the security desk in the airport; the taxi driver in the cab I used; a lady in the shop where I bought a paper; a guy at the…"

"Thank you for your time, Mr Hemmings," Hanson interrupted suddenly as he and Wilkinson stood up. "No doubt you will be hearing from us again in the near future."

"Hey - looking forward to it, Guys!" Frank exclaimed cheerfully as the detectives left the Interview Room. "And I hope you don't mind, but I've always wanted to say this. *Evening all.*"

22

"Don't you ever go home?" Frank said as Manny rolled his fat cigar between his lips.

"Only when I have to," said Manny frowning, "and then for as short a time as possible. The older Sharon gets the more like her mother she becomes."

"Fucking shit!" Frank laughed. "But you only have yourself to blame, Little Brother. Didn't I tell you when you shocked us all by announcing your engagement that she would end up like her mother, and what a bitch she was. If Margaret is in Hell now, I'll bet she's running the place. Before she died, I was never scared of going there, but now…"

"Aaaa, Sharon's probably got the same heart condition her mother had," said Manny sounding hopeful. "That sort of thing is usually genetic. She's bound to drop dead during one of her tantrums, just like her mother did. I only have to wait. Sooner or later it will happen, and what a fucking relief it will be. Sharon could kill with that shrill voice of hers."

"Yea, but how old was her mother when she kicked the bucket?" Frank replied.

"Sixty three," said Manny. "Why…?"

"And Sharon's how old…?"

"Forty nine…I think," said Manny thoughtfully.

"Shit!" Frank laughed. "That's fourteen years to go, Little Brother!"

"Oh Christ, I never thought of it like that!" Manny cried. Then he smiled. "But I'm hoping to move things along a bit."

"How's that?"

"Well, as you know, she's always loved to eat chocolates, but these past few years she's become a right guzzler. And you wouldn't believe the size of her now, Frank. Mind you, she's real touchy about her weight. And you should have seen how she reacted the other week when we were out shopping and this little kid of about four comes up and asks her if she lives in the circus. And I'll bet you don't know what I always get her each birthday, Mother's Day, Father's Day, Christmas Day, Easter, Ramadan, Victory In Europe Day, and every other fucking celebration I can come up with?"

"All together now," said Frank.

"*Chocolates!*" the brothers declared simultaneously with a roar of laughter.

"Seriously though," said Manny as the laughter died away, "do you think the police know anything?"

"They're just fishing," said Frank. "They have a suspicion that there's a link between us and Blade, but they have nothing concrete. So long as you keep your affairs squeaky clean until this investigation is over, I can get back to the States, once I've dealt with Jack Blade. Now, don't you worry, Little Brother, you'll have your dough back, and that landlord out of you hair for good, in no time at all. Brad Jackson could sniff out a peanut in the middle of one of those European grain mountains of wheat, and tell you if it's salted or unsalted."

"Christ, Frank," said Manny, "it's good to have you here! I didn't know if you would come, being so busy in the States. But you're here and I'm grateful."

"That's what family is for," Frank replied. "When a junk yard dog like Jack Blade starts showing his teeth at you, then the only way to handle him is to kick them down his throat and choke him, that's my motto."

23

Brad Jackson was a balding, dumpy little man of fifty, with a large paunch and a passion for Fig Rolls. Wherever he went he had a packet of them in his car and another in his coat pocket. His doctor had told him that those little brown biscuits with the rich filling would probably kill him one day, but so what. At least they wouldn't rot his lungs like cigarettes, or pickle his liver like alcohol. 'Give up my beloved Fig Rolls - no thanks, Doc,' he had replied. 'Death by Fig Roll would be like eating the biscuit itself – soft, sweet and finished in no time.'

Brad's clothes were always a bit on the shabby side, and despite his wealth he never cared much for grooming. He liked to style himself on the poverty-stricken, solitary Private Eye characters that were regularly on TV in the States. That was one of the reasons he always worked alone. The other was that he had never yet come across anyone with even half his talent. And it was his belief that when you send someone less talented than yourself to do a job, the results were bound to be less productive. 'The curse of your brilliance, Brad, is that you have to do everything yourself,' he frequently sighed. 'That was the price of being a genius.'

Brad sat in his white Mini, which was parked a few doors - and across the road from number twenty four Russell Street. It was five thirty in the evening, and a slight drizzle was falling, creating small puddles in the uneven pavement. Few people were about, and that was just the way he liked it, because in reality he hated people and it seemed that they hated him. He was always polite to them, but only because he had to be. He could never be aggressive towards them because his lack of physical prowess made him feel particularly vulnerable to the violence of others. But if it wasn't for this limitation on revealing his true feelings towards people, they would find out what a nasty character he truly was, and he would be proud to show them. However, they didn't have it all their own way. Because whereas he was always vulnerable in a physical way, mentally it was a different matter entirely. For when it came to a battle of the mind he was a supreme predator, and people were his prey. They would try and hide from him, try and conceal themselves in their burrows like rabbits when the fox was prowling near the warren. But whereas the fox would eventually give up and try its luck elsewhere, not Brad Jackson. He never trusted to luck and he never went away and he never gave up. It was a principle...a religion that once he was put on the scent of a particular prey, then he must follow that scent to its only conclusion...*discovery*. And it was of no consequence at all the reason for the prey's desperate desire to hide. It mattered not at all that some of them might be completely innocent of any crime...perhaps only of being in the wrong place at the wrong time. It didn't matter that they might be male or female - old or young – evil or good. All he cared about was that they were found by him and punished. Usually that meant torture followed by death. Of course he himself never participated in the demise of his victims as a predator usually does, for he found the sight and smells associated with it quite offensive. No, he was happy to allow others to deliver the coup de grace. That was Brad Jackson and he hated people. He was their predator and they were his prey. Now he was on the hunt once more and he had already picked up the scent of his prey. That prey was Jack Blade.

As the rain continued to fall, Brad brushed tiny crumbs from the front of his coat. Then he raised his binoculars and stared once more at number twenty four. He had been watching the place since 8am, and except for obeying the call of nature on two occasions, he had not moved the car. He had seen Mr Peterson leave the house at 8.15am, and Mrs Peterson leave at 10.25am. But she had returned ten minutes later with a bag of shopping. But there had been no sign of Jack Blade. Brad was disappointed by this as he was eager to get back to America and take the three month holiday in Florida he'd been promising himself for eight years.

Brad was fiercely proud of the fact that he had tracked down Blade's parents-in-law in such a short time. And when he reported his findings to Frank later on, his employer would surely be impressed; so impressed in fact that perhaps he would even add an additional bonus to his four thousand dollar fee. Frank could be very generous when he was pleased by a job well done. He was that kind of guy – Brad's kind of guy.

"Oh well," Brad muttered to himself. "It looks like a bit of old fashioned leg work is going to be necessary on this occasion."

Brad then put down the binoculars and struggled to get his barrel shaped body out of the car. He cursed the vehicle for it's shortcomings, rather than his own. His next car would have a proper size door.

He knew that John Peterson wasn't at home, but Marion was. Women were far easier to intimidate and were rarely violent.

Doing up the buttons of his coat with some effort, he ran across the road and made his way to the house. He walked up the short drive and rang the bell.

The door opened a few moments later.

Brad smiled as charmingly as he could manage for a serial people-hater. "I do apologize for troubling you so late, Madam, but may I inquire if you are Mrs Marion Peterson?"

"Yes I am," Marion replied cautiously.

"Excellent," said Brad. "Now, would it be possible to come in and have a little chat with you? You see, I have been on my feet all day, and I'm not as young as I used to be. A chair would be very much appreciated?"

"What is it about?" Marion asked.

"Oh, I do beg your pardon," said Brad reaching into his inside pocket and producing an expensive looking business card. "My name is Brad Jackson. I'm a private detective from California, and I'd like to talk to you about your son-in-law, Jack Blade."

Marion's eyes widened in alarm. "I don't know…"

"Let me assure you that there is nothing to be concerned about, Mrs Peterson!" Brad interrupted hurriedly. "Quite the contrary in fact.

And I won't take up more than a few minutes of your time. So if I could just come in and take the weight off my poor feet…?"

Brad moved slowly forwards, and Marion instinctively retreated back into the hall, but she kept one hand on the door.

"This is most civil of you, Mrs Peterson…most civil," Brad cooed once he was in the hall. "And perhaps you could show me somewhere I could sit down?"

Automatically, Marion led the way to the living room. Sally was watching television, clasping a new doll in her hands.

"What a beautiful child you have there, Mrs Peterson," said Brad, dropping into an armchair. "I have two of my own back home in the States."

"She's my granddaughter," Marion replied. "Her mother died a few years ago."

"Oh, do forgive me!" Brad exclaimed. "I shouldn't have presumed!"

"That's all right," said Marion. "Would you like a cup of tea and something to eat?"

Brad smiled again. "Tea will be just fine. You see, I developed a taste for tea when I spent a year in London a while back. Mind you, I think my family would rather I drank it outside the house. They're all hopeless coffee addicts, I fear, but I very much prefer the delicate flavours tea has to offer. It is also better for my high blood pressure – or so my physician tells me."

Marion gave a half smile and went to the kitchen.

When she came back a few minutes later with two cups of tea on a tray, Brad was trying to engage Sally in conversation. "Shy little thing, isn't she?" he said as he took one of the cups.

"She's autistic," said Marion.

A look of horror appeared on Brad's podgy face. "Oh dear, it appears that once again I have put my oversized foot in it!" he declared, shaking his head. "I do beg your pardon! Whatever must you think of me!"

"Don't worry, it's a common assumption," said Marion. "I've even had people coming up to me in the shops when she's been playing up, telling me I should discipline her and not just ignore her bad behaviour."

"So much ignorance in the world, isn't there?" Brad tutted. Then he took a sip of his tea, and his face lit up. "Excellent tea, Mrs Peterson. Truly excellent. I don't know if it is the water over here or the blend, but you just can't beat English tea."

"You said that you were making inquiries about Jack?" Marion prompted. "What kind of inquiries…?"

"Yes, of course," said Brad. "Well, to put it simply, Mrs Peterson, an important client of mine wishes to make contact with your son-in-law regarding a business proposition."

"What sort of proposition?"

Brad smiled. "I'm afraid that is confidential, Mrs Peterson."

"Then who wants to contact him?" Marion's voice took on an edge to it.

Brad sighed. "The identity of my client is also confidential, I fear. My instructions are to find Jack Blade and present him with a proposition from my client."

"You obviously want something from me, Mr Jackson," said Marion coldly, "but you appear to have no intention of returning the favour?"

"Unfortunately I am bound by the rules of my profession, Mrs Peterson," Brad protested. "However, in the spirit of reconciliation, I will say that my client's offer to your son-in-law will present him with an opportunity to make a great deal of money - a very great deal of money in fact."

"Really...?" Marion replied with exaggerated surprise. "And here was I believing that Jack was just your average young man trying to make his way in the world. So tell me, Mr Jackson, assuming that the rules of your profession allows it of course, what hidden talent does Jack have that, up to now, has been hidden from me, but clearly so valuable to your client?"

Brad began to sip his tea. He needed a few moments to think. He felt annoyed. He assumed that the mention of money would have this woman like putty in his hands, but she was obviously no fool. He stopped sipping and smiled once more at her. "I'm afraid to divulge that would reveal the nature of my client's proposition. And, as I said before, I am bound by the rules of my profession. I realize this must be difficult for you, Mrs Peterson, and I confess that when I first set out on my chosen profession, I found secrecy the most difficult of its disciplines to uphold...especially being an open natured person myself. But time and experience has taught me that although unpleasant, it is nevertheless necessary at times to keep certain facts from certain people. However, in time all is usually revealed to those concerned."

"Very well," said Marion. "What exactly do you want from me?"

"The whereabouts of your son-in-law."

"He's in London I believe."

"And would you know exactly where?"

"No."

"In that case," Brad replied putting his cup down on the carpet, "I must ask another favour of you, Mrs Peterson. The next time your son-in-law contacts you, would you please telephone me on a number I shall leave you. And I would be grateful if you would refrain from telling him about my visit. I would like to be the first person to discuss the matter with him."

"Now you want me to keep secrets," said Marion, clearly irritated.

Brad laughed dryly. "Do forgive me, Mrs Peterson, but I have found from experience that first impressions are crucial in such matters."

Brad then stood up. He reached inside his pocket for his pen and notepad.

A large figure shot into the room and made straight for him.

Brad cried out as a long cord whipped around his neck and was pulled tight.

The strong nylon cord bit deep into his flesh with terrible force, cutting off his blood and oxygen supply to his head - turning his podgy face a purple red colour. His brain, sensing the potentially fatal obstruction of the blood to his upper body, kicked in with a signal that sent a massive dose of adrenalin surging throughout his system. His heart went into overdrive in response – desperately trying to restore the blood flow, but against the external force that was killing him, it was a useless tactic. He continued on towards his slow, agonizing death at the hands of his killer.

But Brad Jackson had a desire to live that would have surprised even him. And as he gurgled and gasped for air, his small podgy fists pummelled Jack's face with impressive force.

Jack turned his face away from the assault and closed his eyes tight – determined to maintain his death hold on the private investigator.

Then he remembered his daughter. "Get Sally upstairs!" he shouted at his mother-in-law, his face now almost as red as Brad's from the pounding it was taking.

Marion stared in horrified disbelief at him.

"*Get her upstairs...now!*" Jack roared at the top of his voice.

Suddenly galvanized by the command of his voice, Marion flew out of her seat and grabbed Sally. The child screamed as she was quickly carried out of the room and up the stairs.

The blows from Brad Jackson's fists were growing weaker now, but they still had power in them.

Jack cursed the man's persistence.

A wet patch began spreading between Brad's trouser legs as his bladder emptied itself, but he was beyond caring.

His lungs were on fire and his mind was a cauldron of dizziness, desperation and terror. The cord around his throat had become a knife, cutting through his flesh. He could no longer see his attacker; only feel him as his fists beat against his face. But even those sensations left him and he was hitting a solid wall.

Then something lurched inside his brain and a cloud of complete blackness seemed to expand in the distance – rushing towards him with terrible speed.

Jack sighed with relief when Brad's arms suddenly dropped to his sides.

His face felt raw and somewhere inside him a germ of vanity protested about the damage that may have been done to his looks.

And when Brad's body began to slip downwards, Jack's rigid arms followed – maintaining the pressure – maintaining the strangling hold that was putting an end to his victim.

He held on for a full minute longer after Brad was laying motionless in the armchair. Then satisfied that death had occurred he released his grip and moved away from the body. He was breathing hard and his hands hurt where the thin strands of the bathroom pull-switch had bitten into his flesh. He massaged them for a few moments, then he found a seat and dropped into it. He sat staring at Brad Jackson's body for over ten minutes before he heard Marion's soft footsteps as she came down the stairs.

Marion walked quietly into the room and stared at the body. She was white-faced and her hands were trembling.

"How's Sally?" Jack asked.

"She's sleeping," Marion said in a flat tone.

Jack suddenly jumped to his feet and dashed into the kitchen. He rushed back with a towel and threw it over Brad's distorted face.

"God Almighty, Jack," said Marion, "what have you done?"

Jack placed himself between Marion and the body. He held both her shoulders in a firm grip. "Now listen to me, Mum," he said in a forceful tone. "You know I wouldn't have done something like this without the biggest reason in the world?"

Marion continued to stare straight ahead as if she could still see Brad Jackson's body through her son-in-law's chest.

"Look at me, Mum!" Jack ordered. "Look at me...!"

Slowly, Marion's eyes came up until they were staring directly into Jack's. He could see the shock and confusion in them.

"Now listen to me, Mum," he went on. "I know you just saw me do a terrible thing - something you thought you would never see anyone do except in the films. But that man represented the greatest danger any of us will ever be in. Do you understand. If he had walked out of this house alive, he would have reported back to some very bad people. Then those people would have come here and killed all of us, including Sally. Do you understand what I am saying. In order to protect you dad and Sally I had to stop that man reporting back. And there was only one way to do that, and that was to kill him."

"But to strangle him like that," Marion whispered. "And right here in front of Sally and me..."

"I know, I know!" Jack cried in anguish. "But I couldn't do it outside! I couldn't let him leave the house! Don't you see, Mum, he might have someone else outside in his car! Someone might have seen and called the police! I had to do it in here! I had no choice! Surely you can see that?"

Marion blinked a few times, then she seemed to recover some of her composure. She sat down again in her armchair, her hands clasped between her knees. Jack sat next to her on the armrest. He put an arm around her shoulders.

"What kind of trouble are you in, Jack, that it was necessary to kill a man in front of your own daughter?" Marion asked accusingly.

"The worst kind, Mum," said Jack. "Now I can't get out of it."

"Then why didn't you go to the police?"

"That wouldn't have done any good. Even the police can't get the man who's after me. He always sends other people to do his killing for him. And if they get caught before the job is done, then he just sends more people."

"And is this how it's going to be from now on?" Marion asked. "This man sends people here to get you, and you strangle them, so he sends more people. Could get quite tedious after a while, couldn't it...?"

Jack grinned and shook Marion a few times. That was one of the things he'd always liked about his mother-in-law - her dry sense of humour, even during very difficult times.

"Look, Mum, it's possible that Brad Jackson hasn't reported back to his employer yet. And if that's the case, he won't know about you. But just to be on the safe side, I want you and dad to take Sally to Aunt Miriam's place in Cornwall and stay there; just until this blows over."

Marion turned her pale face up to him. "And will it blow over, Love? I mean, you just said that this man who is after you won't stop sending people? He could hire other private investigators, couldn't he, and they might find out about us too?"

"He'll stop doing all that pretty soon," said Jack. "Don't worry about it, Mum. I have a plan to make sure he never bothers us again."

Suddenly there was the sound of the front door opening and closing. Jack and Marion threw startled looks at the living room door.

"Jack!" John Peterson declared with obvious pleasure as he walked into the room.

Then he saw the expression on their faces. "What's up? Someone forget to put my dinner on...?"

Still receiving no reply, John turned to sit in his favourite chair, and stopped abruptly when he saw the body of Brad Jackson sprawled in it with a towel over his face.

"Who the bloody hell is that?" he cried.

"He's a private detective from California," said Marion in a level voice.

"So what's he doing sleeping here? And why is that towel on his face?"

John moved closer and reached out to remove the towel.

"Don't!" said Marion.

John looked back at his wife. "Why not? What's going on here?"

"He's dead," Marion replied.

John stepped back instantly and frowned. Then he stared at the body once more. "You mean he died - right there - in my bloody chair...?"

"Yes."

"God, the poor bugger. And is the ambulance on the way?"

"No."

John was shocked. "What do you mean no? Didn't you call one? For heaven's sake, Marion, where's your head? You should have called an ambulance?"

"There was no point," said Marion, feeling as if she was trapped in some awful nightmare.

"Why not?" said John. "He might still be alive! Heart attacks are funny things! Someone can look dead, but...!"

"He *is* dead, John," Marion interrupted. "Jack made sure he was."

"Jack's no doctor!" John shot back. "You mean you've left the poor sod lying here, and you haven't even called an ambulance!"

"I told you, Jack made sure he was dead!" A touch of hysteria had entered Marion's voice.

"And I told you he's no doctor so he can't be positive!" John snapped. Then he reached out and whipped the towel off the body.

"Christ Almighty!" he exclaimed in horror, retreating a few steps. "I've never seen a heart attack do that to someone's face before!"

"That's because he's been strangled, you fool!" Marion screamed. "What's the matter with your eyes! Can't you see what's around his neck! Jack strangled him to save us from some terrible people who want to hurt us! Now do you understand!"

"No I bloody don't!" John retorted. "All I wanted to find when I came home from work was my dinner in the oven, and for you to tell me Sally was feeling better! Instead I find a dead man in my favourite chair with the kitchen towel over his face - the cord from the bathroom light wrapped around his neck, and you going on about Jack strangling him because some bad people want to harm us! No, Marion, I don't understand at all!"

It took two solid hours of persuading from Marion and Jack to convince John not to call the police. As far as he was concerned, the police were there to get you out of such trouble, and it would be obvious to them why Jack had to kill the private detective. The man was clearly a criminal himself if he was working for one, and the police in America were bound to have a file on him. But Jack and Marion didn't see it that way, and so he agreed to go along with them. Jack emptied Brad's pockets of everything, including a key, and risked going outside and checking every car until he found one the key fitted. He started the engine of the Mini and drove up to the house. Then, just after three am, he and John put Brad's body in the boot. Jack drove away, and John followed in Jack's car. Two hours later they were in Kent. And as it was just getting light, they abandoned Brad Jackson and his car in a wood - having wiped the vehicle clean of prints, and removed the number plates. They drove back to Chigwell in Jacks car and in total silence.

By ten am the Peterson's and their granddaughter Sally were on their way to Cornwall.

24

Frank Hemmings lifted the receiver of the phone by his bed. "Room service please," he said.

A moment later a voice answered.

"This is room 107," said Frank. "I'd like to order some breakfast please. That's two fried eggs, two sausages, two bacon, tomato and mushrooms. I'd also like three slices of toast...buttered; a small serving of dark bitter marmalade, and a large pot of strong coffee...no milk or sugar. Oh, and a copy of The New York Times."

Frank replaced the receiver and smiled to himself. He didn't know what it was about five star hotels, but they always gave him an appetite first thing in the mornings. Back home he'd have made do with toast or cereal. Perhaps it was something to do with being raised in a London slum area where even margarine on his toast was a treat.

He reached behind his head and straightened his pillow. He glanced down at his dressing gown and smiled. Lynn always did like him to be comfortable when he was travelling.

Twenty five minutes later an elderly waiter delivered his breakfast on a trolley. Then he proceeded to take the breakfast from the trolley and lay it on a glass top table with the speed and professionalism of long service.

"There you go, Buddy," said Frank, handing the waiter three crisp pound notes. The waiter seemed very grateful, promising to help him out if he needed anything at all.

He had just about finished his breakfast when there was a sharp knock at the door. Still in his dressing gown, Frank crossed the room to answer it. He opened the door, then stepped back as eight large men walked in.

"Sorry, Boss," said one of the men when he saw the breakfast dishes. "We didn't realize you were eating."

"Just finished, Boys," Frank said, closing the door. "Now, why don't you make yourselves comfortable while I go and get dressed. Order drinks or something to eat from room service. Just pick up the phone."

"Thanks, Boss," said the man, heading for the telephone next to the bed.

When Frank reappeared half an hour later, the men were sitting around, drinking scotch and bourbon. "Comfortable, Boys?" he asked.

"Sure thing, Boss," came the reply from a couple of the men.

"Right then," said Frank, "I've brought you over to do a job for me. My brother is having a bit of trouble from a pub landlord, believe it or not, and I want him dealt with. Now this landlord - his name is Jack Blade by the way, has already killed Manny's top men, and stolen a crate of very valuable magazines from him, so I want you to contact me when you find Blade. Understand, I don't want you to even question him until I get there...?"

"Got you, Boss," one of the men replied with a casual flick of his hand. "You give us his last known address and leave it to us. We'll find him for you."

Frank looked at the speaker - a blond haired Texan in his early thirties. "You won't have to do the looking, Eddy. I've got Brad searching for him, and I'm waiting for his call right now. All you and the boys have to do is disarm Blade and keep him safe until I get there."

"Jeeze, I wouldn't want Brad Jackson on my trail if I was trying to hide from the world," Eddy said. "That guy could find a rain drop in an ocean."

"With a blindfold on," a New Yorker called Jed added.

"And during a hurricane," said Eddy, and they all laughed.

"OK, settle down," said Frank. "But you're right about Brad. No one can hide from him."

"So, what time are you expecting him to call, Boss?" Jed asked.

Frank looked at his watch. "Nine o clock."

Jed looked at his watch too. "Nine ten now, Boss...?"

Frank frowned. Brad was ten minutes late, and Brad Jackson was never late; it was a principle with him. If he said he'd meet you at the Houses of Parliament at five minutes past ten, and Big Ben struck ten o clock just as Brad showed up, you'd feel obliged to warn those in charge of the famous clock that it was running five minutes slow.

Frank saw the rest of his men glancing at their watches. They were probably thinking the same thing. What had happened to Brad Jackson?

"You sure he said nine, Boss?" Eddy inquired.

Frank walked over to the phone and picked up the receiver. "Reception desk, please. Hello, this is Mr Hemmings in room 107. Have there been any calls for me this morning?"

An anxious wait followed.

"Hello," said Frank. "Right. Thank you."

He put the receiver back.

"No joy, Boss?" Jed asked.

"No. Something must have happened to him."

"It's only been ten minutes, Boss," said Eddy. "A bit early to jump to conclusions…"

"No, Eddy, it isn't. Somehow or other Jack Blade's got him, and that leaves us up Shit Creek."

"Then what do we do, Boss - head back to the States?"

A furious expression twisted Frank's features. "And let some pub landlord rip my brother off! Are you out of your fucking mind!"

"But if the trail's gone cold, Mr Hemmings…?" Eddy replied, alarmed that he had angered his boss.

"I don't care if it's turned to fucking ice! I came here to get Jack Blade and that's exactly what I'm going to do!"

"But how, Boss?"

"By understanding him, that's how!" Frank snapped. "This guy don't want just money, otherwise he'd have sold the magazines and be safe in another country by now, and Manny assures me he's still in the UK. No, Mr Jack Blade wants something else. He wants power, and he'll stop at nothing to get it, even if it kills him."

"How does that help us?" Eddy asked. "We don't know where he is and we can't very well search the whole country. The UK may be no bigger than one of our states, but it could still take years finding him?"

"It helps us a very great deal, as a matter of fact," said Frank calming down a little. "You see, Eddy, I think he's going to carry on with his original plan to kill my brother and take over his organization."

"But that's crazy, Boss," said Eddy. "Don't he know who Manny's brother is?"

"You bet he does. In fact, I made a point of introducing myself to him the day I arrived on this damp little island."

"Then the guy's nuts," Eddy replied. "If he tries anything, we'll get him for sure."

"I wouldn't be so confident if I were you," said Frank. "He's done pretty well up to now."

"Naaa..." Eddy pulled a face. "So he stole a load of valuable magazines, and wasted a few cheap London gangsters. But that's no big deal, Boss. Those London guys are strictly small time compared to us."

"That's true enough. And I take it you have the necessary equipment for the job...?"

"More than enough," said Eddy, placing the suitcase he had brought into the room on the bed. He unzipped the lid and threw it back. Inside were various hand guns with boxes of ammunition and silencers. There were also a dozen leather shoulder holsters."

"Now remember," said Frank, "people in this country are gun shy, so keep those out of sight, and only bring them out when you have to."

"Right you are, Boss," said Eddy, zipping up the case. "What now?"

"I want you and Jed to keep an eye on Manny's office from the smaller office next to it. Reg, you and Hank keep watch from outside the building. I'll give you the address of his office, and a description of Jack Blade in a minute. The rest of you boys stay here until I send for you. And lay off the booze. I want you sharp."

"Is this guy Blade working on his own?" Eddy inquired.

"As far as I know he is now. But he wasted a few of his own guys after they took out the Flynn brothers, and I understand from Manny that those Flynns were pretty handy with their fists, as well as with guns."

"Naaa, small time, Boss, strictly small time!" said Eddy with contempt.

Frank felt his anger rising. "Listen here, Eddy! When my brother says the guys were handy, it means they were handy! And if you're going to be looking out for Manny thinking that Jack Blade is a push over, then you can piss off back to the States and let the rest of us get on with it!"

Eddy raised his hands in defence. "Hey, take it easy, Boss! Of course I'm not going to get sloppy! And don't worry about Manny! I know he's your kid brother! I'll take care of him!"

"See that you do," said Frank, "or I'll take care of you."

25

Jack stared out of the window of the cheap room he had rented. It was three days since he had packed his daughter and in-laws off to Cornwall, and it pleased him that there had been no reports yet about Brad Jackson in the media. He had considered hiring some help, but decided against it. For all he knew, anyone he took on could already be working for Manny Hemmings. No, he had to carry on alone for the time being. He could do the hiring when Manny and his brother were dead.

Jack moved away from the window and sat on the single bed. He picked up one of the two guns on it and began cleaning it with a cloth. He liked the compactness of the Nine Millimetre. It felt snug yet powerful, and even though the Thirty Eight had a bit more punch to it, he would choose the Nine Millimetre every time. Precision over raw power was his motto – something Henry Dane should have understood before taking on one of the Flynn brothers by himself.

Besides the guns there were three boxes of ammunition – two for the Nine Millimetre and one for the Thirty Eight, and two silencers. Tom Smith had been a dab hand at acquiring such items and at a fair price too. He missed Tom - his company, and love of poker. It was a pity he had to be killed. But when he demanded that the money be returned in exchange for Pete, he just couldn't see that he was putting too high a price on the man's life. They were good friends, but no one was worth a million pounds and the plans of Jack Blade – at least no one who wasn't family.

As he cleaned and oiled the guns, Jack gave some thought to Manny's brother Frank. He realized the man was formidable, and the arrival of an American private detective was proof enough for him that Frank had company with him - how many, he didn't know, but he guessed probably not more than a dozen. Just as Manny was being watched by Scotland

Yard, Frank probably had the FBI, or some other government organization keeping an eye on him. And leaving the country with an army of men would certainly draw some interest.

His only advantage at this moment in time was that although they had no idea where he was, he knew where they were, or would be sooner or later. Frank would certainly have The Raven and Manny's office watched, so those were the places he must make a start. One by one they must fall, until the only one left standing was Jack Blade.

It was late. Sean Hellet burped a few times and took another bite of his ham sandwich. How he hated jobs like these. Here he was on a Friday evening, sitting in his car opposite an empty pub, watching out for someone who was long gone. Where was the sense in that. And if Manny was forced to do these jobs himself once in a while, perhaps he would be more understanding towards his employees. But then again, knowing Manny as he did, nothing would ever change him. Manny felt that being selfish was his absolute right.

Sean poured himself tea from a red coloured flask and peered out through the door window. The glass was speckled with rain drops, though it had stopped raining hours ago. The Beatles were playing Twist and Shout on the radio, but Sean wasn't listening. He preferred The Rolling Stones any day of the week. At least they dressed the way rock stars should and were consistent, instead of wearing those ridiculous suits and even more ridiculous range of different haircuts the Beatles were famous for, but which he found irritating.

A shudder ran through Sean's body as he stared at The Raven. How sinister and ancient it looked without people and lights; like some place of sacrificial ritual, where unspeakable acts were committed behind dark windows.

Sean took a few swigs of tea and pulled a face. It tasted like cat piss that had gone off. Why did flasks always ruin good tea? He wound down his window to throw it out, and jumped as something cold and hard pressed against the side of his right temple.

"Make the slightest move, Mate and I'll blow your fucking brains all over the inside of your poxy car!" an unfamiliar voice hissed. "Now reach back slowly with your right hand and release the catch on the passenger door!"

Sean did as he was told. 'Please God,' his mind begged, 'don't let it be Jack Blade!'

"That's good," said the voice. "So far you're staying alive, and let's keep it that way, shall we. Now lean forwards and rest your head and hands on the steering wheel."

Sean carried out the instructions, and heard the passenger door open. The car lurched as someone got in.

'Christ Almighty, he's a big bastard!' Sean said to himself. And at five foot five and nine stone, he realized that even without the gun, the stranger was in no danger from him.

"You can sit up straight now," said the voice. "And I'm going to ask you a few questions. And if I even suspect you're lying to me, I'll put a bullet in your brain – understand…?"

Sean straightened up. Sweat began to bead on his face. Manny wasn't paying him enough for this kind of shit. He had never even seen a real gun, not to mind have one pressed against his head. He hated guns – people used them to kill other people, and he was other people.

Something tapped him on the back of the head. "I said, do you understand…?"

"Yes, I understand!" Sean's voice trembled. "Jesus Christ, Mate what's this all about? I was only sitting here minding my own business…?"

His head was tapped again. "I'm asking the questions. Now, do you have a partner on this watch?"

"What do you mean?" said Sean.

"Trying to be clever will only get you dead," said the voice. "And I'll ask you the question just one more time. Now I know that you are watching the pub over there, so do you have someone to take over the watch from you later?"

"Someone relieves me at two am," said Sean, his one hope of getting some help gone in seconds.

"That's four hours from now. Good. We won't be disturbed. So let's clear up a few points first. You're working for Manny Hemmings – right…?"

"That's right."

"And you know his brother Frank?"

"I don't exactly know him. But I've seen him around the last few days."

"Does he have any help with him - American's I mean?"

"Some blokes showed up with him at his hotel," said Sean.

"How many, and what are they like?"

"Eight tough looking heavies, and a little fat bloke, although the fat bloke came before the others. Someone told me he's a big time gumshoe in America, but I can't remember his name."

"That doesn't matter. Now, do you know who I am?"

Sean hesitated before answering. "Jack Blade...?"

"Correct. And do you know why Manny is after me?"

"Something about magazines."

"Fuck that. What's your name by the way?"

"Sean...Sean Hellet."

"Consider this for a moment, Sean. Do you really think Manny would send for his big shot brother in the States because someone stole some magazines from him?"

"Not just ordinary magazines, Mate," Sean corrected. "I heard they were special ones and very expensive...over a hundred quid each."

"Even special magazines wouldn't be *that* important," said Jack. "Just think about it; going to all that trouble bringing his brother; more than half a dozen heavies, and a big time private eye, all the way over from the States."

"When you put it like that, I suppose it does sound a bit fishy." Sean admitted. "But if it's not about magazines then what *is* it all about?"

Jack leaned forwards and said in a low voice. "I'm going to let you into a little secret, Sean. Believe it or not I stole a million pounds in cash from Manny - that's right, a million pounds that he was trying to hide from the police."

"Fucking Hell!" Sean retorted. "No wonder Manny's so fucking mad all the time!"

"And have you any idea why I'm here in your car, pointing this gun at your head?" Jack asked.

"No...?" said Sean with a start, remembering his situation after having momentarily forgotten it at the mention of a million pounds.

"I'm here because the money is hidden over there in my pub," said Jack. "And if you're willing to help me get it, I'll cut you in for a hundred thousand, and no one will be the wiser. And when your partner turns up, you just say there was no sign of me. And then you can drive away with a fortune in the boot? I take it your partner has his own car...?"

"He sure does," said Sean. Then images of endless cold beers, hot beaches and even hotter women flashed suddenly in his mind. He could hardly contain his excitement, but he must put on his best poker face now because he had some very serious negotiating to do. "Look, Jack, I'll be risking my life helping you, so I think it's only fair that you cut me in for half that money?"

"You've got to be kidding!" Jack retorted.

"I might have to get out of the country in a hurry if Manny finds out," said Sean. "And these private airfields charge a bit more than the usual price. And another thing, I don't ever want to work again and I like only the best. Now you have to admit, Jack, even five hundred thousand might not last me the rest of my life, not the way I intend to spend it."

Jack stayed silent for a few moments. Then he sighed loudly. "OK, I'll up my offer to three hundred thousand, and that's my final offer."

"But I'll need half a million," said Sean.

"Three hundred thousand," said Jack.

"Then I'll drop to four hundred thousand," Sean offered. "And don't forget, you need my help. Without me you won't be able to get your hands on it, and what good will it be to you then."

"I'm still not going to give you a penny more than three hundred thousand," said Jack. "And don't *you* forget, I'm the one with the gun, and what good will four hundred thousand be to you when you're dead."

Sean laughed. His fear was gone. And why should he be afraid - Jack Blade needed his help and he was going to give him an absolute fortune for that help. Of course he knew that Blade might try and double cross him – keep all the money for himself. After all, no one would want to give away that much money. And he must be feeling pretty confident that he could pull a fast one on Sean Hellet, because he was the fierce Jack Blade and he had the gun. But what Jack didn't know about was the five inch knife in his trouser pocket. It was true that he had never used that knife before – never even threatened anyone, but to save his life and to spend the rest of his life in sheer luxury, well that was a different matter entirely. Under those circumstances he could easily see himself driving a knife into someone's back.

"You've talked me into it, Jack," he said with a huge grin. "I'll just have to limit myself to one mansion and two Rolls."

"Good," said Jack "Now before we go and get the money, I want you to tell me everything you know about the building that Manny has his offices in. And don't leave out anything, not even the smallest detail."

"Why do you want to know that?" Sean asked. "Surely you're leaving the country tonight as well as me...?"

"Course I am," Jack replied. "But I intend to come back when everything settles and pay Manny a visit he won't like one little bit."

"Good for you, Mate!" Sean declared. "And give that fat greedy pig a bullet for me will you! He's been treating the lot of us like dogs for ages!"

"I'll even write your name on it," Jack promised. "Now about those details...?"

An hour later Sean finished telling Jack what he knew about the building.

"That all of it?" Jack inquired.

"Everything worth knowing," said Sean, "unless you want me to include the patterns on the carpets."

Jack laughed. "That won't be necessary, Mate. Right then, let's go and collect that money."

"You don't have to tell me twice," said Sean, putting his hand on the chrome door handle.

There were two loud putts, and his eyes stared wide open for a few moments. Then he slumped forwards on the steering wheel - blood running out through two large exit holes in the middle of his chest and down into his lap.

"Sorry, Mate," said Jack. "Couldn't afford to be that generous to you."

Jack searched the dead man before leaving the car. And what he found he put in his pocket for use later on.

26

Jack knew that he had about three hours before Sean's partner turned up and raised the alarm. He had already spotted the unmarked police car a short distance from the tall building containing Manny's office, and the single occupant who occasionally lit up a cigarette - a sure and careless sign of somebody who was pissed off at spending nights parked across the road from a criminal's office, without a single incident to give the shift a little spice. It took no time at all to find the car containing Frank's two heavies. They were parked directly opposite the main entrance to the building, and at least ten parked cars from the police surveillance. They could not see each other, which was a bonus for Jack, considering what he had to do.

Turning up the collar of his raincoat, and discarding the powerful pair of binoculars he had used, Jack slowly approached the green Vauxhall Viva containing the Americans. He realized that they could probably see him in the wing mirror, if they were looking, so he tried to behave as casual as possible.

Soon he was walking past the vehicle.

A sideways glance revealed that the two occupants were young large and fit. He would have to go very carefully.

As he passed the car, Jack pulled out his gun and leaped in front of it. The startled look on the men's faces as they saw someone pointing a gun at them through the windscreen almost made Jack laugh, but the situation called for other emotions. Jack flicked the tip of the long silencer up and down a few times. The men got the message and raised their hands. Then keeping the gun pointed at them, Jack moved slowly to the driver's door. He tapped on the window with his left hand.

The driver wound down the window. "What the hell's going on, Buddy?" he demanded.

"Open up the door behind you, and don't try anything," Jack ordered.

"Look, Buddy," said the man, showing no sign of following the order, "if this is a stick up, then..."

Jack punched the man in the face with his free hand. The punch wasn't particularly hard - just enough to command obedience.

"OK, OK, I get the message!" the man cried, reaching back and unlocking the door.

Jack got in.

"Hey, you're Jack Blade, aren't you?" said the man in the passenger seat, turning his head. "My Boss would like a word with you, Buddy."

"Look straight ahead!" Jack ordered. "Now, the first thing I want to know is are either of you carrying a gun?"

"This is England, Buddy," said the driver. "No guns allowed."

"I'll ask only one more time," said Jack. "Are you carrying guns?"

"You deaf or something, Buddy!" the man growled. "Didn't I just say; no guns allowed!"

"In that case," said Jack, "I'm going to shoot one of you through the head, and search the other one to make sure."

"Hey, take it easy, Buddy!" exclaimed the driver. "Sure we're carrying guns! We're bodyguards, for Christ Sakes!"

"That's better," said Jack. "So where do you keep them?"

"Shoulder holsters," came the reply.

Jack jabbed the driver in the back of the neck through the gap in the head rest. "Which arm do you keep your gun under?"

"Left," said the man.

"You...?" Jack said to the passenger.

"Same."

"OK," said Jack, jabbing the driver once more. "Keeping your eyes straight ahead, I want you to remove your friend's gun with your left hand, and then hold it in your open palm."

The driver slipped his left hand inside the other man's coat and pulled out the Smith and Wesson revolver. Then, as he held it in his open palm, Jack took it from him.

Having put the revolver next to him on the seat, Jack then instructed the passenger to do the same. And soon he had both revolvers. Now he could relax a little. But he would have to watch it. Neither of the men were showing signs of being under stress, and that could only mean they were professionals and probably trained to extract themselves from situations like the one they found themselves in now.

"What next, Buddy?" said the driver. "Do we go for a ride?"

"No thanks," Jack quipped. "Not a nice enough day for it."

"I guess that must be an example of the famous English sense of humour?" said the driver.

"It's an example of our obsession with the weather," Jack replied. "Don't you know that we English make all our decisions based on the weather. I mean if it was brighter out, I might not be here now holding a gun on you."

"Look, Buddy!" the driver declared impatiently. "Tell us what you want or get the hell out of the car!"

"Well, if you're going to take that attitude towards our national pastime," Jack protested, "I suppose I better get on with it. Now I'm going to make this so simple that even you Yanks can understand it. I ask you a few questions – you answer them to my complete satisfaction and I stop pointing this gun at you."

"Bullshit!" the driver growled. "From what I've heard about you, Buddy, you ain't that generous!"

Jack smiled. "I might be nice to you if you cooperate."

"You ain't getting nothing out of us, you fucking Limey bastard!" the driver retorted.

"Good Heavens!" Jack exclaimed in an exaggerated upper class accent. "That's a racist remark, isn't it! I could write to someone about you!"

"Go fuck yourself!" said the man.

"Now you're adding bad language to your crime," said Jack. "But never mind. In a gesture of cooperation between our two great nations, I shall not press the matter. However, I must point out that you have parked this rather excellent English motor vehicle in the wrong gear."

"What the fuck are you talking about?"

"You're in the wrong gear, Yank!" Jack snapped. "Change it!"

"You're fucking crazy!" the driver retorted, putting his left hand down on the gear stick.

Jack fired the gun, and blew a hole through it.

"*My hand - you fucking bastard - my hand!*" the driver wailed.

Blood dripped on to the man's lap as he held the injured limb to his chest. Then he began moaning when even greater pain surged through him.

"I take it I'll have your full cooperation from now on, Mr Bigmouth Yank?" said Jack.

When the driver didn't answer, Jack prodded him with the gun. "You wouldn't want me to make you change gear with your right hand, now would you...?"

"I'll cooperate - damn you!" the man declared through agony-clenched teeth.

"That's what I wanted to hear," said Jack. "Now then, how many of you American gentlemen are guarding Manny Hemmings?"

"We're the only ones," said the passenger, sweat now glistening on his brow.

"Is that so," said Jack. "And does that mean just the two of you came over with Frank on the plane?"

"That's right. Oh, and Brad Jackson, of course. I'd forgotten about him."

Jack switched the gun to his left hand. Then he picked up one of the Smith and Wesson revolvers by the barrel. It was a 45 calibre and quite a heavy lump of metal – perfect for what he wanted to do.

"By the way," he said to the passenger, "what's your name?"

"Hank," said the man, wiping sweat from his forehead with the back of his hand.

"Right, Hank. Now I want you to turn your head and look at me."

Hank turned his head and stared at Jack.

"That's good, Hank. But I want you to lean close to me."

Fear showed in Hank's eyes. "Why...?"

"Just do it!" Jack ordered.

Hank licked his lips nervously and did as he was told.

"Closer..." said Jack.

Hank's face came nearer.

Jack smiled. "Closer still, Hank."

Hank began to shake as he moved his head between the head rests of the two seats.

"That's fine," said Jack. Then he raised his right hand and chopped downwards. There was a thud as the gun butt struck bone. Blood spurted from Hank's smashed nose and he fell back against the dashboard, groaning in pain.

"I refuse to be lied to by a couple of Hillbillies!" Jack spat as Hank covered his bloodied face with both hands. "And the next one who lies to me gets a bullet! So, would one of you gentlemen care to tell me how many of you are guarding Manny?"

"Four," said the driver.

"And where are the other two?"

"In a small room outside Manny's office."

"What floor?"

"Nineteenth."

"And where is Frank at this moment in time?"

"With Manny."

"So tell me?" said Jack. "Is Frank part of the Mafia back in the States?"

"No."

"What would happen if he was killed over here?"

The driver winced as a spasm of pain took hold of him. "What do you mean?" he gasped.

"I mean, would anyone come looking for his killer?"

"Sure they would."

"Who?"

"Family. There's a lot of them, and they're real close."

"Hmmm," said Jack, "I thought that might be the case. Oh well, nobody said it was going to be easy."

"Look, Buddy," said the driver, "we know what you're up to, so do yourself a favour and find a good hiding place, because you don't stand a chance. And even if you do manage to kill Manny and Frank, you'll just be inviting a shit load of trouble down on top of you."

"Thanks for the advise," Jack replied. "Anyway, enough chatter. All I want from you now is for you both to look straight ahead and keep perfectly still."

"What are you going to do?" the driver asked, fear replacing the pain in his eyes.

"Follow my orders and find out."

Suddenly Hank made his move. With a reach that took Jack completely by surprise, Hank's left hand shot back and grabbed the collar of his coat.

Jack grunted as he was pulled head first between the seats and held there.

"Get the fucking gun!" Hank screamed, now pulling with two hands.

The driver turned in his seat and fumbled for the weapon. He cried out as something knocked against his injured hand.

Jack struggled like mad to get free, but Hank was a powerful man. He had all the leverage he needed and the strength to keep up the pressure.

Jack tried to aim the gun, which was pinned beneath his chest, at Hank's legs, but the long silencer kept hitting against the gear stick.

"Get the fucking gun, Reg!" Hank roared. "I can't hold him for much longer!"

Reg obtained a grip on the silencer and pulled, but Jack's grip on the gun handle was too secure. Reg then reached under Jack's doubled up body with his good hand; felt his wrist; then fingers. He managed to prise some of Jack's fingers off the handle. But when he managed to get a grip on the handle himself and pulled, the gun went off.

Reg screamed as a bullet tore along the calf of his left leg.

Hank cursed, and still holding Jack's collar with his right hand, brought his left fist crashing down on the top of his head again and again with stunning force.

"You bastard - you fucking Limey bastard!" Hank roared as he battered Jack.

Jack felt his mind beginning to spin as the battering continued. But he daren't let go of the gun. Then, with a mighty heave, he threw all his weight back. Hank's grip was broken.

Jack aimed the gun at Hank.

Hank chopped at it with his left hand.

The gun was knocked downwards and went off.

A powerful fist hit Jack in the face.

The blow threw him back in his seat.

Blood poured from his mouth.

He was still holding the gun. He aimed it at Hank's head and pulled the trigger.

Hank ducked.

The bullet went through the windscreen, leaving a plate size hole in it.

Hank's door flew open, then he was out of the car and running for all he was worth along the pavement.

Jack fired at him through the hole in the windscreen.

Somewhere a window pane shattered.

Hank was still running.

Jack cursed and shot Reg through the back of the head. Then he got out of the car - pulled open the driver's door, and reaching in, dragged the body out.

Stepping over Reg, Jack slipped quickly into the vacant seat; turned on the ignition, and the car roared into life.

Then he pulled away from the kerb and raced down the road after

Hank. The acceleration slammed the passenger door shut. And as Jack passed the fleeing bodyguard, he fired two wild shots out through the passenger window.

The glass crazed from the holes in it, then fell apart.

Hank stumbled and fell.

Jack grinned and pushed hard on the accelerator pedal. The car responded with a screech of tyres and shot down the road.

Hank rolled over on his back, then staggered to his feet. Blood oozed from a small hole in his right shoulder. He turned and made his way to a telephone box across the road. A call to Manny's office brought immediate help.

The dead bodyguard was collected and disposed of without the police seeing, and Hank's injuries were attended to in Manny's office by a doctor on the books. One of Jack's bullets had passed clean through Hank's shoulder without hitting an artery or breaking any bones, so hospital treatment and awkward questions were avoided.

"The guy's got balls, I'll give him that," said Frank Hemmings as he watched the doctor dress Hank's wound.

"Well I'm glad you admire him when all he's doing is trying to destroy me!" Manny replied testily.

"Aaaa, keep your shirt on, Little Brother," said Frank. "We'll get him, don't you worry."

"But when, Frank...when?" Manny exclaimed. "My men are dying like flies, and Jack Blade seems to have a free hand in attacking my organization? And how are we going to get him now? He knows we're looking for him? He'll disappear for good and I'll never get my property back? Fat lot of help you have been! I'm no better off since you came over...maybe even worse! Have you any idea how all this looks to my competition! They'll think that if Manny Hemmings can't even stop a pub landlord from messing up his organization, it must be ripe for the taking! They're bound to move against me!"

"Thanks for taking care of Hank, Doc," said Frank as the doctor stood up from where Hank was laying on the sofa bed.

"Glad to be of service, Mr Hemmings," said the doctor.

Frank handed him fifty pounds and he left.

Frank then looked down at his bodyguard.

"You did well, Hank - phoning in instead of staggering through the front doors of the building and leaving a trail of blood for the cops to follow."

"Thanks, Boss," said Hank, beginning to feel drowsy. "I know the cops are watching, and I don't want to give them an excuse to come sniffing around in here."

"That decision just made you an extra two grand as a bonus," said Frank. "So, what did you make of Blade?"

"He's one tough son-of-a-bitch!" Hank declared. "At one point I was sure we had him, but he's a cool bastard, and never lost his nerve for a second! He was determined to kill us no matter what it cost, and I'll tell you something else, Mr Hemmings, this guy's big trouble - and he's crazy!"

"You just rest up," said Frank. "And I'm sorry about Reg. I know you two go back a long ways."

Hank's gaze dropped and his voice lowered. "Been friends since High School, Boss. I'm sure going to miss the guy."

"Never mind him, Frank!" Manny complained. "You still haven't told me what we're going to do about Jack Blade!"

A look of irritation appeared on Frank's face. "Stop whining will you, Little Brother. I thought you knew how to handle yourself in a crisis. All I see is you beginning to fall apart."

"I can handle myself all right!" Manny cried. "How do you think I built up this business! And I've dealt with plenty of bastards who tried to cause trouble for me! But this man doesn't know when to stop! He's obviously obsessed with taking over my business, even if he dies trying! How do you stop someone like that!"

"By making sure he *does* die trying," Frank answered. "Now I want you to hole up here for the next few days. Send out for anything you want, and don't have anything delivered. If the fire alarm goes off, wait until you see flames coming under the door before you get out. And keep away from the window. Eat only from cans, and don't open any packages."

"I'll be a fucking prisoner!" Manny retorted.

"A live one," said Frank.

"You sure he'll try again?" Manny said, feeling the walls of his office begin to close in on him.

"You bet he will. You see, Little Brother, deep down this guy knows that even if he succeeds in taking over your organization, he won't hang on to it for more than a week."

"So why the bloody hell is he doing it then?"

"I'm not sure; maybe to prove something to himself, or someone else - living or dead. Or maybe it's as Hank just said – the guy's crazy. Who knows why a guy will keep going against impossible odds when common sense dictates that he cuts and runs. He already has your dough. He could make a very good life for himself with a million pounds."

Then Frank remembered Hank. He hadn't told any of his men about the money. Such a large amount could well have an adverse effect on their loyalties.

He looked at the injured bodyguard again. "Hey, Hank, you OK, Buddy…?"

Hank's eyes were closed. He made no reply.

"Sedative the doc gave him must be doing its job," he then said to Manny.

"Did he hear about the money?" Manny asked.

"Naaa, dead to the world, Little Brother. Now sit tight, I've got to go out for a few hours. Get a few of your guys to sit outside this office with Eddy and Jed. And don't forget, stay in here. I don't want mom attending your funeral. Her heart wouldn't take it."

"Neither would mine," said Manny with a sigh.

27

Jack popped three aspirins into his mouth and swallowed them with a gulp of whisky. He had a fierce headache and the back of his neck was sore. 'Dumb bastard - getting caught like that!' he berated himself as probing fingers examined his scalp. Next time he would do less talking and more shooting.

He stretched slowly out on the bed with a drink in his hand, and cast his gaze around the cheap room. He owned his own pub and had a million pounds hidden under it, and yet here he was, stuck in a dive that a tramp would turn his nose up at. Somewhere there was humour in that irony, but his headache and failure wouldn't let him see it. Maybe tomorrow he would, but not today.

He didn't know if he had managed to kill Hank or not. It didn't really matter. If he was dead, his body would be found soon enough; if he was alive, what could he tell Manny that he didn't know already.

Fortunately he had parked his own car in another street. He would have to go and get it sooner or later. And having wiped his fingerprints from Eddy and Hank's car, he had left it down a side street, and walked back to his room. In a way it had been an exciting day, and certainly very productive. He knew how Manny was being guarded and the layout of the building. His next plan was to hire some help and go after Manny again. It didn't matter now if he couldn't trust the men he hired in the long run, just so long as he could short term. All he needed were tough men - greedy men who would do anything for money. And with the wages he was offering, he didn't expect to have any trouble finding them.

The following evening, at just after seven o clock, Jack was sitting at a table in a pub called The Cockerel. The pub had a reputation as a place where most things illegal could be bought and sold, and usually at a low price, although that term was always subjective.

Sitting at the table with Jack was Jimmy Spooner - a wiry looking man of about fifty, with a weasel face and a toothless smile that would put most people off their dinner. His cloths were tatty, and he smelt of stale sweat and drink. But despite his appearance, he was a well know figure in the Underworld. Jimmy Spooner was proud of the fact that he had been in prison twenty seven times in his life, and what he didn't know about crime wasn't worth a damp fag end.

"Cheers, Mate," Jimmy said, then he took a large swallow of his double scotch.

"So…?" said Jack. "Can you help or not?"

Jimmy finished his drink and stared longingly at his empty glass.

"Another?" said Jack.

Jimmy's scraggy, unshaven face lit up. He turned in his chair to look at the bar. "Hey, Sal, same again, Love!" he called out.

"Well…?" There was an edge to Jack's voice.

"Well indeed…" said Jimmy. "You see my problem, don't you, Jack Mate. Here you are, landlord of The Raven, asking for my services in matters way beyond your experience."

"What do you know about my experience?" Jack demanded.

"Enough to know that you ain't had so much as a parking ticket since you took over The Raven five years ago," said Jimmy. "Why, you're so clean, Jack, I'll bet that if I was to reach out and touch you, my hand would burn up, just like those vampires in the films when they touch something pure and holy."

"That's a crock of shit!" Jack snapped.

"Is it…?" Jimmy asked suspiciously. "Tell me something, Jack Mate, why are you here in my local talking tough after all these years? Everyone in the business has dealings with me sooner or later, but five years, Jack; it's a long time? What have you been doing with yourself?"

"I've been working a few scams," Jack replied. "Not that it's any of your business."

"Like hell you have!" Jimmy snapped, pointing a bony finger at Jack. "I know when a fifteen year old is thinking of stealing a packet of fags from a shop, or an old lady has left a store with a tin of Kit e Kat hidden in her pocket for her little moggy! So when I ain't heard about it, Jack Mate, it ain't happened!"

"OK," said Jack. "You're right, I have been keeping my nose clean. I left some trouble behind when I moved to London, but now something's come up and I need a bit of help with it."

Jimmy grinned. "You can say that again, Mate. Manny Hemmings is big time."

The shock showed on Jack's face.

"I told you," said Jimmy, his smile becoming smug. "If it's happening, I know about it."

Jack's hand slid slowly inside his coat, and his fingers curved round the handle of his gun.

"But if you want to go up against Manny, that's your business," Jimmy went on. "All we have to do is come up with a price - but I warn you, the calibre of the blokes you'll need won't come cheap."

"I've got the cash," said Jack.

"Then we're in business," said Jimmy, rubbing his hands.

"Thanks, Sal," Jimmy then said when a tall redhead of about thirty placed a drink in front of him. Then he watched as she made her way back to the bar, her hips sending out all kinds of messages.

"Fuck me!" Jimmy exclaimed, looking at Jack once more. "What I wouldn't give to spend just one night with her! But she's only gone and hitched herself to that boxer bloke Billy Pond, and he's got a mean disposition, if you know what I mean. Still it might be worth it."

"Can we get on?" said Jack, amazed that Spooner thought he actually had a chance with a good looking girl like the barmaid.

"OK then, Jack Mate, lets get down to details," said Jimmy. "So what's your pleasure?"

"I want three men who know how to use guns," said Jack. "They have to be able to handle themselves as well as be willing to go all the way."

"Everyone is willing go the full mile if the pay is right," said Jimmy. "Now, it will cost you thirty quid per day, per man. My fee is three hundred and I want an extra two hundred as an insurance - mine payable in advance of course."

"Bit steep isn't it?" said Jack.

Jimmy shrugged. "You want cheap I can supply you with a couple of winos who used to be in the army. But quality comes at a high price, Jack Mate – always has and always will."

"OK," said Jack. "But what's this insurance you mentioned?"

"Insurance against you grassing on me to the cops," said Jimmy. "Two hundred quid will do wonders for me if I end up inside."

"And if I don't grass on you?"

"Then your two hundred will be returned to you, less fifty of course."

Jack frowned. "What's the fifty for?"

"Why, for looking after your two hundred for you, Jack Mate. At least with me you know your money's safe. So, have you got it or not? And I never supply on credit so don't bother asking. I've been stung too often to get involved in that crap again."

Jack pulled out a large brown envelope, and slid it across the table. "There's a hundred. You can have the rest tomorrow. And you better understand something righ now. If you try and stitch me up you'll soon find out what experience I have when it comes to payback."

"No worries there, Jack Mate," Jimmy grinned, putting the envelope in his pocket. "If I tried anything with the people I deal with, I'd have been fish food years ago. I'll see you back here tomorrow night about the same time. And don't be late – I get real nervous waiting for blokes I don't know that well…especially Snow Whites."

28

When Jack returned to The Cockerel the following night, Jimmy was sitting at the same table, but this time with three men. The men looked capable enough Jack decided as he dropped into an empty chair next to Jimmy.

"Glad you could make it, Jack Mate," said Jimmy with a toothless smile. "I'd like you to meet Len Sennet, Gerry Binkley and Nigel Swan."

The three men nodded as Jimmy introduced them.

The one called Len was a short but powerful, foreign looking man of about thirty five – Jewish, Jack guessed. He had regular features except for his eyes which were small and appeared half closed. He looked like the kind of bloke who didn't seek out trouble, but could handle it when it came his way.

The man called Gerry was much taller and thinner than Len, but about the same age. He had a certain calmness about him that Jack liked; a calmness that said, a job needs doing so lets do it and move on. This bloke wouldn't panic if things went wrong, Jack thought.

Nigel was a bit harder to fathom; about twenty five; average size; average height, and giving nothing away. Jack couldn't even tell if he was really interested in the job. He simply stared with large green eyes at whoever was speaking - smoking his cigarette with slow deliberate movements. Jack didn't like Nigel, but he didn't have to. All that mattered was that he could do the job he was being paid to do.

"Right," said Jimmy, rubbing his hands with childish glee. "Let's get on with it. Now, I've explained to the lads what they're taking on, and they're more or less willing to work for you, Jack Mate. But..."

"How much?" Jack interrupted. He thought this might happen – Jimmy Spooner looked like a greedy little sod.

"Well you see...?" Jimmy spread his hands.

"Stop fucking around and tell me how much more it's going to cost me?" Jack spat.

"A straight talker," said Jimmy. "I like that, Jack Mate. Cards on the table and no messing; just the way I like it. Now the lads here want an extra twenty quid each; after all they are putting their lives on the line taking on a big fish like Manny Hemmings, so you can see their point in wanting a little more dough for their troubles. And I want an extra hundred, because, as I......"

"I'll pay the lads the extra," Jack interrupted coldly, "because they weren't here yesterday to negotiate for themselves. But you're not getting a penny more, you greedy bastard."

A hard look appeared on Jimmy's face. "Is that so. Well, for your information, I'm the only one who can set up a deal like this. And if I give the word then it's fucking dead. And you won't be able to hire a fucking ladder once I put the word out about you. So what do you say to that...*Mr Jack Blade...?*"

Jack glared at Jimmy for a moment. Then he looked at each of the men with him in turn. "How about it lads? I'm willing to pay you fifty pounds a day, and I'd say I will need you for a week...that's three hundred and fifty plus a seventy five pound bonus at the end of it. Are you really going to pass up that kind of money because this greedy pig is trying to fleece me? And don't forget, I've already agreed to pay him three hundred and fifty, and the only risk he will be taking is that he might get a paper cut while he's counting it...?"

"Too right we ain't!" Len growled, throwing a hostile glance at Jimmy. "In fact, maybe you should cut him out altogether! He ain't got the clout he thinks he has! He's all mouth when it comes down to it!"

And when Gerry and Nigel announced their agreement with Len, Jimmy became desperate. "Now wait a minute, Lads! There's no need to take that attitude! OK, maybe Jack's right! I am getting a little too greedy!"

Jimmy then stared pleadingly at Jack. "Tell you what, Jack Mate! Your original deal with me stands...OK...?"

Jack considered his options before answering. Cutting Jimmy out of the deal could cause problems. He might even warn Manny.

"OK, Jimmy," he replied. "But don't fuck with me again or you're out."

The relief on Jimmy's face was clear. "Sure, Jack Mate...anything you say! And no hard feelings, Eh...?"

Jack ignored him.

"So what's the plan?" said Len.

"Not here," said Jack. "And there's something I have to insist upon right now. You three are working for me, so you don't have any contact with Jimmy or anyone else until the job's done. Agreed...?"

"Now hold on a minute!" Jimmy protested.

"Agreed...?" Jack repeated.

"You're the boss," said Len.

"Good. Now get yourselves some sleeping bags. You're kipping down at my place for the time being."

Jack then handed Jimmy another envelope. "Here's the balance. But I want my one hundred and fifty back when the job's finished. Understand...?"

"Sure I do, Jack Mate," Jimmy said, grinning all over his face. "Don't worry, you can trust me."

"I hope I can...for your sake," Jack replied.

A few hours later Jack was back in his room with his hired help. He spread a large sheet of paper on the bed. It was a map he had made of the building containing Manny's office, based on information gained from Sean Hellet before he was killed. Fortunately the man had been a regular visitor, being required to run personal errands for Manny on quite a few occasions. The map was detailed and Jack hoped - accurate.

"I see there's someone at the reception desk all through the night," said Len, reading some of Jack's notes. "We could have done without that."

"Some of the biggest companies have offices in that building," said Jack. "Seems they're willing to pay extra on their rent for the security it provides."

"So how are we going to get up to Manny's office? I ain't no mountain climber you know...?"

"I've got Sean Hellet's pass," said Jack. "It was simple to replace his photo with mine."

"But what if the bloke in reception knows this Sean Hellet?" Len asked.

Jack scowled. "And what if he has a machine gun hidden under the counter and a dozen men armed with hand grenades in the kitchen making the tea! We improvise of course! Now according to Hellet, the lifts are to the left of the reception desk, and they go all the way up to the twenty third floor. Manny's office is on the nineteenth and looks out from the back of the building. So long as you don't shoot out any of the windows, we shouldn't draw any outside attention. But to get to his office you have to go through his secretary's office and another room beyond that...a sort of waiting area. I doubt Manny will have any bodyguards in his actual office, because even the best bodyguards blab occasionally. That means we can expect all the trouble to come from the middle room, and possibly the secretary's office."

"What kind of bodyguards are we dealing with?" Nigel asked.

"Difficult to say," said Jack. "I do know that Frank Hemmings brought four over with him. At least one is already dead...possibly two. That leaves Frank's two and any Manny might have."

"Well, if this Frank Hemmings is some big time gangster in the States, his bodyguards must be able to handle themselves."

"Is that a problem?"

"No," said Nigel. "But it is a consideration. And I suppose they'll be tooled up?"

"Goes without saying," said Jack.

"What about the secretary?"

"We'll have to tie her up if she's still there, and disable the phone," Jack answered. "But as for anyone else, I don't want any survivors...understand...?"

"If that's the way you want to play it, Jack, then that's the way it's going to be," Nigel replied grimfaced.

"That's the way I want to play it. And that goes for any of you who can't walk out under your own steam."

The three men glanced at one another.

"Is that understood?" said Jack.

"You mean any of us that are injured gets a friendly bullet?" Len exclaimed. "Why for God Sakes...?"

"Because the police have someone watching the building round the clock, that's why. If we come staggering out with blood all over us they'll be buzzing around the building like flies around a shit pile. So, before we go any further we have to agree on that. And leave any ID you have on you here."

"Fuck that for a game of soldiers!" Gerry retorted. "There's no way I'm getting blasted by both sides! Any bastard who points a gun at me - friendly or not, gets his balls shot off!"

"Then you're out," said Jack. "I'll pay you for today and you can piss off back to Spooner. But keep your mouth shut."

"But it's ridiculous!" Gerry protested. "And I didn't say I wouldn't agree, did I...but you have to admit it wouldn't be an easy thing to do...?"

"Easy or not that's the way it has to be," said Jack. "Now, last chance, Gerry – in or out...?"

Gerry considered his position for a moment. Then he came to a decision. "In. But I don't like it."

"Neither do I, Mate. And how about the rest of you?"

"I guess it's OK by me," said Nigel.

Everyone looked at Len. "I don't know." he replied hesitantly. "To just shoot someone I know as well as you two..."

"Sod off," Nigel laughed. "You'll probably be the one that gets injured, You know how careless you are,"

"OK," Len grinned. "So, when do we do it?"

"Tomorrow night," said Jack, "at eleven o clock. Now clean your guns, and check the silencers. I've put a couple of sandbags in the bath. And don't forget to flush the toilet just before you fire."

"Christ, Jack!" Len declared. "Your neighbours will think you must have eaten the most dodgy curry in England."

Jack laughed with the others, but his mind was already on a different problem. Except for about two thousand, all the cash he'd taken from one of the knapsacks was gone. And if he needed more he would be left with no choice but to go back to his pub for it...and that could be very dangerous indeed. However, if tonight was a success it wouldn't be a problem, so he had to make sure that it was.

29

DCI Mandell received another visit to his office from DI Hanson. Mandell could tell from his officer's expression that he was going to hear something he didn't like.

"What is it this time?" he asked.

"Last night a resident of Plumley Street reported her front window being smashed, and a painting hanging on the wall being damaged," said Hanson.

Mandell frowned. "Plumley Street? That's where Manny Hemmings has his office, isn't it?"

"Yes, Guv. But the thing is, when the investigating officers examined the painting, they found a bullet embedded in the plaster wall behind it."

"A bullet?" Mandell exclaimed. "How the hell did that happen? And don't we have that office block under twenty four hour surveillance?"

Hanson looked suddenly uncomfortable. "Yes, Guv."

"And didn't whoever was on duty report the incident? He must have seen something going on?"

"No, Guv. It was the home owner who reported it. And when the investigating officers checked on the surveillance car, they found the driver fast asleep with his windows closed and the radio on. And there's something else, Guv, a blood stain was found on the ground near a pile of broken windscreen glass. And further along, a bullet was found embedded in someone's front door."

"What the blazes is going on!" Mandell snapped. "I want the officer on surveillance duty pounding the beat for the next six months! That should teach him to keep his eyes open! And how do you think this will look when the Commissioner hears about it – he'll probably think that we're not doing our jobs properly and he will be damn right, Hanson! Any more cock ups like that and there will be a few demotions around here! Do you understand me, Detective Inspector Hanson...?"

"I understand, Guv," Hanson replied, wondering how he could make the surveillance officer's life a misery for the next two years at least. "And what do you want us to do about the incident, Guv?"

Mandell seemed to calm down. "Nothing, for now. If we go filling the street with forensics teams, it could jeopardise the Hemmings investigation. Nothing must get in the way of that or I'll be pounding the beat with that other idiot! And from now on I want a two man surveillance team on that building at all times!"

"Yes, Guv."

"What about the bullets?" Mandell asked. "Any match?"

"Working on it right this minute, Guv."

"You know something, Ken," Mandell declared looking straight at his officer. "I sometimes wonder why I bother coming in to this office every day."

Hanson smiled. "To let the criminals understand that their days are numbered, Guv. Isn't that a good enough reason."

Mandell smiled also. "Perhaps. But somehow it seems less good as the years go by."

"You'd miss it, Guv," said Hanson. "You know you would."

"I suppose so, Ken. But if I don't come up with something special in the Manny Hemmings case, and pretty damn quick, I just might find out."

"We'll get him, Guv," said Hanson. "Don't worry about that."

"But not by standing around in my office, Ken. You better get on to forensic about those bullets."

"Right you are, Guv," said Hanson, and he quietly left the room.

Mandell glanced at the phone on his desk and mentally ordered it not to ring; not to bring more grief down on top of him.

It didn't take Jack and his team long to spot the unmarked police car that was parked across the road from Queensbury House. But this time there were two men watching, not one.

"Right, Lads," said Jack, "let's get going. And for Christ Sakes try and look natural. We're just four business men paying a visit to Manny's office, so relax. OK?"

"OK, Jack," said Len, "relaxed and natural it is."

A few minutes later they were walking up to the reception desk. "Good evening," said Jack with a smile, showing his pass. "We're on our way up to Manny Hemming's office for a late night meeting."

The grey haired male receptionist stared at the pass for a moment, then he looked at Jack. "I know Sean Hellet, and you certainly are not him."

The man then reached for the phone next to him.

Jack pulled back the left side of his coat to reveal the Nine Millimetre in its holster.

The man paled and stepped back in alarm.

Jack leaned on the counter. "What's your name?" he inquired.

"James...Mantle," said the man in a quivering voice.

"Pleased to meet you, James. Now, may I ask if you are a sensible sort of chap?"

The man nodded.

"And would you by any chance be a reasonable chap as well?"

"I think so..." James stammered.

"And tell me, James, how long have you worked here?"

"Twenty three years."

"And is it compulsory retirement at sixty five?"

Jack saw a momentary hardness appear in the man's eyes before the fear returned. "Yes it is."

"And you are what...sixty two...?"

The hardness returned for a moment. "Sixty four as a matter of fact."

"Christ, Jack," Nigel hissed, "can we just get on with it!"

"Shut up!" Jack snapped. "Can't you see I'm talking to a sensible and reasonable man here. Now, James, I take it the company will be generous in your retirement?"

The hardness came back and stayed. "A clock and a cheque for fifty pounds," he replied.

"I thought so," said Jack. "Its been my experience that after giving the best part of your life to a company...*any* company, when you are no longer of use you go from being a valuable asset to a nuisance that must be removed as quickly as possible. And to get to the point, James, what would you say if I was to offer you something to supplement your pension, so that you and the little lady indoors can have those holidays you've always wanted? I take it there *are* holidays you have always wanted...?"

"Italy is a country Margaret and I are very keen to visit one day," James replied. "Especially Venice and Rome."

"Then Italy it shall be," said Jack. "Want to hear more, James...?"

"Go on?" said James, stepping nearer to his desk.

Jack reached inside his pocket and discretely produced a thick envelope. "Listen to me carefully, James. Now that we have built up an understanding, I believe I can be brutally honest with you. My friends and

I are here to punish a very bad man who ruins innocent young lives with drugs and prostitution. But because you are obviously a danger to us, my friends here want me to shoot you through the head so that you won't be a danger any more. However, I believe that you, being sensible and reasonable, will take it into your head to keep out of our business, and go about your own as if nothing untoward is happening. And no matter what does happen, I know you will see nothing, hear nothing, and most of all remember nothing. And in return for your cooperation, I intend to leave you this envelope. And do you know what this envelope contains, James?"

James shook his head and stared at the envelope with greedy eyes.

"Twelve hundred pounds in crisp new tenners," said Jack. "Surely that's better than a bullet in the head any day, wouldn't you say, James?"

James licked his lips nervously. Then he reached out and slowly took the envelope.

"Good man," said Jack. "Now, just one last question, James. Do you know if Frank Hemmings is with Manny in his office?"

"Mr Hemmings left the building some time ago and he hasn't been back as far as I know."

"Thanks, James. And you think of me when you and the little lady are strolling on some Italian beach next year."

"I will," James replied, slipping the envelope into one of the pockets of his coat that was hanging on a hook.

"Twelve hundred quid!" Nigel hissed as they walked towards the lifts. "You're fucking crazy! A bullet would be a hell of a lot cheaper!"

"Maybe...maybe not," said Jack. "I want everything down here to look normal, and a reception desk without a receptionist for more than a few minutes does not look normal."

"It's your money I suppose," said Nigel. "But I still say a bullet would be cheaper. And if I'd known you had cash to throw away, I'd have asked for double. We couldn't renegotiate could we...?"

"Sorry," Jack replied with a grin. "Terms are fixed until the beginning of the next financial year."

"We're taking orders from a fucking comedian, God help us," Nigel muttered, shaking his head.

Just as Jack and his men finally entered the lift, the reception desk phone rang. Jack put his foot against one of the lift doors to stop it closing. He listened as the receptionist answered the phone.

"Yes, Mr Hemmings, I'm absolutely sure," said James. "Your brother hasn't left any messages for you. Yes, Mr Hemmings I most certainly will. Thank you, Mr Hemmings."

Jack smiled and allowed the lift doors to close.

The four men were silent as the lift ascended to the nineteenth floor of the building. What they were about to do was extremely dangerous, and there was a good chance that not all of them would be coming down again. It was a sobering thought, but it focused the mind beautifully.

The lift finally stopped at the nineteenth floor with a lurch and the two doors parted. Jack led the way out of the lift, turning instantly left into a very long corridor. At the end he turned left again, and left for a third time before making his way down another very long corridor.

"We should have brought fucking bicycles with us!" Nigel complained, a thin sheen of sweat covering his face.

"Be there in a sec," said Jack.

The building was pretty much empty since it was after eleven pm, and they passed twelve locked office doors before coming to the one with the name 'Manny Hemmings Ltd' painted in black letters on its white, frosted glass.

Each man pulled out his gun, and then taking a deep breath, Jack quickly opened the door.

Instincts more than actual awareness threw Jack face down on the floor as he stepped through the doorway.

Bullets from seven guns passed over his head.

Gerry Binkley staggered backwards across the corridor and slid down the opposite wall with his chest haemorrhaging blood from three holes in it. Jack levelled his gun and fired, hitting one of the seven gunmen in the room. The man spun away with the side of his face shattered.

Suddenly Jack felt his legs grabbed and he was pulled out the door backwards, followed by another spray of bullets.

"Thanks, Len!" Jack panted, climbing to his feet.

"You ain't paid us yet," Len growled as he flattened himself against the wall next to the doorway. Then he reached round the doorframe with his right hand and fired into the room a few times. There was a scream followed by swearing. More bullets shot out of the room and embedded themselves in the opposite wall above the body of Gerry.

"The poor sod's had it," said Nigel who was on the other side of the doorway to Jack and Len.

"Fucking obvious I would have thought!" Len declared, staring at the body of his dead friend. "Well, this has become personal now! No Yank

bastards are going to come over here and put holes in my friends! Not one of them is going to leave this building unless they're on their way to the morgue, that's for sure!"
!

Then Len reached around the doorframe again and let off three more shots. A dozen answered him as he jerked his arm back.

He quickly reloaded his revolver, and put the empty shells in his pocket as ordered by his boss earlier. "How the fuck did they react so fast, Jack?" he demanded.

"They were waiting for us, that's how," said Jack.

"That fucking receptionist!" said Len. "I knew we should have put a bullet in his head!"

"It wasn't him," said Jack.

"Then who? He was the only one who knew that we were on our way up. They had their guns actually pointed at us the instant you opened the door. Pretty good timing wouldn't you say."

"I agree that they must have known down to a few minutes when we were going to attack," said Jack. "But how they knew, that's what's bugging me. Somehow it had to be that rat Jimmy Spooner."

A few more shots came out of the room, but Jack wouldn't let his men answer them. They didn't have ammunition to waste firing blind.

"Couldn't have been, Jimmy," said Len. "I'm not saying he isn't capable of ratting on people, but although he knew you were going after Manny, he knew none of the details. He didn't even know what day."

"Unless someone told him after I had laid out my plan to you lot," said Jack.

"You're kidding," said Len.

"They knew the exact time," said Jack. "And only the four of us knew that."

"Well you can forget that shit for a start!" Len retorted. "The three of us have worked together for years, and I'd trust Nigel and Gerry with my life, which is more than I can say for you!"

Jack glared at Len. "I don't give a fuck how long you three have known each other! One of you informed on me to Jimmy Spooner, and none of you are getting a penny until I find out who it is!"

"Then you're on your own," said Len.

"I wouldn't try running out on me if I were you!" Jack warned.

Len's face was hard as he glared back at Jack. "And I wouldn't try stopping us, if I were you, Mate!"

"It was me!" Nigel wailed suddenly.

Jack and Len looked at him.

Nigel became defensive. "I didn't know Jimmy would go to Manny Hemmings! Honest to Christ I didn't, Len!"

"You fucking bastard!" Len roared. "So that's what you were doing when you said you had gone out for a packet of fags early this morning - phoning that weasel about our plans!"

"Jesus, Len," Nigel cried, "how was I to know he would grass on us to Manny! All he asked me to do was let him know when you were going to make your move! I didn't see no harm in it!"

"Try telling that to Gerry!" said Len. "I'm sure he will understand even with a chest full of lead in him and an appointment with the morgue!"

"So why did you do it?" Jack asked, resisting an impulse to shoot the man out of hand. "More money...?"

"Of course not!" said Nigel.

"Then why?"

Nigel's features twisted with frustration and shame. "Because he asked me to!"

"You could have said no, couldn't you?" said Len.

Nigel screwed his eyes up tight. "I owe him, Len...big time! He said if I kept him informed he would knock two hundred off the IOU! But honest to God, I didn't see any harm in it! And when I asked him why he wanted to know, he told me that he likes to be informed what his boys are up to!"

"And you believed him, you stupid bastard!" Len snapped. "No one in their right mind would pay out two hundred quid for a bit of information unless they were going to make a lot more than that! I'll bet you Manny paid him at least five hundred to know exactly what time we were going to show up here!"

"Hey - you out there," an American voice called out. "Having a bit of a tiff are we, Girls,"

"What do you want, Yank?" Jack answered.

"I want to talk to Jack Blade."

"You are."

"Great. My name's Eddy. So how you doing, Buddy?"

"Better than you, *Buddy*!"

Eddy laughed. "You know something, Jack, I think we underestimated you. If everything had gone to plan, you and your three buddies would be turning our carpet a nice shade of red by now."

"Oh, I don't know about that," said Jack. "One out of four after setting up an ambush is pretty poor shooting if you ask me."

"Yea, well you know what they say, Buddy. If at first you don't succeed. Anyway, why don't you be reasonable about this. We have you outnumbered."

"True enough," said Jack. "But we're out here, and you're in there, trapped like lobsters in a pot."

"Yea, but lobsters have pretty powerful pincers, Jack, and the kind in here could easily put you on a cold slab. Now, what I propose is that we talk about this. Manny has instructed me to agree to your terms - assuming that they're reasonable of course."

"That seems fair enough," said Jack. "So here's the deal. How about you all die and I take over Manny's business."

There was a long, low whistle. "Boy, you sure don't want much, do you, Buddy."

"*Look out!*" Nigel shouted.

Jack turned just as a man with a gun stepped out into the corridor from a door further along.

Jack, Nigel and the gunman all fired at the same time. Nigel grunted and collapsed on the floor. Jack fired again as the gunman darted back into the room.

"Fuck, we should have expected something like that!" Jack snapped. "Make sure he doesn't do that again!"

"Don't worry, he won't," said Len, training his gun on the doorway.

Jack then examined Nigel who was sitting with his back against the wall. There was a small hole in the left shoulder of his coat, but only a little blood was oozing out of it. It didn't look too serious.

"You going to be able to walk out of here?" Jack asked.

A sheen of sweat had appeared on Nigel's pain contorted face. He grinned. "If you're thinking of putting a bullet in my brain, then forget it. I've had worse injuries from that sod of a dentist I use..."

The *putt putt* of Len's gun and a cry of pain drew Jack's attention.

"Got the bastard!" Len declared, staring down the corridor. "He won't be using his right hand again, that's for sure!"

"You're not having trouble out there are you, Buddy," Eddy called out.

"Nothing we can't handle," Jack answered. But he knew this wasn't true. Gerry was dead, and Nigel was injured. That left just him and Len. They had to get out of there before Manny's men decided to rush them, or others arrived from elsewhere.

"Can you stand?" he said to Nigel.

Nigel struggled to his feet, using the wall as a support.

"Right, time to go," said Jack. "Len, give me some cover while I help Nigel to the lift."

Len looked suddenly worried. "What sort of cover...?"

"I mean stay here for a couple of minutes and keep them busy. I'll hold the lift doors open for you."

"OK," said Len, and he fired two shots into the room. A number of shots came back at him. Len then emptied the chamber of his gun and inserted six fresh bullets.

Jack put his left arm around Nigel, and the two of them staggered back along the long corridor.

As Jack and Nigel finally approached the lifts, they could just about hear the constant explosions of guns being discharged. Obviously Len was doing a good job, and Jack felt a touch of admiration for the man. It took real courage to stay behind as your companions made their way to safety.

Then the firing stopped. Jack reached out and pressed the lift button. The doors opened. He helped Nigel into the lift, then he kept his finger on the open button. He leaned out into the corridor and shouted for Len. A couple of seconds later he heard the sound of running feet and more shots. Eventually Len came tearing along the corridor.

Three men were running behind him firing their guns.

"Come on, come on!" Jack roared.

Then he aimed his gun and fired past Len. One of the pursuing men stumbled and fell.

A bullet yanked at Jack's shirt collar and he pulled back into the lift.

"Come on, Len!" he shouted. "We can't wait any longer!"

The footsteps grew louder and so did the sounds of the shots. Len had to be still alive.

Someone screamed but the shooting continued and so did the footsteps.

Then Len flew into the lift. "Close them!" he cried. "Close the fucking doors!"

Jack took his finger off the hold button, but the doors stayed open.

Jack jabbed desperately at the close button. Nothing happened.

"Close them...close them...!" Len screamed.

The sound of pounding feet grew much louder.

"Come on! Come on!" Jack cried, slamming the heel of his right hand time and time again on the button, but the doors remained open.

Suddenly a man appeared in front of the lift.

Len fired instantly.

The man's gun went off as he fell dead.

The bullet ricocheted from the metal floor of the lift and tore through Nigel's left calf.

Nigel screamed.

Another man appeared and aimed his gun.

Jack shot him through the forehead.

The lift doors slowly closed with a long hiss, then rattled as bullets slammed into them. The inner metal lining bulged inwards in places but no bullets got through. Then the lift was dropping down.

"First my fucking shoulder, now my fucking leg!" Nigel complained through tight lips.

"Getting yourself shot once is acceptable, but twice is downright masochistic," Len laughed, extremely surprised and relieved to be alive. How he managed to avoid being shot as he belted through those long straight corridors had to be divine intervention as far as he was concerned. And he would no doubt be expected to atone for his rather colourful past, and he would, but not just yet...not until he was a little bit older and his life had become a little bit more colourful.

"Now what?" Nigel asked wincing as his leg throbbed. "I thought the idea was that we would stroll from the building having left a pile of bodies in Manny's office?"

"Considering the part you played in causing this fiasco," said Len. "I'd keep my mouth shut if I were you."

"I didn't know Jimmy would contact Manny!" Nigel protested. "How many more times do I have to say it!"

Len then began spinning his gun sideways against the palm of his hand.

"Cut that out," Nigel ordered, "or you'll drop the bloody thing and I'll get another bullet somewhere!"

"It would be no more than you deserve," said Len, and he continued spinning the weapon in short bursts.

"I mean it, Len!" Nigel warned.

"Stop fucking around you two," said Jack. Then he frowned and placed his right ear against the side of the lift.

"What's the matter?" Len asked.

"Schhh!" Jack hissed, closing his eyes in concentration. Then he looked at Len. "We're not out of the woods yet. The lift next to this one is being used."

"Shit!" said Len. "I'd hoped they might have given up after we just shot at least three of them and with the police watching the place! Persistent bastards!"

"Then they're only just behind us," said Nigel. "What are we going to do?"

"Make a run for it of course," Jack replied. "What else can we do."

"But they will get us in the back as we cross the foyer!"

"Shut the fuck up will you, Nigel!" Len growled. "You're giving me a headache!"

"Stop the lift, for Christ Sakes!" Nigel cried. "I can't run!"

"I'll give you a hand, so stop whining!" said Len.

Nigel tried reaching for the emergency stop button.

Jack pushed him away. "Try that again and you're dead."

"But they'll shoot us down like dogs as we try to leave! Even with Len helping me I won't be able to run fast enough!"

"Well you better," said Jack. "It's the only option you have, and remember what we agreed. Anyone who can't keep up gets a bullet."

Nigel stayed quiet after that, but Jack and Len could feel the panic coming off him like stale deodorant.

"Nearly there," said Jack. "Check your guns."

Each of them reloaded their weapons, and then the lift stopped. The doors opened and Jack placed his finger on the open button.

"Wait!" he hissed as Len made to leave the lift.

Then they heard the other lift doors opening just a few feet from them, but they could not hear anyone getting out.

"It must be empty," Nigel whispered, with a half laugh.

"Wait," Jack whispered back.

"But they might be using the stairs instead of the lift…trying to catch us out," said Nigel. "We could be wasting valuable time."

Jack knew that anyone in the other lift would have to pass him to get to the foyer. And since no one had, as far as he was concerned, that could only be for one reason; they had set a trap - waiting for him and his companions to step out into the open. He decided to risk having a look.

Carefully he edged closer to the doorway, still keeping the index finger of his right hand on the open button.

He quickly stuck his head out and looked to his right.

For a split second he saw an unfamiliar face staring back at him, then it was gone.

Jack withdrew into the lift.

"Well...?" said Nigel.

"They're in the other lift," said Jack.

"Fuck...fuck...fuck!" Nigel cried. "We're never getting out of this place alive! Fuck Jimmy Spooner! Fuck that bastard!"

"They're in the same position as us when it comes down to it," said Len.

"How the fuck do you figure that!" Nigel retorted. "All they have to do is wait for reinforcements to arrive! Then we're fucking dead!"

"Shut up and let me think!" Jack snapped.

"What's the point in thinking!" said Nigel. "We're fucking finished! It doesn't take a degree in physics to figure that out!"

"I have an idea, Len," said Jack. "I'll go first, then you and Nigel can follow."

"What do you mean...?" said Len suddenly suspicious.

"I mean what I said," Jack replied. "I'll go first, and you cover me. Keep your gun trained on the other lift, and if anyone pokes his nose out, shoot it off."

"That's great for you," said Len. "But how do me and Nigel get out?"

"I'll set up a position over there behind that large jardinière and keep them from leaving the lift," said Jack. "That should give the both of you time to get to the front doors. Once you're there you will be safe. They won't dare follow you out with that surveillance team parked across the road."

"Why am I always left behind?" Len protested.

"You want to go first?" said Jack.

Len's mouth opened, but no words came out.

"That's settled then," said Jack. "Now get ready, and don't forget to keep the open button pressed."

Jack reached down and removed his shoes. The floor of the foyer was marble and would warn the bodyguards that someone had left the lift. In his stocking feet, and with a bit of luck, he should be at the jardiniere before they twigged what was happening.

Holding his shoes in his left hand and his gun in his right, Jack risked a quick glance. There was no one looking.

"I don't trust him!" Nigel hissed to Len. "Once he's out he'll be off!"

"Oh shut up, Nigel!" Len hissed back.

"Right, I'm going," Jack said to Len. "So keep me covered. And when I wave to you, the two of you make a run for it. And don't forget to take your shoes off. OK...?"

Len nodded.

Jack looked once more, then he ran from the lift.

Halfway to the Jardiniere he heard two putt putts, and cringed as he ran. Since all the guns used in the battle had silencers, he didn't know who was firing. He hoped it was just Len.

A few seconds later he was crouching behind the giant pot that was standing on a column. Both the pot and stand were extremely thick and heavy looking and hopefully bullet proof.

Then he heard a sound from the other end of the foyer, and saw the receptionist running into a back room. Jack couldn't help smiling. James was clearly determined to live long enough to enjoy those holidays in Italy, and who could blame him.

"Jack?" Len whispered as loud as he dared from the lift doorway.

Jack looked over. From his new position he couldn't exactly see into the other lift, but he certainly had a good view if anyone poked their head out.

"You ready to cover us?" Len mouthed silently.

Jack saw a hand appear in the doorway of the other lift. There was a gun in it. He shook his head vigorously.

"We haven't got all fucking day!" Len replied.

Jack aimed his gun at the hand and fired. The bullet clanged off the edge of one of the outer lift doors. The hand withdrew instantly.

Jack waved at Len, who immediately staggered out of the lift with Nigel.

It became clear to Jack that Nigel was much weaker now, and he was leaving a heavy trail of blood with his left leg which was dragging, and making things very difficult for Len.

"Come on, come on!" Jack hissed, urging the two men onwards.

Suddenly a figure darted out of the other lift; fired twice; then darted into the now vacant one.

Jack cursed. It would be difficult to keep both lifts covered at the same time.

Len and Nigel moved slowly away from the lift area.

Then two figures appeared simultaneously in the doorways of both lifts and began firing. The bowl of the Jardiniere hummed when three bullets struck it.

The two figures fired again.

Len cried out and fell against Nigel.

Then they both went down.

Jack emptied his gun at both lifts and pulled back to reload. He could hear Nigel and Len groaning. He cursed. It was all Nigel's fault - the stupid git.

Having inserted a fresh magazine in his Nine Millimetre Automatic, Jack aimed his gun once more, but the figures in the lifts withdrew.

He then pointed the weapon at Len, who's shirt front was stained with blood. Len saw and stopped groaning. His expression of agony turned to desperation. "Jack, what the hell are you doing! You've got to help us! Nigel is still alive and I'm not hurt too bad! We can make it if you just give us a hand!"

Jack's face was devoid of all emotion as he stared at his companions. "Sorry, Mate, you know what we agreed."

"Fuck that!" Len snapped. "We're nearly there! At least make them keep their heads down until I can get Nigel outside! Then you can drop us at the nearest hospital! You know we'll keep out mouths shut! You won't be involved!"

"OK!" said Jack. "But make it quick! I've only got two magazines left!"

Relief showed on Len's sweat-covered face. "Cheers, Mate! You won't regret it!"

Len then renewed his grip on a semi-conscious Nigel. "Come on, Mate!" he prompted. "This ain't no time to take a kip!"

The first bullet from Jack's gun smashed into Len's head, killing him instantly.

Nigel also died instantly..

"The bastard's only gone and shot his own men!" Jack heard someone from one of the lifts cry out.

Jack quickly slipped his shoes back on and weighed up his options. He would have to run about fifty metres to reach the exit. But there was no cover along the way so there was a good chance he would get a few bullets in the back before he made it. His second option was to shoot out one of the main windows at the front of the building to attract the attention of the police surveillance team. The down side of that was that he would probably spend twenty years in prison. He decided to risk making a run for it.

Jack removed the empty clip from the Nine Millimetre and placed it with the others in his coat pocket. He knew that fingerprints could be taken from them and he had no intention of leaving any for the police.

Having reloaded, Jack fired a single shot into each lift, then he took to his heels.

He heard a shout from behind and the *putt putt putt* of bullets exploding out of long silencers. One whizzed past his ear and shattered the glass of a framed print on the wall to his right.

"He's getting away!" someone shouted. "Bring him down!"

Jack flew across the foyer towards the main doors of the building. The sounds of running feet joined the sounds of gunfire as he fled. Then a streak of hot lava seared his ribs on the left side of his body. The agony threw him off balance. He stumbled; regained his balance and ran on.

The doors were only ten metres away now.

His breathing became laboured as his brain tried to ignore the agony - tried to keep itself focused on just one purpose - to escape the certain death that was bearing down on him from behind.

He screamed when a second bullet sliced through his left calf. He crashed to the floor and rolled over on his back.

Through blurred vision he saw a dark, shapeless figure rushing at him. He aimed his gun and fired. There was a scream and the figure was gone. Another appeared and the floor next to his head exploded. Shards of marble ripped through his left cheek.

He aimed and fired again. The figure stopped; tottered, then fell.

"Get the fucking bastard!" a voice roared.

Jack pulled himself up and staggered towards the doors. Bullets flew past and a plate glass window shattered. Then he was through the doors and out into the night.

Two men ran towards him from across the street.

Recognizing them as police, Jack fired a shot over their head's. The men turned and ran back the way they had come.

His car was parked just a hundred metres from the building; a long way for an injured man to run. But despite his situation, Jack was still determined to get Manny Hemmings, no matter what it cost. And in order to do that he had to be free.

Hobbling as fast as he could, he made his way towards the car. After what seemed a lifetime it came into view. He fumbled with his keys - managed to get the door open, and then dropped into the driver's seat. A wave of dizziness and a powerful desire to sleep swamped his brain. He slammed his fist repeatedly on the steering wheel. "No...no...no! Stay awake, you fucking bastard!" he shouted.

The pain in his hand cleared his mind.

He rammed the key in the ignition lock. The engine roared. Then the vehicle accelerated away from its position.

He spotted the two police officers standing by their car as he shot past. He saw one writing something on a note pad.

They had his registration number, so he would have to dump the car.

He parked as near to his room as he dared, and having wiped his fingerprints off everything he could, he made his way to his temporary home. And the room he had bemoaned earlier, now contained the most enticing bed that had ever been created by man.

He had been lucky, very lucky. Both bullets had only grazed his flesh. And after bathing the wounds and bandaging them with a few strips from a clean sheet, he began to feel a little better. He then fell into a deep sleep that lasted twenty seven hours.

Three days of resting up had passed and Jack was lying on top of the bed; his head propped up by two pillows. He had a bottle of scotch in his right hand - taking occasional swallows as he considered his situation. The plan had ended up a complete disaster, and all because that stupid sod Nigel owed Jimmy Spooner. Well, now Jimmy owed him, and it would cost him every bit as much as it had Nigel.

Finally, exhaustion and the effects of half a bottle of whisky took their toll, and Jack drifted into yet another prolonged sleep.

30

There was a click.

Jack opened his eyes.

There was another click.

He raised his head and looked around the semi-dark room. The street light provided just enough illumination for him to see. Everything was as it should be.

A brief scratching sound drew his attention to the door. He sat up. Then he slipped off the bed and moved to the other side of the room. He pressed himself between the wardrobe and an old, disused chimney breast. The Nine Millimetre felt comforting in his hand.

The door opened very slowly. Two shadowy figures stood in the doorway for a moment, obviously scanning the room. Jack pulled his head back. They couldn't see him, but he couldn't see them either. Then a creak from a floorboard told Jack that the visitors had stepped inside. His grip tightened on the gun.

"The fucking bastard ain't in!" one of the men hissed. "So what do we do now?"

"Search the room of course," said the other man. "Jimmy said that he was loaded and might have some of it stashed under his mattress."

Jack heard soft footsteps, then the sound of the mattress being moved. Curses followed.

"Let's try the wardrobe," said one of the men. "I have no intention of leaving this dump empty-handed."

Jack stepped into view as the men approached. "Evening, Gentlemen," he said in a calm voice.

"Fuck!" the taller of the men exclaimed.

"Stay exactly where you are," Jack ordered, edging past the men towards the door. Then he closed it and switched on the light.

Two tall, heavy set men stared back at him. One was about thirty; the other being in his early fifties and had a slight stoop..

"Look, Mate," said the older man, licking his lips nervously, "we don't want no trouble, so we're going to leave now - OK...?"

"Fuck OK," Jack replied. "What you *are* going to do is tell me what you came here for."

"We heard you had a bit of cash stashed here, so we decided to have a look; that's all, Mate," said the man.

"But you expected to find me in?" said Jack. "What plans did you have for me?"

The older man glanced at his younger companion who was looking very frightened. "Me and Phil weren't going to hurt you or anything like that, Mate. We were just going to put the frighteners on you so that you would hand over the money without any trouble. From what we heard, you have plenty more somewhere else so you could afford to lose a bit."

"I don't believe you," said Jack.

"It's the truth, Mate, honest it is," said the man.

"I'll decide what is the truth," Jack warned. "And I can tell you now, I don't like liars."

Jack kept the Nine Millimetre pointed at the younger, fitter looking man as he continued to question the older man.

"So what's your name?" he asked.

"Alec," came the reply.

"And his? Oh yes, it's Phil isn't it. Right then, Alec, you and your friend Phil here had no intention of hurting me. Is that correct?"

Alec nodded and he began to sweat. He looked as guilty as hell to Jack.

"But what if I had refused to hand over the money, Alec? What would you have done then?"

Alec gave a sickly smile. "OK, so we might have leaned on you a little; nothing serious mind you; just a few slaps."

"I see," said Jack thoughtfully. "And I suppose you two are just a couple of blokes down on your luck - looking for a bit of easy money?"

Alec visibly relaxed. "Got it in one, Mate. Me and Phil, well to put it bluntly we both lost our jobs and we couldn't find anything else. And since we have families to support the pressure was on us to find a bit of cash PDQ. And when we heard that you were a bit flush...well...I know we shouldn't have tried to steal from you, but we didn't mean any real harm. We were just desperate."

"Then you won't have any guns on you, if as you say you're only a couple of blokes down on their luck?" said Jack.

The sickly smile vanished from Alec's lips.

"The way I see it, Alec," Jack went on, "you two are in my room, either looking for a bit of spare cash, or to put a bullet in my brain. Isn't that right?"

"How do you mean, Mate?" Alec replied.

"I mean take your coats off one at a time," said Jack. "You first, Silent Phil."

The younger man slipped off his overcoat and held it in his right hand.

"Drop it on the floor," Jack ordered.

Phil dropped the coat, and there was a loud thump as it landed on the carpet.

"Now that's what I call heavy duty material," Jack said with a smile. "And you, Alec, if you don't mind."

There was a similar thump when Alec dropped his coat next to Phil's.

"I see you both shop at the same place," said Jack. "What friends you must be."

"OK, so we brought along a couple of knuckledusters..." Alec admitted.

"Or guns," said Jack, "which would put quite a different slant on your reasons for being here in my room. I'm afraid it would mean you came here to kill me, and then I would have to become very angry. And I even frighten myself when I'm angry."

"Jesus Christ, Mate!" Alec exclaimed. "We ain't gangsters you know!"

"Of course you're not," said Jack. "Because only gangsters would carry guns, and as you just told me, you only brought along a couple of knuckledusters to give me a few slaps if I didn't cooperate."

"That's right, Mate!" Alec shot back.

"We shall see about that," said Jack. "Now, why don't you reach down and pick up your coat. Then you can turn it upside down - give it a few shakes and we shall see what falls out."

Alec stared back at Jack for a moment, then he threw a glance at the Nine Millimetre which was now pointing at his belly. Then he bent down and picked up his coat. A few shakes later and a Snub Nose Revolver landed on the carpet.

"Funny looking knuckleduster," said Jack. "Must pack quite a punch."

"What are you going to do with us?" said Alec.

"Answer my questions and see. Now both of you back up and sit on the bed, and sit far enough back so that your feet are not touching the floor."

Jack watched as his captives complied.

Jack then collected a wooden chair from next to the wardrobe, and positioning it in the middle of the room, sat astride it. "This is cosy," he said. "So start talking. Who sent you?"

"No one," said Alec. "I told you, we were just looking for a bit of…"

Alec screamed when a bullet smashed through the shoe of his left foot.

"Oh, I am sorry," said Jack as Alec rocked back and forth in agony, cradling his injured limb. "Didn't I explain. When I ask you a question and you are rude enough to lie to me, I shoot you somewhere."

"You fucking maniac!" Alec screeched through gritted teeth.

"Don't be such a cry baby," said Jack. "I've been shot twice recently and you don't see me whining. Just be a brave boy and tell me who sent you…?"

"Jimmy Spooner," Alec replied between gasps of breath.

"To do what?"

" I said to do what?" Jack repeated when Alec said nothing.

"You know bloody well what!" Alec retorted. "To fucking kill you!"

"I see. But why would he want to do that? I mean, Jimmy and I have a deal, so why would he want to kill me?"

"Because you were after Manny Hemmings."

Jack sighed. "So, Jimmy set me up. But what about Len and the others? After all, they were his lads?"

"Jimmy don't care about nobody except himself. He looks out for Manny's interests and does his best to make some extra cash along the way. Manny don't mind because that way he can pay Jimmy less and still keep him loyal."

"And where does Jimmy live?" Jack asked.

"Twelve Orpington Street," said Alec. "It's a four bedroom terraced with a bright red door. You can't miss it."

The first bullet that then left the gun went through Phil's forehead; the second through his chest. He was dead before his head hit the mattress.

Alec cried out in terror and dragged himself across the bed. Jack gave a sneering laugh and shot him through both legs, then through both shoulders before finally shooting him through the heart. Jack didn't like Alec, and when he didn't like someone, he wanted to make them suffer before they died.

It took Jack an hour to clean his fingerprints from every part of the room.

And by five am he was gone, leaving behind two dead bodies, and a load of fresh questions for the police.

By ten am he had rented another room in Stepney. If anything, it was even worse than the one he had left, but he didn't really mind. He had other things to think about besides creature comforts; namely pay back time for Jimmy Spooner.

It was Tuesday. Jack had to wait for four hours opposite Twelve Orpington Street before he saw Jimmy Spooner pull up outside in a brown coloured Mini.

'Must be keeping a low profile driving around in a car like that with the money he must be making,' Jack thought as Jimmy let himself in through the front door. Then the movement of a curtain two doors along drew Jack's attention. He saw a face appear at the window for a moment, then it was gone. He decided to give Jimmy about ten minutes to make himself comfortable, then he would make his move.

At exactly four pm Jack crossed the street and stood at Jimmy Spooner's door. He pressed the button high up on the middle of the door and the ugly clatter of a bell in need of rewinding came from within. Jack tightened his grip on the gun that was in his right pocket.

Then the door opened.

"Come on in, Jack Mate," Jimmy Spooner ordered with a smile.

Jack stared in surprise at the large WWII Army Service Revolver that was pointing directly at his belly.

Jimmy stepped back, and Jack moved passed him into the hall.

Jimmy closed the door without taking his eyes or the gun off his prisoner. Then he ordered Jack into the living room.

The place was a tip. Newspapers; pornographic magazines, and unwashed cups lay scattered all over the place.

"That's far enough," said Jimmy. "Now keep your back turned to me and put your hands out in front of you. And if you're thinking of having a go - *don't*. I know how to use this, and you wouldn't be the first man I've killed with it."

Jack stood still and held out his arms as he felt the gun muzzle pressed hard into his back and a hand searching his coat pocket. His Nine Millimetre was removed, then the pressure on his back was gone.

"Sit over in that armchair," said Jimmy.

Jack did as he was told. The chair was old and a spring twanged as his weight settled into its thick cushion.

"Good so far," Jimmy said with a grin. Then he sat on a faded settee - the revolver not for a second moving off the centre of Jack's belly.

'This bastard knows what he's doing,' Jack said to himself. He was in big trouble.

"Well, Jack Mate," said Jimmy, laying Jack's gun down beside him. "I bet you didn't expect this…did you…?"

"No," said Jack.

"Ain't life a bitch," Jimmy laughed. "And you know something, Jack Mate, you really should have stuck to serving drinks to your customers in that great pub of yours, because when you cause trouble for the big boys, they fight back one hell of a lot harder than any drunk that needs chucking out."

"I suppose I should have," said Jack. "So, what happens now?"

Jimmy arched his eyebrows. "Do you mean, before I kill you, or after I kill you?"

"Oh, before you kill me, of course," said Jack casually. "I'll probably have lost interest after."

"You know, you're a calm bastard if ever I saw one," said Jimmy with obvious admiration. "And I do believe I'm going to hate shooting you."

"Well, I'm not twisting your arm," Jack replied.

Jimmy laughed. "So, Jack Mate, what's all this shit about? You had a great pub, and you were obviously making money. So why jeopardize it all and take on someone like Manny Hemmings? If you thought to ask, anyone would have told you that it's been tried before, and everyone who has tried has ended up dead."

"I knew that already," said Jack.

"So why do it?"

Jack shrugged his shoulders. "I was bored; it was raining out, there was nothing on the Telly, and since I didn't fancy joining the library…"

"OK, OK," said Jimmy. "Your reasons are your own; I can respect that. But can't you at least tell me how you planned to hang on to the organization if you had killed Manny and taken over? Surely you know that his brother Frank is big time in the States - maybe even connected to the Mob?"

"I planned on being big time myself," said Jack. "I have the money, all I had to do was hire the help I needed."

Jimmy let out a long whistle. "You mean you've got that kind of cash! Where the hell did you get it?"

Jack shrugged. "Manny asked me to look after it for him, so I decided to look after it for myself instead."

Jimmy shifted in his seat as excitement grew inside him. "So, Jack Mate, how much are we talking about; twenty thousand; thirty thousand…?"

"A million pounds."

"Fuck off!" Jimmy replied. "No individual has that kind of money except them millionaires…and I ain't ever seen a millionaire - not to mind a million quid!"

"Well you have now," said Jack. "And for your information Manny Hemming's operation is worth at least twice that."

"Christ Almighty," Jimmy whispered to himself. "I knew Manny was big time, but I'd never have guessed he was into that kind of money."

"Mind you, he's not worth that now," said Jack, "not since I nicked half of it."

Jimmy focused his eyes on Jack with great intensity. "Are you really telling me that you have *one million quid* stashed away somewhere?"

Jack nodded. "Less a few thousand I had to spend hiring some help."

"Fuck me…*fuck me!*" Jimmy cried, his eyes glowing. "A million quid! Christ Almighty, Jack Mate, what does it look like?"

"Like what it is - all the dreams you've ever had, in one place – cars, beautiful women, booze, soft beaches, yachts, cruises, and most of all power, the power to spend the rest of your life doing exactly what you want, without one single bastard telling you what to do. And I can't even begin to describe what it was like going through a hundred thousand crisp new ten pound notes."

"One hundred thousand tenners," Jimmy whispered, as if suddenly in a dream. Then he left his seat and made his way to a drinks cabinet. With one hand he poured scotch into two glasses. And all the time the gun stayed on Jack. Jack cursed the man's efficiency.

Jimmy approached and handed Jack one of the glasses. Jack noted that Jimmy made him reach out for it - keeping him off balance.

"You know, Jack Mate, there is a rumour going round that Manny has had some terrible upset about special magazines being nicked. And according to one of my sources Manny is treating everyone around him pretty bad since the stuff went missing. It did strike me as odd that he reacted so badly. I thought he was probably losing his grip a bit, you know…too many of those stinking cigars of his rotting his brain, and that was why he sent for his brother Frank. But what you've just told me explains it all. I'd go ape too if someone pinched a million quid of my money."

Jimmy then went back to his seat and sat down. "So, where have you hidden the money? I mean, a hundred thousand tenners must take up a bit of space?"

Jack tasted the scotch. It was very good.

"Oh come on!" Jimmy exclaimed with a grin when Jack didn't reply. "It won't do you any good now!"

"You've got a fucking nerve," Jack replied, "expecting me to hand you a million quid just before you kill me."

"Then how about I make it worth your while?" said Jimmy.

"You mean you'll let me go?"

"No can do, Jack Mate," Jimmy replied. "What I mean is, tell me where you've stashed the money and I'll put a bullet in your brain. It will be quick and painless."

Jack's eyes narrowed. "And if I don't...?"

"Then I'll put one in each of your kneecaps, your shoulders, your ankles and your arms – not to mention one in your privates."

"That's nine bullets," said Jack. "Your gun only holds six."

"So I'll reload," Jimmy replied shrugging his shoulders. "I mean, you will hardly be in a position to stop me."

"I suppose not," said Jack. "But I'm curious, Jimmy. How did you know it was me at the door, or do you greet all callers with a gun?"

"That's down to good old snoop Mrs Williams at number sixteen - just two doors from here," Jimmy replied. "I told her that I was hiding from a violent love rival and she agreed to phone me when anyone like you called."

"Clever," Jack admitted. "But why did you inform on me to Manny Hemmings? I paid what you asked, didn't I? Surely it wasn't so that you wouldn't have to hand back the extra cash you were looking after for me?"

"You're right there, Jack Mate," said Jimmy, taking a drink. "It wasn't the money. Manny pays me the same fifty quid each week whether I have something to report or not. But let me tell you a story about something I read in a book a couple of years ago. The book was all about sharks. Now, as you probably know, sharks are one of the most dangerous fish in the oceans. They have no natural predators except for man, and their speed and strength is incredible. Very few creatures are safe when a shark is hunting. Now, with certain species of shark, a very much smaller and more harmless fish follows the sharks wherever they go - I mean swimming real close to them. And the marvellous thing is that the sharks don't eat them, and why, because despite the shark's tremendous power, it can't scratch itself. Imagine, Jack Mate – being the most dangerous bastard in your environment, and you can't even have a good old scratch. And was God having a laugh or was he having a laugh when he made them. Anyway, that's where the little fish come in. They provide a cleaning service for the sharks - picking off parasites that would otherwise irritate the sharks or burrow their way into the shark's bodies - causing all kinds of trouble. And in return for this most valuable service the sharks protect the little fish. Now, in that great ocean we know as London, Manny Hemmings is a very big shark indeed, and I'm one of his little fish. I watch out for him - getting rid of the parasites that might cause him trouble. And when the parasites are too big for me to cope with - you for instance, Jack Mate, then I give Manny a ring so that he can get other little fish, but just a bit larger than me, to do the job. In other words, Jack Mate, without the protection of Manny Hemmings, some bastard would have done away with me long ago."

"And Len, Gerry and Nigel…?" Jack asked.

"Good lads, but ten a penny. Manny phoned me about your failed attempt, and I must say, Jack Mate, that you and the lads gave a good account of yourselves. You left five bodyguards dead, plus your own three of course. I heard you finished Len and Nigel off yourself."

"Better than twenty years in prison," Jack replied.

"For you or for them?"

"Both."

Jimmy sighed. "You're a cold bastard, Jack Blade. Anyway, the cops were all over the place. Manny managed to keep out of it, but some of his bodyguards are spending a few nights in the cells. And of course they're looking for you, Jack Mate. You would probably get life without parole for all that killing. But as you've just said, you're better off dead than doing a long stretch."

"I may have been a little hasty there," Jack muttered.

Jimmy laughed out loud. "You know, you're really something! Look at you, sitting there on the wrong end of a gun and you can still crack a joke! But to more pressing matters. How about telling me where the money is?"

"How will you know if I'm telling you the truth?" said Jack. "You might go there and find nothing - unless you plan for me to take you to it…?"

"Sorry, Jack Mate. Orders from the man himself. There's no way you're leaving this room alive."

"Then you're prepared to risk that I'm lying?"

A sheepish grin appeared on Jimmy's face. "I'm afraid I'm the one who's lying, Jack Mate. You see, I have no choice but to force the truth from you, so I'm going to shoot you just as I described, and I won't stop until I'm convinced you're not lying. Manny's orders too. Although I'm disappointed he didn't trust me enough to tell me the truth about what you had stolen from him."

"And now that I have told you, do you really think Manny will let you live?" said Jack. "That money is his future. I don't see him risking the police finding out about it by letting you sit here itching for more cash?"

"I considered that the instant you told me," said Jimmy. "And once you tell me where it is, I can decide what to do. You can go a very long way on a million quid, Jack Mate."

"Not long enough to hide from Manny and Frank," said Jack.

"Maybe," said Jimmy. "But you let me worry about my future. Now let's get on with it."

The grip of something ice cold was on Jack's heart as Jimmy's words sunk in. Suddenly he was out of options. He finished his drink in one gulp.

"Help yourself to another from the cabinet," said Jimmy. "And don't try anything stupid like chucking the bottle at me, or I'll shoot you a few times in the belly and leave you in my cellar to die slowly."

Jack poured himself a full glass of scotch and returned to his seat.

A certain look that suddenly came into Jimmy's eyes told Jack that his captor was about to set events in motion, and his mind began to race with desperation. He just had to do something. He couldn't let it end like this. His eyes cast hurriedly around the room, but there was nothing anywhere that he could use as a weapon, except the glass in his hand. But Jimmy was expecting him to use that.

Jack spotted half a dozen black and white photographs displayed on the shelf above the fireplace. "I see you were something of a sportsman?" he said.

Jimmy looked at the photos, and his shoulders straightened. "I was a pretty good weightlifter in my time, although you wouldn't think it to look at me now."

"What was your best event?"

"The Snatch," said Jimmy. "My trainer said I could have been chosen for the Olympics if I trained hard enough."

"So why didn't you?"

A look of sorrow appeared on Jimmy's face. "Hurt my back. Knocked me out of competitions for years. Eventually my back recovered, but it was too late. Weightlifting is a young man's game, but I'm still one hell of a strong bloke. Just last year I got into a fight with a rugby player- big bastard he was, but I still gave him the hiding of his life. Why, you fancy your chances with me, Jack Mate?"

"No thanks," said Jack. "It would be like beating up my old dad."

Anger glowed suddenly in Jimmy's eyes.

Then it was gone and he smiled. "I do believe you're trying to rile me, Jack Mate."

Jack smiled back. "Can't blame me for doing something to get myself out of the mess I'm in, can you?"

"Course not," said Jimmy. "But this is a nasty game we're playing, Jack Mate. There are no rules and definately no fair play. You lost the minute you rang my doorbell. Tough luck but there it is. And believe me, I'm not going to enjoy this, but it has to be done, so let's do it."

Jack's heart raced in his chest as desperation began to swell in his belly. There must be something he could do...'something!'

Jimmy finished off his whisky and placed the glass on the cushion next to him.

'Something!' Jack's mind demanded. *'Anything!'*

"Put your glass down will you, Jack Mate," said Jimmy, his expression now as hard as the blue metal of his gun.

Jack slowly placed the empty glass on the carpet.

"Now sit back and hold still. I don't want any bullets going wide of the mark."

Jack's breath began to catch in his throat, and sweat broke out all over his body.

Jimmy aimed the gun at Jack's left knee. "Hold still now."

'Do something!' Jack's mind screamed.

"Jesus Christ, Jack Mate!" Jimmy exclaimed, squinting as his finger began to tighten on the trigger. "I really don't fancy doing this! But orders are orders, and a million quid is a million quid!"

'Do it now!'

The fingers of Jack's right hand dug into the thick cushion he was sitting on. He instantly recognized what the filling was.

Hope surged up inside him.

He threw himself out of the chair, bringing the cushion around in front of him as he rushed towards a startled Jimmy Spooner. Jimmy fired twice, then Jack was on top of him.

Jimmy's gun-hand was grabbed.

He fired again. Old ceiling plaster showered down on top of them.

The two men struggled for control of the weapon.

Jack pinned Jimmy's right arm against the back of the settee. Jimmy punched with his left fist. Jack grunted as the blow caught him on the mouth, knocking him off the settee. But as he fell to the floor he pulled Jimmy down on top of him. The gun went off again and the television screen crazed.

Despite being smaller and lighter than Jack, Jimmy was proving to be a powerful adversary. He aimed the gun down towards Jack's face with both hands.

Jack struggled to push it away.

For a few moments it seemed he would succeed, but then the barrel moved back towards his face, and at the instant Jimmy squeezed the trigger, Jack moved his head to the right. The bullet tore through his left ear and the floor. Pain flooded his brain.

Jimmy cursed and tried to aim and fire again.

Jack let go of his left hand and jabbed his fingers into Jimmy's eyes.

Jimmy screamed and fell away.

Jack rolled on top of him and wrestled for the gun.

But Jimmy's grip was like a vice on the weapon.

"You fucking bastard!" Jimmy cried through clamped lips. "You fucking rotten bastard! I'm going to kill you!"

Jack shoved his left elbow down on Jimmy's throat.

Jimmy gurgled and grabbed Jack by the hair.

Jack's head was jerked backwards, but he held on to Jimmy's right hand, which was still holding the gun.

Across the floor the combatant's then rolled, each trying for control of the weapon. But they were evenly matched - Jack's youthful energy against the older man's strength and experience.

Then a vicious punch to the side of Jack's face cost him his vital hold on his adversaries gun hand.

He shook his head to clear away the mist that had suddenly formed in front of his eyes.

Jimmy shoved Jack off him and leaped to his feet. "Got you now, you fucking bastard!" he roared, pointing the gun at Jack with both hands. "Got you now! And whereas I didn't really want to hurt you before, now I'm going to enjoy watching you suffer!"

Jack stood up slowly. His eyes began to clear and he stared back at Jimmy with utter contempt. "Do you know something, Spooner," he growled, "a scrawny bastard like you could never have achieved Olympic standard in anything, unless it was for some kind of 'treacherous little weasel' event!"

"Well, you're wrong there, Jack Mate," Jimmy growled back, "because I'm a first class shot with this, as you're about to find out!"

"Fuck you , Spooner!" Jack retorted, then he dived at the settee.

Jimmy pulled the trigger of his revolver.

Jack felt something pull at the hair on the back of his head, then he felt the hard metal of the Nine Millimetre in his hand.

He spun around - aimed and fired, just as another explosion sent a bullet blasting into his left shoulder.

The shock stunned him, but he fired again, sending four bullets flying at Jimmy.

The force of the bullets smashing into his chest sent Jimmy staggering backwards. He collided with the damaged television, and they both went over with a tremendous crash.

Then there was total silence in the room.

"Fuck!" Jack cursed, examining his injured shoulder. "How many more times!"

On this occasion the bullet had managed to stay in his body instead of passing through it. But he would live – at least for the time being.

Then the precariousness of his situation focused his mind. He picked up his empty glass from where he'd left it and wiped away his fingerprints. He also cleaned the whisky bottle. Then he examined the cushion he had used as a shield. On one side there were two small entry holes, but no exit holes on the other side. He had been very lucky to remember at such a crucial moment that a thick stuffing of horse hair will stop most bullets. A spinning bullet will wrap horse hair around it so that its momentum is stopped. Yes he had been lucky, but for how much longer could such luck last? 'Long enough to get that bastard Manny Hemmings,' he concluded.

Then he left the house and crossed the street to where he had parked his latest second-hand car. And as he drove away he heard the ringing bell of a police car. It shot past him a couple of seconds later.

31

Jack returned to his new room at sixteen Pigeon Road and examined his wound. Although the bullet hadn't severed the main artery or broken any bones, it was still embedded deep in his shoulder. This time he was going to need surgery, but that was out of the question for the moment. He bandaged his shoulder and popped three aspirins into his mouth. The pain was strong but bearable. He could put up with it for now.

After a good night's sleep, he felt a bit better in the morning. His bandage had only a small patch of blood on it, which was a good sign. There was obviously no serious bleeding going on.

He made himself a pot of tea and a couple of slices of toast. The radio announced that police were at the scene of a vicious murder that had taken place at number twelve Orpington Street. A police spokesman, when asked by a reporter if this new killing was related in any way to the killings at Queensbury House a few days before, had replied 'At this moment in time we cannot rule out any possibility. Once forensics have examined the cause of the victim's death, a clearer motive may be established.'

Jack munched thoughtfully on his buttered toast as the spokesman continued to answer questions from the media. He was certainly making news these days, and in some small way he liked it. But there was still much to do if he was to achieve his goal. And why was he so desperate to achieve it; especially now when the police and his victim-to-be, knew his identity? This was a question that had been bugging Jack lately. He had nearly a million pounds hidden in the pub; easily enough to pay for his daughter's treatment in America and to give him a very comfortable life abroad. The sensible thing to do would be to get the money and leave the country. Yes, that would be the sensible thing to do, but not the Jack Blade thing to do. It was as if he was a deposed monarch; determined to return to his throne no matter what the cost. And he was going to sit in Manny Hemming's chair, come what may. And any bastard who got in his way would end up like Jimmy Spooner - with more holes in him than a colander.

Two days later, and wearing a raincoat and hat he had bought, Jack walked by The Raven a few times. There was no signs that the place was being watched. Obviously the police and Manny Hemmings had decided that he would never return there, and was probably making desperate attempts to leave the country.

Jack let himself in by the back door of the building, and a few minutes later he was positioning the grab of the hoist over the flagstone cover. And removing the cover certainly took its toll on him. Nevertheless he was determined to carry out the task he had set himself so he carried on.

The sudden blow to the back of his neck sent him spiralling into a black void.

Something was hitting his face. He felt lots of individual sensations on his skin, and although they didn't hurt, they were irritating. He lifted his right hand to brush them away, but they wouldn't go. Angry, he opened his eyes. There was a drizzle of rain. He sat up.

"About fucking time," an American voice announced. "I was worried there for a while that you had snuffed it from that karate chop to the neck I gave you."

Jack turned his head and saw a soaked figure sitting a few feet from him on an up-side-down galvanize bucket. "Who the hell are you?" he asked.

The American; in his early thirties, grinned. "Don't you remember me, Buddy? The name's Eddy - Eddy Hickock."

"Never met you before," Jack grunted, massaging the back of his neck. Then he realized his Nine Millimetre was missing.

"Sure you have, Buddy," said Eddy. "We had a little chat at that shindig at Manny's office."

Suddenly the man's voice was familiar to Jack. "You were one of the lobsters with the pincers."

Eddy laughed. "That's me. But look at you now, Buddy - sitting on your butt in the rain.

"And you're sitting on a bucket getting as wet as me, so what's your point, Mate?" said Jack.

"Boy, you sure do view every situation from a positive point of view, don't you," said Eddy.

"Yes, well I gave up whinging about life when everyone I told always came back with a sadder story than my own," said Jack.

"You got that right," said Eddy. "And I see that you have got up to some new tricks since we last met. Two of Manny's hired help found dead in a flat you rented, and some other guy called Spooner found with half his back blown away. You know, I don't know who wants your hide most, Manny or the cops."

"So how did you know where to find me?" said Jack.

"I had a shrewd idea you would come back here," said Eddy, looking around him. "After all, this place has been your life for five years. And it's been my experience that a wounded dog always returns to where he feels safe – his lair. And I also believed that this was where Manny's million pounds was hidden."

"You know about the money then," said Jack.

"Sure I do," Eddy replied. "And do you know how I know? Well let me tell you. I have Frank's office bugged back in the States. And when his little brother phoned him to complain that someone had run off with a million quid of his money and was killing his top men, sneaky old me was listening."

"I'll bet Frank would like to know about that," said Jack.

"Sure he would," said Eddy. "But you know something, Buddy, Frank thinks he's untouchable. And what he doesn't realize is that when you think that way you become the very thing you think you're not. Now something else Frank doesn't realize is that there is not one organization but two under the banner of Frank Hemmings Inc, and that he runs only one of them. I run the other. And when the time is right, Frank Hemmings Inc will become Eddy Hickock Inc. Has a much better ring to it don't you think, Buddy?"

"I think, as a certain English poet once wrote 'a rose by any other name would stink just the same,'" Jack replied. "So what happens now?"

Eddy stared at the hole next to Jack. "It's my guess that the million is down there."

"Didn't you look?" Jack inquired.

"And have you bash my skull in as I came back out if you recovered," said Eddy. "I didn't get to where I am by taking stupid chances like that."

"You could have killed me first?"

"And then found only some of the money down there."

"So you want it all?"

Eddy's eyes narrowed. "I need it all, Buddy – every dime. You see, although I'm just about to put a great big hole in Frank's armour, I can't do it without far more ready cash than I have. And a million quid placed in the right hands will make sure that when I make my move, I will have all the backing I expect to have. So down the hatch you go, Buddy, and see what we can find."

It was then that Jack saw the gun in Eddy's right hand. It was small – a two shot Derringer that was popular with gamblers in the Wild West.

"And don't try anything," said Eddy. "This will put two very nasty holes in you if you misbehave."

Jack began lowering himself down the shaft.

"Make sure you stand still at the bottom," Eddy ordered as he began to follow.

Finally Jack was standing on the floor and he waited.

Still five feet from the ground Eddy pointed the gun at Jack. "Step back," he ordered.

Jack moved away and Eddy dropped the rest of the way – expertly bending his knees as he hit the floor to cushion the impact.

'Fit bastard!' Jack said to himself.

Eddy pulled a torch out of his pocket and shone the light around the room. "Cosy little place, if you were a rat that is."

"But one in a million," Jack quipped.

Then the beam from Eddy's torch fell on the table supporting the eight knapsacks.

Jack heard the American's sharp intake of breath, and rage flared up inside him, but he fought it down.

Eddy whistled. "Is that it, Buddy...a million pounds in cash?"

"See for yourself," said Jack.

Eddy kept the gun pointed at Jack as he edged towards the table.

Jack felt an involuntary movement of his muscles.

"Hold it, Buddy!" Eddy snapped and the beam of light swung around, dazzling Jack for a moment.

Jack put his hands up to cover his eyes.

"Put your hands down and keep your eyes wide open," said Eddy.

"The light is blinding me!" Jack protested.

"That's the idea," said Eddy. Then he laid the torch on the table so that the light continued to illuminate Jack.

Jack heard Eddy opening one of the knapsacks and heard another intake of breath.

"Holy Shit!" Eddy cried. "I have never admired a single thing on this island of yours, Buddy, but this million pounds has educated me real quick!"

"We could split it?" Jack offered "Fifty-fifty…?"

"Sorry, Buddy, no can do," Eddy replied staring at a thick bundle of ten pound notes in his hand.

"Twenty five-seventy five in your favour?" said Jack.

"Need it all, Buddy. I'm just a greedy bastard like you. Only one hundred percent will do. Negotiations are for the United Nations."

"And I suppose you're going to leave me down here?"

"Wouldn't dream of it," said Eddy, putting the money back into the knapsack with his left hand. His right hand held the Derringer. "I need someone to carry these sacks upstairs. I can't climb up with one of them and cover you at the same time. So you're doing all the carrying, Buddy. And forget about trying to drop one on me. I'll always go first. so grab one and start climbing."

It took Jack and Eddy over twenty minutes to take the knapsacks up into the courtyard due to the narrowness of the shaft. And when the task was completed, Jack was just as relieved as his captor.

"So?" said Eddy, keeping the Derringer trained on Jack. "You've had this dough for a while now and you're still here? And what gives with the campaign against Frank's brother? He do something bad to one of your family?"

"I don't have a family," Jack replied, wiping water from his face.

"Then why all the killing?"

"Maybe I don't like the ties he wears."

"Maybe it ain't about the money, and maybe it ain't personal?" said Eddy. "Maybe it ain't even about power?"

"What else is there?" said Jack.

"Something very few people understand. But you do, don't you, Buddy. I saw something in you back at the office, and again when you wasted your own guys. But you ain't no Psycho…are you, Jack?"

"You tell me," Jack replied. "After all, you're the one doing all the talking."

Eddy grinned as the rain ran down his face. "OK, Buddy. You are what they call a Toberosch in some North American Indian cultures."

"Never heard of it," said Jack, part of his mind trying to work out a way for him to get the better of a large and fit man with a gun, while he was trying to recover from at least three recent bullet wounds.

"Few have," said Eddy. "But I have studied the legends of the different Indian tribes, and the Toberosch crops up in quite a few of them. Anyway, it seems this…creature if you like, although that isn't an accurate description, is neither man nor beast."

"A spirit you mean?" Jack offered, desperate to keep the man in front of him talking – anything was better than shooting.

Eddy shook his head. "Not really a spirit either, but something between all three. The Indians believe that the Great Spirit had a son by an Indian princess, and although the child looked human, he most certainly wasn't. It seems that as he grew up, he began terrorizing the other children, and in adulthood started fights that often ended in death. Eventually the tribe drove him from the village."

"So what has that to do with me?" Jack asked.

"The modern Indians believe he is still wandering the Earth, killing for reason's we wouldn't understand," said Eddy.

"I'm still asking what it has to do with me?" said Jack.

A strange look entered Eddy's eyes. "In 1864 twenty members of the Hickock family were slaughtered by one man as they were making their way to California."

"Not another history lesson!" Jack admonished.

Eddy was clearly annoyed by the interruption. "And when some local Indians were questioned, they claimed that they saw the man who did the killing, and it was Toberosch."

"Oh I get it!" Jack declared. "You think I'm this…Toberosch character, and you are here to take revenge for the slaughter of your ancestors!"

"That's right, Buddy."

Jack was astonished. "I was only joking, Mate!"

"Were you…" said Eddy.

"I think you have been eating too much of that Texan beef," said Jack. "I hear it can interfere with the blood circulation to your brain."

Eddy reached into his jacket and pulled out a large silver coloured object. He then held it out in the palm of his hand for Jack to see. "Know what this is?" he asked.

Jack stared at the ten inch long object. "That's a real difficult question but I'll have a go anyway. I think it's called a knife…correct…?"

"Not just any knife, but a very old Bowie knife," said Eddy, ignoring

Jack's sarcasm. "Made around 1834, and maybe even by Bowie himself. It has a few nicks and scratches but still in good condition."

Eddy then stooped down and slowly placed the weapon on the wet paving, but all the time keeping his eyes and the Derringer fixed on Jack. Then he straightened and produced a similar looking knife.

"Another one made by Bowie?" said Jack. "Just how many of them do you have?"

"This one was made after his death…about 1865. But it will do just as well."

"Just as well for what?" Jack asked.

Eddy took half a dozen steps back, then he tossed the Derringer into the open shaft. The gun clattered a great deal on the way down.

"You just threw away your advantage," said Jack, "unless you have another gun…?"

"The only other gun is your Nine Millimetre," said Eddy, "but that's in the cellar."

"And I suppose all this rubbish has something to do with you believing that I'm Toberosch," said Jack. "Just how fucked up can a bloke from Texas get."

"Now you pick up that knife, Buddy!" Eddy ordered. "Because whether you're ready or not, I plan to skin you alive."

"You're not serious?" Jack declared.

But the look on Eddy's face answered his question.

Jack then moved slowly forwards, half expecting Eddy to attack. But whatever was going through the American's mind, it wasn't trickery. He simply watched when Jack picked up the knife retreated a few steps. The weapon felt heavy and cumbersome in his hand.

"Take a few moment's to get the feel of it," said Eddy.

"It's a bloody knife," said Jack. "I've seen better ones in the kitchen section of my local Woolworth's. What's there to get used to."

It was clear to Jack that the American was obsessed by the Wild West and unable to take any criticism of the period. He hoped his jibes would unsettle him enough to make him careless.

"OK then, "said Eddy. "A fair fight to the death, and let the best man win. And you know something, Buddy, you're soon going to find out why Jim Bowie is so famous for inventing these knives."

"Just a minute!" Jack exclaimed. "You call this a fair fight! I've been shot in my left shoulder and the fucking bullet is still there! How can it be a fair fight!"

Eddy looked thoughtful for a moment. Then before Jack's disbelieving eyes he plunged the knife into his left arm, just below his shoulder.

Eddy staggered and stifled a cry. Then he pulled out the knife and composed himself. Blood seeped out through the cut on the material of his coat.

"Christ, you *are* a sick bastard, aren't you," said Jack.

"Just giving you an even break, Buddy," said Eddy. "Now are you going to stand there in the rain and let me butcher you like a pig, or are you going to show me what the great Jack Blade is really made of?"

Jack stared back at the man standing before him and wondered if he was completely insane. But whatever the state of Eddy Hickock's mind, one thing was certain. He was standing in the courtyard of Jack Blade's pub, threatening to kill Jack Blade. And there was no way Jack Blade was going to let him get away with that.

"OK, Eddy," he replied. "I don't know what this crap is really all about, but you are obviously determined to have this fight. So let's get on with it."

Eddy grinned. "That's more like it, Buddy. And none of your Queensbury Rules. This is a Texan Slice And Dice. Everything goes."

"Fine by me," said Jack.

"Here we go then," said Eddy, instantly adopting the crouch of the knife fighter.

Jack followed suit, but as with Eddy, his left arm was pretty weak, so only the right hand could be used to hold the knife.

Eddy began to approach Jack, his body gently swaying from side to side and the long blade extended in front of him.

Jack instinctively retreated at first, but then stood his ground.

Eddy came ever nearer, then he lunged at Jack.

Jack instantly side-stepped and stabbed at Eddy as he rushed past.

But Eddy turned and the blades of both knives clashed together.

"Good move, Buddy," Eddy grinned.

Then he rushed again. But when Jack side-stepped once more, Eddy's knife sliced through his shirt, and a thin stain of blood turned his chest red.

"We call that one *The Thin Red Line*," said Eddy, still grinning. "Don't hurt much and don't do any damage, but it serves as a marker for all the rest that are coming your way, Buddy."

"I didn't realize this was a talk fight," Jack replied. "If I had, I would have brought along a pair of ear plugs, because that Prairie Dog squeaky voice of yours is getting on my nerves now."

The grin left Eddy. Then he charged.

Jack tried to fend off the swing that sent Eddy's blade towards his left side, but he had only partial success. An inch of metal stabbed through Jack's flesh and split one of his ribs. Agony exploded from the area.

"How did you like that, Buddy!" Eddy laughed. "It's one of my own specialities. I call it a *Two For One!*"

Then Eddy came at Jack again, but this time jabbing his knife before him, forcing Jack to retreat.

And when Eddy then lunged, Jack swung his injured left arm and caught Eddy full in the mouth. The force of the blow stopped Eddy in his tracks, and blood gushed from between his lips.

"We call that *One In The Gob*," said Jack smiling. "And how do *you* like it, *Buddy.*"

"You fucking bastard!" Eddy roared. "I'll cut you to pieces for that!"

Jack managed to hold his smile despite feeling as if his left arm had been twisted off at the shoulder. The arm had now gone partially numb and he doubted it would be much use to him again.

Eddy wiped the blood from his mouth and then attacked.

For ten minutes the two men fought one another with all the vigour of two hated enemies. Each received dozens of minor cuts that proved painful but not serious. Eddy was certainly an expert with a knife, but Jack, though inexperienced with the weapon, clearly possessed an instinct that allowed him to anticipate Eddy's moves a fraction of a second before he made them. This kept him alive for far longer than would be expected.

Then everything changed. After one particular clash, the blade of Jack's knife snapped off at the hilt.

"Tough luck, Buddy!" Eddy sneered.

Jack backed hurriedly away and Eddy followed; licking his damaged lips and grinning. He had his man now and it was simply a matter of cornering him and finishing him off.

Jack's eyes were casting around desperately looking for another weapon; anything with which to fend off someone very good with a knife.

Then realizing he was still holding the hilt of the broken weapon, he flung it straight at Eddy's face.

Eddy simply leaned to the right and the missile flew harmlessly past.

"Pathetic!" Eddy declared. "You will have to do a lot better than that, Buddy!"

Jack spotted the metal bucket Eddy had been sitting on and shot towards it.

Eddy ran after him.

Jack suddenly slipped on the wet surface and cried out when his injured shoulder slammed down against the hard paving.

He turned over as Eddy bore down on him then kicked out with his feet.

Eddy's legs were shoved from under him and he fell on top of Jack.

Jack then grappled with Eddy who was trying to drive the blade of his knife into his body.

Over and over they rolled in an awkward tangle since Jack had a grip on Eddy's right hand with his own. Neither man could use his left hand.

Suddenly Eddy broke free and shot to his feet.

He spun the knife in the air. Then it was in his hand once more but reversed; throwing position.

Jack saw the danger, then the bucket, which was lying on its side just a couple of feet away.

Eddy raised his hand to throw.

Jack's right hand shot out and whipped the bucket towards Eddy.

The bucket crashed into Eddy's chest. He staggered backwards, and stepping on an uneven surface, began to lose his balance.

For a few desperate moments his arms spun wildly, then he fell backwards.

The middle of his body slipped down into the shaft that led to the room below the courtyard, but his legs and upper back prevented him from going in all the way.

Eddy struggled like mad to lift himself out of the shaft but his left arm refused to take his considerable weight.

Jack got to his feet, feeling as if he had been trampled by an elephant. He walked slowly towards Eddy.

"Looks like you got yourself into a right fix there, Buddy," he said to his stricken opponent.

"Fuck off, Limey!" Eddy growled, struggling to extract himself.

"And I see a Texan always hangs on to his weapon whatever happens," said Jack, seeing that Eddy's knife was still in his hand in a throwing position. The man was still dangerous.

Eddy attempted to throw the knife, but as his arm lifted he slipped further into the shaft. His arm shot down to prevent him going any further.

"Hang on a sec, Mate," said Jack. "I'll get you something to help you."

Eddy continued struggling as Jack walked towards the cellar.

A minute later Jack was back carrying one of the special crowbars, and he positioned himself so that he was facing Eddy and standing at the end of his legs.

Eddy eyed the crowbar. "What are you going to do with that?"

"Help you out of course," said Jack. "But I have to admit, this *really is* going to hurt me every bit as much as you."

Eddy was puzzled for a second, then understanding hit him. He screamed in terror at the same moment Jack screamed in agony. And holding the crowbar high above his head, his injured left shoulder becoming a site of pure agony, Jack plunged the weapon down with every ounce of strength in his battered body. The thin blade sliced through Eddy's right leg a few inches above the ankle.

Both men continued screaming as the crowbar was raised once more, then plunged downwards for a second time.

Suddenly Eddy was falling, his body slamming against the rungs as he dropped twenty feet to the floor. His screaming quickly changed to moaning.

Jack stood looking down. He could just make out the American. "Hey, you OK, Buddy!" he called out. "When I told you I would help you out, I meant to say I would help you in! Sorry about that! And no hard feelings I hope!"

Ignoring the pain that seemed to be trying to tear his body apart, Jack brought one of the knapsacks to the shaft, and opening it, he began dropping large bundles of ten pound notes down on top of Eddy.

"Hey, Buddy!" Jack called out again. "Look after my money will you!"

And having half emptied the sack, he closed it and put it on the ground. Then he collected the other seven knapsacks and threw them in.

"Fuck you, Blade," came a faint reply.

Jack grinned; then he turned his focus on the two severed feet at the edge of the shaft and shoved them in.

Half an hour later the shaft was covered once more, and Jack was on his way back to his room with sixty thousand pounds in a knapsack.

Three hours later he was in his rented room, and a large package was on the bed, tied up with string. The temporary address of his in-laws was written in bold letters on the brown paper that covered the cardboard box containing sixty thousand pounds. Also in the box was a letter explaining how the money was to be used. If all went well, his daughter would be on her way to America within a month.

Having posted the package, Jack rested up for another nine days. His powers of recovery truly amazed him. His split rib was healing very well, and so were the various wounds on his body. However, although the hole in his left shoulder seemed to be also healing well, he knew all was not right. He felt strange - as if he was coming down with a dose of flu. But he knew it was not flu, it was an infection - probably in the tissue that was surrounding the bullet. He didn't have much time left if he wanted to complete the task he had set himself five long years earlier.

32

Manny Hemmings sat in his office talking to Frank. His mood was upbeat, and it showed itself by the smile on his tubby face.

"You're looking pleased with yourself, Little Brother?" said Frank. "Any particular reason why you should be?"

Manny settled more comfortably into his chair. "The best reason in the World. And that is that after weeks of stress and worry, things are finally looking up."

Frank was puzzled. "Are they...?"

"Course they are," said Manny.

"Well, not wishing to put a damper on your new found optimism," said Frank, "I don't see that the situation has improved any?"

"That's because your big time bodyguards got their arses kicked by an East End boy," Manny chuckled, genuinely pleased that it had happened.

"What the hell has that got to do with it?" Frank growled.

Manny's smile turned into a scowl. "I know what you think of us on this side of the pond, Frank. You think we're all just small fry, with small fry problems; relying on you big fish from the States to come over and sort things out. Now you know better."

Frank shot out of his seat. "You ungrateful bastard! I put my business on hold to help you, Manny! I don't need to hear that kind of shit!"

"Say's you!" Manny retorted. "Do you think I'm stupid or something, Frank! Do you think I don't know that the real reason you're here is to keep an eye on what you see as your investment!"

"Bullshit!" Frank snapped. "I'm here because you sent for me! Don't forget that! You came to me - remember!"

"Maybe I did, because I knew you'd jump at the chance to come over here and show me how it's done! You know something, Frank, you're still the greedy little bastard you were when you were a kid!"

"What the hell are you going on about?" said Frank in some confusion.

"You know damn well what I'm talking about! That time with the new bicycle I got for my sixteenth birthday! You convinced mum that I would kill myself with it, so she took it off me and gave me a pair of new trousers instead! Then you ended up with my bike, and you knew how much I wanted it!"

"You would only have killed yourself, "Frank replied in a subdued voice. "Look at that time you nearly went into the canal. And you can't swim."

"It was raining!" Manny declared. "The brakes failed! They were too loose!"

"They weren't too loose when you hit that car. You were lucky to get away with only a scraped leg. Nearly gave mum a heart attack. Even then her heart wasn't good."

"That wasn't my fault!" Manny roared. "That fucking driver wasn't looking where he was going! He was opening a packet of fags! Anyway, you just had to tell mum, didn't you, because you knew what a worrier she was! And since she always thought of you as the more careful out of the two of us, she was bound to give you the bike!"

"What the fuck has this to do with now!" Frank retorted. "It was over thirty five years ago, for Christ Sakes!"

"Yea...well some things never change," said Manny calming down a little. "But at least you'll be on your way home now."

"Why's that?" Frank asked.

"Because there's no reason for you to stay," Manny replied. "All right, so we haven't caught Jack Blade yet, but we will soon. He's all beat up and he's probably hiding in some dive waiting for the heat to die down. Well it won't. I have over fifty people checking every place in London he might be. And when they find him, then I'll have my money back. He's on the run from the police as well, so he can't go to them for help. As I said, things are looking up."

Frank stared at his brother and frowned. "Look, Manny, I know when you are keeping something from me. And this over-optimism of yours is a sure sign. So spit it out...?"

Manny sighed. "Alright. If you must know I have an ex copper on the payroll and I think he's done a bunk."

"Is that a serious problem?" Frank inquired.

"It is if it's a case of rats and sinking ships," said Manny. "I rely on that bastard to keep an eye on what the cops are up to. Now I can't get in touch with him. And if he opens his yap, he could put me away for twenty five years minimum. So far the cops can't prove I was involved in the gun battle that happened here. But if they ever get their hands on him, that will change. That coward could be successfully interrogated with a feather."

"Don't worry about him," said Frank, glancing at his watch. "I've sent for a few more of my boys from the States. They'll be here soon. They'll take care of things for you."

"The last lot weren't much cop when it came down to it," said Manny.

"Yea, well, we know what to expect now. Mind you, I'll say one thing for Jack Blade. He's got more balls than anyone I've ever come across."

"He's a fucking psycho!" Manny snapped. "Why did he have to pick on me. What did I ever do to him. Five years I let him operate that pub of his without demanding so much as a packet of free crisps from him. So why come after me the way he did. And if stealing a million pounds from me wasn't enough, the bastard kills all my best men. Now he's sent Phil Braddon scuttling for cover like a terrified rabbit, leaving me to face the cops alone. Why me, Frank, why me…?"

Frank shrugged. "Ambition I'd say, Little Brother. You got; he wants. It's as simple as that maybe."

"Well fuck him!" Manny growled. "No bastard achieves his ambition off my back! All he'll get is a whole load of pain and then a bullet in the brain when I get bored with listening to him scream! Jack Blade is finished, and waiting for me to just reach out and pick him up!"

"So you said," Frank answered. "But I wouldn't write him off just yet, Little Brother, if I were you. His kind don't give up just because things have become difficult. He reminds me of an English bulldog. I've heard you have to use a crowbar to break their grip once they have their teeth into you."

"A bullet is quicker," said Manny. "And I've got plenty of those for Mr Jack Blade if he's stupid enough to come after me again."

"Aaaa…maybe you're right," said Frank, slapping his thighs with both hands. "After all, he must be pretty shot up by now, and I doubt he has had any medical help. So, if he does leave the country, we'll have him. I've got contacts in every country in Europe. Sooner or later he'll surface, and when he does I'll post him to you a piece at a time."

"Only after a great deal of torture, I hope," said Manny. "I want that bastard to suffer for putting me through all this. And I'll bet you that missing million that my major competitors are having a field day reading the newspapers lately, and it's all down to Jack Blade."

Frank grinned. "He'll suffer, don't you worry about that. One of my boys, Eddy Hickock knows a few Indian techniques that would hurt just talking about them."

"Glad to hear it," said Manny. "So, when *are* you going back?"

"Thought I'd hang around for a few more days," said Frank, "visit a few of our old haunts...that sort of thing."

"Just so long as you remember that a few of the blokes from your old haunts are now major competitors," said Manny.

Frank laughed. "Don't you trust me, Little Brother?"

Manny pulled a sour face. "I trusted you when I loaned you my bike. I never thought you were planning on keeping it."

"Not that shit again," said Frank, heading for the drinks cabinet. "Seems I'm going to have to buy you a new one or you'll never shut up about it."

"You can't," said Manny. "The company closed down ten years ago."

Frank poured himself a generous scotch. "Then I'll start up another bicycle company and all it will do is make the model you want so that you can have a new one every day for the rest of your life."

"Look, Frank," said Manny, rolling his unlit cigar between his lips a few times. "What I said about you only helping out because..."

"Forget it," Frank interrupted. "And don't get me wrong - you've got quite a piece of action going on here. But compared to what I have in the States, it's strictly small change. You enjoy your success. And any time you need help, you just give a holler."

Emotion entered Manny's voice when he spoke. "Thanks, Frank. I really appreciate your help."

"Course you do, Little Brother," said Frank sitting down once more. "Glad to be of service."

An odd sound reached Frank's ears that was almost imperceptible.

He turned his attention to the door.

"What's the matter?" said Manny.

Frank stood up and put his fingers to his lips for silence. Then, as he walked softly to the door, he pulled out a small revolver from a shoulder holster.

Holding his body close to the door, he slowly turned the handle and opened it a couple of inches.

Looking through the gap he saw the bodies of three men on the carpet. It was clear that each one had been shot in the head.

"Phone the cops!" Frank hissed to his brother.

Alarm appeared on Manny's podgy face. "Why...?"

"Do it!" Frank ordered.

Manny lifted the receiver of the phone on his desk and held it to his ear. And when he began frantically tapping one of the contact buttons, Frank knew that the line was dead.

Tightening his grip on his revolver, Frank opened the door a few inches more. There was no sign of movement in the other room. Nor was there any sound.

Suddenly the door flew open, throwing Frank backwards. And before he could recover, something hard slammed into his face and he went down.

"Keep your hands where I can see them," Jack said to Manny as he locked the door and put the key in his pocket. Then he reached down and took the revolver from Frank's hand.

"You've killed him!" Manny cried. "You've killed my brother!"

"He'll come round in a couple of minutes," said Jack, "for all the good it will do him."

"What the hell do you want, Blade?" Manny retorted. "You have my money, what fucking more do you want?"

"Everything you have," came the reply. "And everything you ever will have."

"But why pick on me? This fucking city is full of people with money? What did I ever do to you? Did I kill your father or something? Did I rape your mother; run over your kids; kick your dog - what for Christ Sakes...?"

Jack walked to the drinks cabinet and poured himself a large scotch. He swallowed it in one gulp. It made him feel a bit better He poured himself another and made his way to the settee. His drink spilt as he flopped into it. The infection within his body was getting stronger.

"Nothing like that, Mr Hemmings. You were the one that came within range, that's all."

"What the fuck are you talking about?" Manny cried. "Within range of what?"

"Me," said Jack. "Look, it's a long story. It concerns this South American snake that I've always admired. It waits for weeks sometimes, just for its..."

"You're fucking crazy!" Manny exploded. "You should see a Shrink instead of giving me all this fucking hassle! Now, you've already taken me for a million quid, so leave me alone will you! Just keep the money and get yourself some help! I won't come after you! All I want is to conduct my business in peace! It's a good offer! Take it!"

Jack took another drink and smacked his lips. "You keep only the best of everything, don't you, Mr Hemmings."

Manny spread his hands. "So what? Is that a crime?"

"No - just makes it all the more worthwhile for someone to come along and take it from you."

Manny's eyes flared with sudden outrage. "Listen to me you fuck-brain, no one takes anything from me and lives to boast about it - especially not some fucking landlord with a death wish!"

Jack smiled. "Strange thing to say when that fucking landlord has a bullet aimed at your belly button. I wonder if I could put a bullet through it from here without making the hole any larger. Bet I could with a Nine Millimetre. So let's have a go shall we..."

The reality of his situation came back to Manny with the speed of an express train and his anger evaporated. "Look, Jack," he said, trying to smile, "what is it you really want? Is it to show what a big man you are? Well, you've done that. You've killed all my best people; done something to my brother I've longed to do since we were kids, and taken me for a fortune in cash. Why not quit while you're ahead. And as insurance that I won't send anyone after you, you can keep that list of my transactions you took with the money. While you have that, I'm not going to cause you any trouble."

"Sorry...no deal," said Jack.

"But why not?" Manny pleaded.

"Because deals aren't in my plans. Anyway I chucked that book in the bin when I transferred the money into sacks. I intend to make my own contacts when I've taken over your organization. I don't need a ready made list."

"But they're your plans, Jack? Surely you can change them if it was worth your while...?"

"A friend tried to do that recently, Mr Hemmings, but I didn't want him to, so I had to kill him. Surely you don't expect me to let you do it now. My friend would turn in his grave, and rightly so."

"I have more money you know!" Manny pleaded. "Not quite as much as you took from me, but enough to make you very rich indeed!"

"Sorry, no deal, Mr Hemmings."

"But...?"

"Mr Hemmings!" Jack interrupted forcefully. "If you won't listen to me, perhaps you will listen to a bullet! Now I said no deal and I mean it!"

Manny's shoulders slumped. "So what now?" he asked.

"We wait for your brother to wake up," said Jack, taking another gulp of whisky.

The minutes past in silence. Then Jack lost patience. "You can get up now, Frank," he said.

There was no response.

"I said you can get up now, Frank," Jack repeated in a louder voice. "And I think you should know that there's no way I'm coming over to check on you and give you an opportunity to try your luck, so you might as well stop pretending to be out to the World."

There was still no response.

Jack sighed. "If you are still unconscious, Frank, then you won't feel the bullet I'm going to put through your right ankle."

Frank climbed slowly to his feet.

"Hi there, Buddy," said Jack. "Why don't you come over and sit on the desk next to your little brother."

Frank made his way to Manny's desk and sat on one corner of it. There was a red swelling just above his left eye.

"What the fuck do you want, Blade?" Frank growled, feeling the lump.

"Surely a smart Yank like you must know that already," said Jack.

"You crazy bastard," said Frank. "You won't last five minutes once my boys get here."

"Your boys...." Jack shuddered in mock fear. "Heavens, that's scary. But you know what they say, don't you, Frank. Never send a boy to do a man's job."

"You cocky little shit!" Frank retorted. "You'll never leave this building alive! And look at the state of you! You'll probably keel over and die within an hour."

"Well I did have a run in with a Texan called Eddy a while back, and I got cut up a little."

"You had a set to with Eddy?"

"A knife fight as a matter of fact," Jack replied. "He had the drop on me with a gun, but for some strange reason he wanted us to go at it with a couple of Bowie knives."

"I wondered where he had got to," said Frank. "So where is he?"

"Can't tell you that," said Jack, "because he's guarding the million pounds for me."

Frank's eyes were wide in disbelief. "You took Eddy Hickock in a knife fight! I'll be damned!"

"I cheated," said Jack. "I used a bucket."

"Fuck off!" Frank exclaimed.

"That's what he said to me," Jack answered. "Now how about pouring us all a drink, Frank."

"Get it yourself! I ain't no fucking waiter!"

Jack aimed the Nine Millimetre at Frank's right leg. "Come on now, Old Buddy, you wouldn't want me to put a bullet in your kneecap for being rude to me, would you."

Frank immediately went to the drinks cabinet and poured whisky into two glasses. He then handed one to Jack and the other to his brother, who took it with a trembling hand.

His face was white with rage when he sat down once more.

"Not joining us?" said Jack.

Frank glared at his captor. "I'm particular who I drink with."

"Can we please get on with it," said Manny. "What are you really after, Blade?"

"Your chair," said Jack, taking a sip of whisky from the glass in his left hand. He kept the Nine Millimetre on Frank at all times.

"Then take it!" Manny declared, standing up and moving back from his desk.

"I want to earn it, not steal it," said Jack.

"Just take the bloody thing!" Manny exclaimed, becoming desperate once more.

"Sit down, Little Brother," said Frank. "He means that he can only own it if you're dead. Ain't that right, Buddy?"

"Spot on, Frank."

Manny sat in his chair once more and gulped down his drink.

"So," said Frank, "why do you want my brother's organization when you must know that you won't be able to hang on to it?"

"Because your brother and all he owns are prey," Jack replied.

"I see," said Frank, touching the lump above his eye. "Then that must mean you consider yourself a predator?"

Jack nodded slowly.

"And what kind of predator are you exactly?"

"A patient one."

"Which means that you've been planning this for some time?"

"Five years."

Frank whistled. "Five years! That sure is a hell of a long time in this business. And during those long years, did you not give any thought to what happens after you destroyed your prey?"

"No."

Frank was surprised. "Why not?"

"Once the act is completed, a new one begins."

"But you must know the outcome of this - second act?"

"I have an idea," said Jack.

"Manny believes you're insane. Are you insane, Jack?"

Jack smiled. "We're all in this together. If I'm insane, so must you be."

Frank smiled too. "Good point. But, you know something, I could use someone like you in my organization back in the States. I could start you off on five hundred dollars a week, and who knows how far you could go with my backing."

"I already have a million pounds," said Jack. "Why would I want to work for someone else for five hundred dollars a week?"

"Because you might have the money, but you don't have the power," said Frank.

"I feel pretty powerful at the moment," said Jack. "I mean, between the two of you, you control a great number of people. And little old me with my little gun has control of you."

Jack saw the anger that entered Frank's eyes for a moment. Then it was gone.

"You've got the drop on us, that's all," said Frank. "And that situation could change in the blink of an eye."

"Then I better not blink," Jack quipped.

Suddenly there was a knock on the door, and the handle rattled.

"Boss...Boss?" said an urgent sounding voice with an American accent. "What's going on in there?"

"May I...?" said Frank to Jack.

"You may," Jack replied. "And feel free to say what you like."

"Boss...Boss, it's Jed?" said the voice, and more door knocking and handle rattling took place.

"It's OK, Jed," Frank called out. "A situation has developed in here that need's careful handling."

"But who the hell killed the boys out here?" Jed demanded.

"That would be the work of one Jack Blade, I'm afraid to say, Jed."

There was a pause. "You mean Blade's in there with you, Boss?" Jed finally asked.

"He is indeed, Jed. And have the boys I sent for arrived yet?"

"Sure they have, Boss. They're waiting at your hotel like you said they should. I'll have them here in half an hour."

"You do that, Jed," said Frank. "And you can have a thousand dollar bonus if you make it twenty minutes."

"Sure will, Boss. And don't you worry, I'll get you out of this mess. But you tell Jack Blade that he won't leave that office alive. I'm leaving Hickey and Chuck here to make sure he don't leave before I get back with the boys."

"He heard you, Jed," said Frank. "You get going now."

"Sure thing, Boss. And you hang on in there."

"Have you ever had that kind of loyalty?" said Frank to Jack.

"Loyalty is just a product like anything else," said Jack. "The more you pay, the more you get, until the money runs out that is."

"I see you're a cynical bastard as well," Frank replied.

"Just realistic," Jack replied.

"So how about reconsidering your decision? I could make it worth your while?"

"No thanks."

"But you ain't heard my offer yet?"

"I don't need to. And the answer is no."

"You could at least listen," said Frank.

"I already gave you my answer," said Jack.

"But that was before, Buddy."

"Before what, Mate?"

"Before Jed turned up."

"But Jed has gone away again."

"Only to bring my boys here."

"The answer is still no," said Jack.

"Why not?"

"Because I've already got what I wanted."

"But you can't keep it!" Frank snapped. "Can't you get that through your thick Limey head!"

"We've been through this already, and I don't like to repeat myself," said Jack feeling the relentless progress of the infection as it moved throughout his body.

"You know, we never fully get what we want," said Frank. "If we're very lucky, we can get most of it – but never all of it."

"I have," Jack replied.

"So you say. But I'm guessing that you don't know what you want. I'm guessing that you have no more idea why you're here than I have. And I'll bet you have asked yourself why you're tearing around like a maniac, causing all sorts of shit for everyone else."

"You finished...?" Jack's voice was cold.

"So you're going to kill my brother?"

Jack nodded.

"What about me?"

"You fucking bastard!" Manny exploded at Frank. "You better not try and make any deals, or I'll kill you myself!"

Frank stared at his brother. "You mean if you die you want me to die along with you. Well shame on you, Little Brother. What would mum say if she could hear you now."

"We're in this together, Frank!" Manny snapped. "Don't try and wriggle out of it!"

"I came here to help you, Manny," Frank replied sternly, "not to die for you. And all I'm trying to do is establish whether I'm on Jack's prey list or not. I see no reason for me to end up with a bullet in me unnecessarily."

"Don't let him talk his way out of it!" Manny declared to Jack. "He was always trying to get the better of me when we were kids, and he's still at it! And remember, if you take over my organization, Frank will be the one to take it back!"

"Thanks for that, Little Brother," Frank replied calmly.

"There was no need to remind me," said Jack. "I've already decided to kill the two of you."

"Happy now, Little Brother," said Frank, with a half smile.

The anger left Manny and he ran his fingers through what was left of his hair. "It can't end like this - it just can't!" he wailed. Then he stared at Jack. "Look, there must be some way around this? What if I was to step down - hand over the whole organization to you...?"

"No deals," said Jack.

"Why not, for Christ Sakes...?"

"Didn't you understand the man earlier!" Frank snapped at his brother. "He can only own it if you are dead. Isn't that right again, Mr Blade?"

"That's right again, Mr Hemmings," said Jack.

Jack told himself he should be enjoying this moment immensely, but he wasn't. It was as if he was simply re-enacting an event that had taken place many times before. It felt flat and familiar. And he wondered if it was the infection affecting his mind.

Manny suddenly began to weep. "Do something, Frank...please! I don't want to die!"

Frank's eyes narrowed. "Pull yourself together, Little Brother! You're carrying the Hemmings name! Don't disgrace it now!"

There was a clicking sound and the door suddenly opened.

Jack aimed at it and fired.

A man staggered backwards and vanished. There was a soft thump.

Jack made his way to the door and peered into the outer room. A fresh body had joined the others. Jack didn't recognize the man, but from his build he was probably a bodyguard.

Jack then closed the door and locked it with the key the other man had left in the lock. He put the key in his pocket and sat down once more.

There was a furious look on Frank's face and he was glaring at his brother. Manny was looking shame-faced. Jack twigged straight away.

"Manny," he said in a low voice. "Why don't you take that gun out of your desk and throw it over here."

"I don't have a gun," Manny stammered.

"Do I have to shoot you to make you tell the truth?" Jack warned.

Manny opened a drawer and threw the small pistol to Jack.

Jack caught it and put it in his pocket.

"I bet you would have gone for it," Jack said to Frank.

"You bet your ass I would!" Frank snarled. "And so would anyone with balls!"

"He'd have heard me opening the drawer!" Manny protested.

"What difference would it have made, you moron!" Frank retorted. "He's going to kill you anyway!"

"Right," said Jack, "it's time to get on with it."

"You mean you're going to kill us without giving us a chance?" Frank asked.

"Would you give me a chance if our positions were reversed?" said Jack.

"Not on your life, Buddy," Frank grinned. "But it was worth a try, wasn't it?"

Jack grinned back. "It certainly was. And for that bit of honesty, Frank, I will give you and your brother a chance. Now, I'm going to place Manny's gun between us on the carpet, and I'll put my Nine Millimetre back in my pocket. And when I count to three, then, as they say in the films, *go for your gun, you Son Of A Bitch!*"

Frank laughed out loud. "You like Westerns, Buddy. Well so do I. And I'll say one thing for you, Jack Blade, you sure have style. And I want to thank you for giving me the opportunity to relive the Old West. Eddy Hickock would have given his right arm to be here watching right now. He styled himself on Jim Bowie you know. "

"He's already had his Alamo," said Jack.

"I still appreciate it," said Frank.

Happy to oblige," said Jack, putting the pistol on the carpet and taking a few steps back.

"You're crazy - the both of you!" Manny exclaimed.

"Ready?" said Jack.

"Just one thing," said Frank. "Which of us is the good guy in this shoot-out?"

"Think of it as a fight between outlaws," Jack offered.

"OK by me," Frank replied.

"At the count of three then," said Jack.

"Stop this!" Manny shouted, moving away from his desk.

"*One!*" said Jack, fighting off a wave of dizziness.

Frank fixed his eyes on the gun lying on the carpet, and tensed his body. With anyone else he would have wondered if the safety was on, but having met Jack Blade he had a shrewd idea that it was off and still loaded.

"No...no...!" Manny's voice rose to a scream.

"*Two!*"

Manny whimpered and stared desperately at the locked door.

"*Three!*"

Frank dived for the gun.

Jack's right hand dropped into his pocket and came out with the Nine Millimetre.

Frank's fingers tightened on the gun handle.

Then his hand whipped up and he squeezed the trigger at the exact same time as Jack.

Both bullets left their guns at the same instant in jets of smoke and flames.

Manny cried out in terror.

Frank fell back with a red hole in his forehead, and Jack winced as a bullet tore a path along his right cheek.

Manny cried out again and ran for the door.

The aiming sight on Jack's Nine Millimetre followed him.

Then two bullets smashed into Manny's back and his run turned into a stumble before he fell face down on the carpet. He didn't move again.

Jack picked up the gun Frank had used, then made his way to Manny's chair and sat down. The chair was leather covered, with broad arm rests, and a high back. It felt very comfortable to sit in, and Jack savoured the experience by stroking the arm rests and swivelling the chair in a half circle a few times. He put the revolver on the desk. Then he reached inside his coat and pulled out three more revolvers two of which he had taken from two of the dead bodyguards in the outer room. They had no silencers, but it didn't matter. Noise would be the least of his troubles.

He checked that the chambers were full, then he placed the weapons on the desk in front of him. The last to go on the desk was his Nine Millimetre. His fingers stroked the cold metal for a moment. He had taken the weapon from a former boss seven years ago. It had been with him ever since and had saved his life more times than he could remember. And it was only fitting that it was here with him now, joining him in the final chapter of the first act.

He didn't have any spare ammunition, so what were in the guns would have to do. Somehow he knew there would be just enough.

Then he settled back and fixed his attention on the locked door. His eyes began to glaze over, and his breathing dropped so low it would have alarmed a doctor.

He would certainly have presented a gruesome image to anyone seeing him. Blood was oozing down the right side of his face, and his skin had taken on a deathly pallor. Yet there was something that projected barely-contained energy about him: in his stillness: in his posture, as if the merest touch would send him exploding into action. It was as if he now existed somewhere between the living and the dead – allowing something strange within him to reveal itself for the first time.

And so the minutes passed, and Jack Blade waited; his breath less than the softest touch of a butterfly wing, but his concentration as tangible as a battering ram.

Fifteen minutes from the time he had killed Frank and Manny he heard the sound of voices in the other room. Then the door handle turned.

"Boss, it's Jed and the boys?" a voice said.

"Frank can't talk to you right now, Jed," said Jack.

"Is that you, Blade?" Jed demanded. "What's been going on, and where's Mr Hemmings?"

Jack peered over the desk to look at Frank's body. "He's busy staring up at the ceiling, and his brother is staring at the carpet - must be thinking of redecorating."

"Open this fucking door, you murdering bastard!" Jed roared.

"Can't do that, Yank," said Jack. "You'll have to do it yourself."

"Step aside, Jed!" a bullish voice declared. "I'll open the fucking thing!"

Jack picked up two of the revolvers.

Then the door crashed open, and Jack began firing.

A crowd of people had gathered outside Queensbury House. A line of police were keeping them back as they struggled to see what was going on. Seven police cars were parked close by, along with four ambulances, and there was a great deal of confusion amongst all concerned.

It was midnight, and a cloudy sky was in the process of disgorging a fine drizzle of rain. Detective Chief Inspector Mandell climbed out of the police car and turned up the collar of his Tweed coat. DI Hanson came to meet him.

"It's a bloodbath up there, Guv," said Hanson. "Bodies all over the place."

"Manny Hemmings?" Mandell inquired.

"And his brother, Frank - along with Jack Blade and seventeen others."

"Jesus!" Mandell exclaimed. "What about survivors?"

"Not a single one, Guv."

"Witnesses?"

"Not to the actual shooting. But the receptionist at the main desk said that Jack Blade arrived at about ten o clock. Said he had an appointment with Manny Hemmings. Then about an hour later a crowd of Americans turned up. They said they were working for Frank Hemmings so the receptionist didn't think anything of it. And it was only when he thought he heard shots that he discovered the slaughter."

Mandell frowned. "Is the receptionist the same one who was on duty the last time Blade paid a visit to this building by any chance?"

"Yes, Guv. But the building has only two of them, so there's a fifty fifty chance of him being there at the time of both shootings."

"Surely he recognized Blade?" said Mandell. "After all, his face has been plastered all over the newspapers. So why didn't he give us a call when Blade showed up?"

"You think he was in on it, Guv?" said Hanson.

"Not sure. But bring him in for questioning, just in case."

"Right, Guv."

"Any idea how it happened?" Mandell asked, wondering if the Commissioner would ask him that very question in such a calm and civilised manner.

"Well, it seems that Blade must have killed the bodyguards in the outer office, and then killed the Hemmings brothers in the main office. And I know this sounds crazy, Guv, but we think Blade just sat at Manny Hemming's desk and waited for the rest of Frank's bodyguards to show up. Then he shot them as they came through the door."

"What - all of them - with just one gun?" Mandell exclaimed.

"Five guns, Guv; four revolvers and a Nine Millimetre automatic."

"Christ Almighty," said Mandell, moving towards the entrance of the building. "Must have been quite something."

"You can say that again, Guv."

Hanson then looked away and he seemed to pale a little.

"You all right, Ken?" Mandell inquired.

Hanson looked at his superior. "I don't know, Guv. Being in that office gave me the creeps. Blade's just sitting there in Manny Hemming's chair with at least twelve bullets in him, and…"

"Try not to let it get to you," said Mandell as Hanson's voice trailed away. "A scene like that is enough to give anyone nightmares; all those bodies in one place. I remember the first time I went to a bad pile up. It made…"

"I don't mean the bodies, Guv," Hanson interrupted, holding the lift doors open for his superior. "Though, God knows, I've never seen anything like that slaughter before."

"Then what…?"

Hanson's expression seemed to take on a haunted look. "It's Blade himself, Guv."

"What about him?"

"I know you'll think I'm crazy, Guv, but the way his eyes are wide open…"

"That happens sometimes," Mandell replied sharply, suddenly impatient at the slow progress of the lift to the nineteenth floor.

"Yes, I know, Guv. But his are different. To me they look like – well they're just like…"

"Spit it out, man, for God's Sake!" Mandell snapped.

"The eyes of a snake, Guv," said Hanson, "staring right back at me - following my every movement as I checked the office."

"What utter nonsense!" Mandell scoffed, looking at the younger man.

Then Mandell's impatience vanished. He laughed and put his hand on the DI's shoulder. "I think you need a spot of leave, Ken. Anyway, death can do strange things to a body. You should know that by now."

"Yes, Guv," said Hanson in a low tone, "I suppose I should."

■ ■ ■

Printed in the United Kingdom
by Lightning Source UK Ltd.
120085UK00002B/28-54